"Oracle is a fantastic read. It had me from page one and a real page turner..."

— S. JOESTEN

"Jaw Dropping!"

— AMAZON REVIEWER

"I'd recommend it to anyone who enjoys mystery, psychics, and Greek mythology."

— JULIE WEEKS

"It didn't take long for me to become invested in the story with Diana the main character, it hit the ground running and I was hooked."

— PAMELA MCK

"Almost a scarily good book."

— AMAZON REVIEWER

"I really hope the series continues because it's an addicting read!"

— SHANTELLE HAZELTON

Copyright © 2018 Carissa Andrews

Published in 2018 by Carissa Andrews

Cover Design by Carissa Andrews ©2021

All rights reserved.

ISBN-13: **978-1-953304-01-8**

ACKNOWLEDGMENTS

Special thanks to the amazing beta-readers I have on my team. All of the insights you bring to the table makes every one of the books I write even better. I don't know what I'd do without you and thank you doesn't even begin to cover it.

Sherry Dumpprope
Colin Andrews
Twila Belton

DEDICATION

*After years writing one series, knowing which direction to go next can be a challenge. That was certainly the case for me after finishing up the **Pendomus Chronicles**.*

Oracle is dedicated to all of my fans who voted in favor of Oracle's concept so it would be the next to come into being. Diana's first story is finally complete and it's all because of you. Thank you!

ORACLE

A DIANA HAWTHORNE PSYCHIC MYSTERY

CARISSA ANDREWS

*W*HY THE HELL do I even bother being polite to people?

Pretty sure I'd fall over from disbelief if even one of them could care about anyone beyond their own godly selves. Truth be told, being around most of them, really kinda pisses me off.

The arrogant ass who cut me off on the already-narrow sidewalk continues on his way, oblivious to the rest of the world. He doesn't even spin his dark head of hair around to grace the woman he nearly toppled into the busy street with a passing look of apology.

I oughta kick him in his annoyingly perfect-shaped ass.

I give my sopping wet foot a shake, hoping it will alleviate the inevitable squish in my running shoe for the next three blocks. Of course, it doesn't.

There is simply no way I can be part of the human race.

The thought makes me snicker.

By the time I reach my office, I'm ready to peel my shoe off and throw it against the wall—just to see if it sticks like a wet noodle. Unfortunately, my first appointment is already pacing outside; hands wringing, and hair frazzled like she's been pulling on it. Her eyes are wide as I walk up to my private entrance at the back of the building I rent out and shoot her a half-smile.

Why do they always wait to hijack me at this time of the morning?

"You must be Amber," I state, matter-of-factly.

She looks like an Amber. Tallish, blonde cropped hair, wide blue eyes, and pouty lips.

Amber nods, her hair flopping up and down frantically.

"Cool. Come on in," I tell her, nodding to the black abyss inside. I push open the door, flick on the low lighting, and take a seat to unlace my shoe. "Sorry about this, but I'm gonna need to go barefoot, or my foot's gonna transform into a regurgitated prune."

I toss the shoe aside and fling the sopping wet sock over the radiator in the corner, before starting on the other foot.

Amber still hasn't said anything, not even a chuckle at my lame attempt at a joke. Instead, she stands awkwardly in the middle of the room, tugging on the frayed end of her sleeves and looking around.

This is about a man.

I sigh deeply. Why does it have to always be so obvious? Just for once, I'd love a challenge.

"Okay, Amber…have a seat," I say, pointing to the chair beside her.

I walk around the small table to position myself directly opposite her. If I had more time, I would have set out the ambiance—a little incense, some crystals. Maybe even a little Enya going on in the background. Who doesn't love Enya?

She sits quickly, biting her lip, and grimacing like she chewed on a box of nails.

I brush the bright pink chunk of bangs from my face and tuck it behind my right ear. With a deep, cleansing breath, I close my eyes and clear my mind. Images rush in without restraint; faces, places. Hands holding hands. Steamy sex with a dark-haired, green-eyed man. The green expands from his eyes, turning into flashing green lights.

Green means go.

I open my eyes, already well aware of the answer.

"Go ahead. What's your question?" I ask.

"Is he the right one? Should I stay with him? Does he really love me?" The woman blurts out her first words of the day in one big jumble. Her eyes are glossy as she pleads with me, searching my face for her answer.

Knew it.

I grin, searching for the best ambivalent words.

"He can be, if that's what you choose. I'm seeing green lights. They sorta mean universal energies are open to going forward confidently. However, the ultimate path will be decided by the actions you and he make…beginning now."

"Is that a yes?" Her tone is desperate as she scrunches her face and leans forward, digging her fingertips into the table's edge.

"It is a yes, at least for now. Free will has a way of course-correcting, though. So be careful. However, that said, what I see presently is he is very clearly meant to be in your life—as you are in his."

She nods, tugging her eyebrows in, clearly hoping for more.

"What I want you to do," I begin, "is remember to take things one step at a time. Be present with him in this moment, without jumping to the next. It's your job to ground the two of you because he can't. He isn't to your level, yet. Do you understand?"

I've found assigning a job helps ease a person's mind and gives them an active role to focus on.

Her eyes gloss over, and I reiterate, "You need to enjoy

each other. Be happy where you are in each stage with Jason because if you—"

Amber gasps. "I... How did you know his name? I swear, I didn't say it. I was trying not to give too much away."

I wince.

Even after all these years, I can still slip. As much as people want to believe what I say is real, they kinda don't want to know for sure, either. I mean, what if it means I can sense everything, you know? Like that extra piece of pizza they ate when they shouldn't, or the name of the man they cheated on with last night. The thought of it all wigs them out.

And it should. Because I can.

"I'm sure you mentioned it in our phone consult," I lie, with a cheesy smile plastered on my face.

"Yes, yes... I must have. Thank you, Diana," she sighs, nodding to herself. Amber stands, shaking my hand absently.

"You are most welcome," I tell her. "Now relax and enjoy the ride."

"I will. I mean, I'll try. Thank you."

Our exchange comes to an end and I find myself alone. Blissfully—peacefully—alone.

Unfortunately, it's not meant to last long.

My assistant, Renaldo bounds through the door moments after Amber exits. If he weren't so damn good at his job, I'd fire his flamboyant ass for being late every day.

"Well, hey there, sunshine. How's the most ah-mazing boss in the world?" he says, doing a flourish of his hand as he takes the seat recently vacated by Amber.

With my face deadpan, I slowly blink from him to the clock on the wall.

He ignores me. As he always does.

I sigh. "I'd be even more amazing if I had a decent

assistant who could tell time. Or at least bribe me with coffee."

"If that's what you really wanted, you would have foreseen someone different to hire, honey. Instead, you're stuck with me," Renaldo says, his pearly whites shining broadly. "Besides, you know you love me. Warts and all."

I roll my eyes. Damn if he isn't right. All signs pointed to having him by my side, though I'm still not sure why. The universe has a funny way of making paths clear for everyone but me. All I can figure is it must be a sick cosmic joke because I'm sure as hell not clued in.

"So how many lovesick birds have you dealt with in my absence?" he asks, gathering his hands up by his chin and fluttering his eyelashes.

"Just the one." I laugh, giving him a knowing look. "So far."

"And I'm sure there will be many more for the day. It's almost Valentine's Day, after all. I better get the front stocked up with lovers' potions and scented candles. I'm telling you, we need some blindfolds and whips on display with the whole Fifty Shades of Spanking obsession still sweeping the nation. We'd make a killing," he winks, dashing to the front of our small store entrance.

The instant he says it, I know he's right. We'd make a ton of money, but that would mean dealing with more people. I have enough to deal with, thanks. Then again, I suppose it's why I hired him. He can deal with it.

"You're not paid on commission," I call after him, shaking my head. "You get that, right?"

"Maybe the idea of lust-bunnies having passionate kinky sex is enough mental payment for me," I hear him call back.

"Brody withholding again?" I say, chuckling.

"Oh, honey, do not get me started," Renaldo says, walking to the doorway with his hands on his hips.

5

"Darling, I have already foreseen it," I say, watching his bright face freeze. I wait just long enough for the color in his cheeks to drain before adding a final, "Kidding."

He lowers his eyebrows and spins on his heels. "There's a special kind of hell for people like you, Diana Hawthorne."

"Don't I know it," I chuckle.

Honestly, he has no idea how right he is. Whatever this is, this life I lead, it's like a Groundhog Day loop of hells especially crafted for me. I mean, ironic much? I can't stand people, but here I am working in close proximity daily as I try to do for them what I've never been able to do for myself. It's kinda messed up, actually.

If I ever meet God—or whatever—I'm gonna give him a piece of my mind.

The bell of the shop door dings, as a man and woman walk in. The man's a closed book; apprehensive and skeptical. His aura exudes disdain, while the woman on the other hand is drowning in grief and worry.

Renaldo shoots me a sideways glance before trotting over to them in his signature walk.

"Why hello there, is there anything I can do for you?" he says, cocking his head slightly to the side. His perfectly groomed, dark hair flops slightly with the gesture, showing off his accentuated part he's had his stylist carve in.

The man's left eyebrow twitches upward, but his lips tip down.

I walk back into my reading room. There's no question, they're heading my way and I need to cleanse myself first. There's a helluva lot of grounding I need to do before they invade my space.

Standing in the middle of my mental circle of light, I call upon the universal energies to wash away all the shit no longer serving me, so I can become an open vessel to help those who need my gifts. The white light washes through my system, taking away anything unwanted, or clinging to me from the previous encounter with Amber. Not to mention, discarding any of my own BS from perfect-ass-man.

"Eh-hem." Renaldo clears his throat, but by the time he knocks on the doorframe, I've taken my final cleansing breath before releasing the light.

Turning around, I grin as genuinely as I can.

"These lovely folks would like a word with you, if you have a moment, Diana," he says, swinging his hand out to put them on display. "It's important."

"Absolutely. What can I do to help?" I ask, widening my arms to suggest they take a seat.

The woman moves quickly, clutching something small in her hand. The man stays behind, his eyes scrutinizing my every move. I hold my ground, waiting for him to finish comparing dicks.

Finally, he moves to the open seat beside his wife.

I catch Renaldo's eye as he diva air snaps and walks out.

Moving slowly, I extend my energy out, getting a feel for the situation before they even say a word. This situation, the reason they're here, is more important than most. It's about a child.

Missing? Dead?

I light a white candle and take my seat opposite them.

Watching both closely, it doesn't take a rocket scientist to know the wife is distraught—outta her mind worried. The husband has reserved himself for the worst. Oh, and he thinks I'm complete bullshit.

"So, where would you like to start?" I say, simply.

"I—well, I mean we—" the woman begins, blinking wildly as she searches for words.

"It's okay. Let it come out as it should," I say, leaning in and waiting for the oncoming storm.

"How old are you?" The man blurts out.

If it wasn't written all over his face, I'd be taken more aback.

The left side of my mouth quirks.

"Honey," the wife warns, her eyes wide and forehead scrunched.

"It's a reasonable question," he says, his voice deeper and nostrils flaring.

I lean back in my chair.

"Ted, it is Ted, right?" I say, crossing my fingers over my knee, and watching his expression shift slightly when I get his name right. "How old were you when you realized you could breathe?"

He shifts uncomfortably in his chair, his eyebrows tugging in.

"I thought as much," I say, not letting him define his answer. "Look, what I do comes from outside myself. I'm not the one in charge. Something much bigger is. I don't presume to understand it fully or even try to. So, either we can get down to business so we can find..." I close my eyes searching for the name. "Esther?"

I open my eyes to see his lips press into a thin line.

"—or we can have a philosophical debate about age," I finish.

His wife, Lacy, I gather, grabs his right hand in her left, clutching it so tightly her knuckles turn white.

She whispers, "I told you she was the real deal."

Ted's nostrils flare, but he keeps his trap shut.

Finally, we can get somewhere.

"Lacy, I need the necklace in your other hand, if you don't mind," I say, pointing to her free hand.

With a shaky extension, she reaches out and lets the dainty silver necklace tumble into my palm.

Instantly, I'm inundated by flashes of a blonde, brown-eyed eight-year-old girl. She's playful, artistic, incredibly intelligent. She loves reading, dogs, and more than anything else, her parents. This is no runaway.

"Can you—do you sense where she is?" Lacy asks, her voice cracking.

I take a deep breath and shake my head.

"Unfortunately, it doesn't always work like that. Objects hold energy, yes, but they're not necessarily tied to her present, future, or even the event itself. I get snippets, but I need context. How long has she been missing?" I ask.

This isn't the first missing child I've dealt with, but this one is more urgent somehow. Of course, they're all urgent, but this one holds some sort of importance and I can't put my finger on what it is.

"Three days," Lacy says breathlessly. "The police—they can't find any leads. They're frantically searching but it's not fast enough. She's only eight."

Tears stream down her face as she reaches out for the necklace. I place it gingerly into her palm and she clutches it to her chest.

I take another cleansing breath and try to settle into the energy. Esther is alive, that much is for sure—but beyond that, everything is slightly obscured.

"Were there any clues or items out of place at the scene?" I ask, knowing full-well the police never declared an actual scene. They didn't have enough to go on.

"We don't know. Not for sure. We have some guesses as to where, or even who may have done this, but the police are having trouble making a connection. We were hoping—" Lacy looks tentatively at Ted, who sits stone-cold in the chair, still processing.

"Okay, what do you think you know?" I ask, trying to open their minds enough for me to dig around.

Ironically, it's Ted, not Lacy who begins to relay the most information. Despite his stoic stature, he thinks about the day of the event and all of the situations leading up to her disappearance. The people he suspects. The whys.

I catch a flash of a man with a litter of puppies—the one thing Esther would love to get her hands on. It's also the one thing Ted and Esther could never agree on. She wanted one in the worst way, and Ted couldn't deal. One more mouth to feed when he was worried about losing his job. His company is downsizing and he's afraid they don't need him. A puppy right now was the last thing they needed. Especially since he hadn't voiced his concerns with his wife.

"Good, good," I say, nodding at Ted.

His eyes widen, and he glances at Lacy, "What in the hell is this woman doing? What in the hell have you dragged us into?"

"The man, the one with the puppies—who is he?" I say, standing up and leaning with my fingertips pressed on the glass table between us.

"He—uh—" Ted blinks rapidly, clearly reaching his max-spook point as his chair screeches backward when he stands up and backs away.

I hold my hands up apologetically. It can be a lot to take in when you're expecting a fake.

"Tell her, Ted. Please," Lacy begs.

Ted glances from Lacy, back to me. His mouth gapes open slightly as his eyes search the not-so-distant past.

"I dunno. He's a guy who peddles puppies in the park. He's always creeped me out, but I thought he was harmless. Esther and I—we talked about him, though. She knows she isn't supposed to talk to him without me or her mom. Lately, I dunno, he's been persistent with us. Esther wants a puppy in the worst"—he looks up, his eyes full of fear—"anyway, he wouldn't take no for an answer."

"Okay, I need you to take a seat and hold out your hands," I tell him, pointing at the chair he'd kicked aside.

He does so without question, though I can tell he doesn't understand why. His brain is on overload, but curiosity and a glimmer of hope starts to take seed.

As he holds out his hands, I slide mine underneath—the receiving mode—so our palms touch. Instantly, I see the man's face, the last interaction between the three of them. Through the energy transfer, there are glimpses of truth behind the puppy peddler, not the assumptions made by Ted. His name is...

I tilt my head slightly, as I reach out for it.

Burt? Brent?

Yes, Brent.

He's in his mid-forties but has a developmental delay of some sort. His mental age is still much younger. He loves puppies. And he loves little girls. Only recently has he learned to use one to get the other.

My eyes flip open.

"We don't have much time. Your suspicions about Brent are spot on. He has a thing for little girls. He wasn't a bad guy, not at first, but something has snapped. Maybe he's off meds or something. We'll need to act quickly before the trail goes fully cold," I say.

Lacy's eyes widen and she clutches the necklace to her chest as she holds back tears.

Ted nods, "He always comes out of the small apartment complex by the park. It's possible he lives there but the police found nothing when they canvassed."

"This helps, though. Now we have a name. You need to get to the police department and tell them to find Brent for questioning. I wasn't able to get a last name. I think he must go by a few different names... It's too muddy. But it should help them narrow it down when they talk to the landlord. I'll call my guy at the PD and give him a heads up. Ask for Detective Radovich when you get there and tell him you've just been to see me. He'll know what to do," I say.

Goosebumps flash up and down my body and the last thing I want to do is follow the line of energy further.

I hate people.

I hate knowing good people turn bad. Bad people pretend to be good.

I hate knowing sometimes there's nothing I can do to stop bad things from happening.

And if they don't hurry, bad things are definitely going to get worse.

2

I WISH I COULD SHUT MY MIND the hell up sometimes. Instead, my thoughts refuse to stray far from the couple who came in earlier in the day and the little girl still missing. I gotta know if they've raided the apartment building yet. Has the detective been able to ascertain anything useful? Did they find the girl? During the slower moments of my day, I reach out, trying to sense what's happening, but nothing is certain. I take it as a sign things are more complicated than anyone would like.

In all honesty, if it wasn't about a child, I couldn't care less. But as much as I hate to admit it, there are actually some things in this world that can melt this ice-queen's heart. Even though I've never had any of my own, kids hurt or missing happens to top the list.

After a long day of saying most of the same old bullshit over and over—because, let's face it, most humans aren't all that complicated—Renaldo finally manages to cut off the stream of those wishing for a word.

"I ordered those chains and whips," he grins enthusiastically, as he clicks the deadlock into place. "They'll be in on Thursday."

His perfectly plucked eyebrows wiggle in rhythm with his butt.

I shake my head and smirk. At least he's able to be upbeat.

"Whatever you say. I trust your judgment with all this nonsense," I say, walking back into my reading room. He follows as I grab my previously soaked stocking off the radiator and pull it over my foot. "Thanks for doing it, though. Do you have any plans tonight?"

Renaldo sighs dramatically.

"Oh, I wish. We'll probably be staying in with a bottle of wine and Netflix on the ready. Again. How about you?" he asks, his eyes rolling to the back of his head.

"Absolutely nothing, and it's going to be glorious," I say, exhaling.

"Any news on the little one?" Renaldo asks, his tone edging on serious, as he scrunches his nose and squints nervously in my direction.

I shake my head.

"Nothing yet, but give it time. The police are on it," I say.

"Yeah, 'cause they're so great at finding the bad guys these days," he snickers. "That's gotta be hard for you—knowing bad things are happening or could get worse—and not being able to personally intervene. At least, not without going all vigilante."

Images of Batman flash through my mind.

My eyes widen and my lips purse to cut off a snicker. As much as I say I hate the mundane bullshit most days bring, he's right. I hate knowing when something is really wrong and not being able to step in. Turning it over to the authorities can be one of the most difficult things to do. But then again, I've seen what happens the other way around, too.

"Yeah, it pretty much sucks," I finally admit. Biting my lip, I cast my gaze to the floor.

"Hey, you could become a superhero or something. Can I make a costume? Ooooh, tights. A cape," he says, clapping.

"M'kay, on that note… See you tomorrow, Ren. On-time, this time. Yeah?" I say, quirking a smile.

I catch his gaze, then lower my eyebrows and squint at him, knowing it will make absolutely zero impact.

"You bet, super boss o' mine." He tips his chin, grinning sheepishly.

"Thanks for closing up shop," I say, casting a final wave.

"Oh, wait. That's my job?" he says in mock surprise, fingertips pressing against his chest.

"Goodnight," I call out without another glance back.

I slip out the back door of the small cottage I rent as my place of occupation and take in the aroma of dusk. There's a magic in the air during these twilight hours. This is my favorite time of day. The earth's scent is sweet, and the cool breeze of evening is starting to settle in. It's similar during dawn, but there's something enchanting about the coming of night and the rising of the moon. The beautiful crescent is already peeking through the clouds and acknowledging it makes me smile.

"Waxing phase," I mutter to myself.

Just a week and a half to the full moon.

I like to keep tabs on where the moon phase is. It helps me to orient myself to the cycles of nature. Besides, it's kind of my job as a psychic, I suppose. There are plenty of people who have expectations of such things, as dorky as it might sound. All it takes is one Wiccan to walk in and ask when the best moon phase is for starting a ritual or some damn thing. Besides, there are instances where moon placement truly is crucial.

Already, the energy of the moon pulls on me, but the last

full moon's events seep in, dragging on my already burdened mind. I wish I could release them and be done with it. My body tenses with the anguish tied to the memory of that night. It certainly didn't go as planned.

Mental note—I better check in with Demetri again.

I wish he'd answer my damn calls. We never should have attempted diverting the Violet Flame invocation...

Talk about stupid.

"This is ridiculous, Diana. It's happened—there's nothing you can do now," I whisper.

Taking a deep breath, I press onward.

The walk home is surprisingly enjoyable, despite the cooler, early February air. Could certainly be worse. I could be in one of those godforsaken places where the wind hurts your face and white shit covers the ground this time of year. I've never figured out what would drive a person to live where there's seven months of snow. Who signs up for that willingly?

Shuddering to myself, I pass the neighborhood park where kids are still out and about, squealing as they chase one another. Ordinarily, I would continue to hurry on my way so I can wrap myself in the silence of my living room. But today, I stop and really watch—my eyes scanning the children playing and running about.

Casting my gaze to the tufts of brownish-green grass and puddles, I can't help but see the little girl's face. The family never divulged a photo, but I didn't need it. She's as clear to me as if she were standing beside me. Her bright brown, inquisitive eyes are what haunts me most.

I'll check back in with Detective Radovich when I get home.

Turning on my heel, I pull my sweatshirt a bit tighter. Before I know it, I climb up the front steps to my small, but adorable house. You'd think it was a granny's house from the outside, but I don't care. I love the pink embellishments and ornate ironworks. They remind me of something I can't quite put my finger on. Perhaps it simply reminds me every day the universe is still a mystery on some levels—even to me. Because why else would those two things ever go together?

With my key in hand, I reach for the door, only to have the handle ripped from my grasp. As the intruder flings it open, he pushes me aside with a sweep of his broad arm. I slam hard against the iron railing adorning the front stoop, and pain radiates from the middle of my back, down my left leg. Oddly enough, I get no impression of who he is— nothing about him at all, as I instantly push my abilities out in search of who the hell would be in my damn house without permission.

Nothing. A big fat zilch.

Twisting around, I catch a glimpse of him before he disappears from sight. I might not be able to ID him with my gifts, but I recognize his perfectly shaped ass as it runs away.

It's the same guy from this morning. Clearly, he has a thing for trying to topple me over.

Wow. I'm really off my game.

Either that, or he's deliberately warded from me.

Had I not been so preoccupied with my own thoughts, maybe I would have been able to do something to apprehend the dude. Then again, who expects someone to come bounding out of their house when they live alone?

What in the hell could he possibly have been looking for?

Truthfully, nothing I own would be of any consequence to me if it were stolen—not being allowed to have a true past will do that to you, I suppose. However, the idea someone bothered to break into my house—and not just someone— the same guy who nearly knocked me into the street. Now, that makes me curious.

I push forward, gaining a more solid footing in my entry-way, and try to focus. The guy's scent is familiar, but off somehow—like he's tried to alter it with too much cologne.

Pushing past the empty darkness as I attempt to play in his mind, I start seeing glimpses—flashes of knives—ancient ones with runes or something written along the side, an explosion—blood. Lots and lots of blood. The images are old, like they belong in an ancient memory; blurred and obscured. I take a deep breath, letting the world fall away.

Reaching out with all of my senses, I search the impending darkness as it threatens to consume me for going where I'm not wanted. A moment later, the door to the memories slams shut. My abilities shut down, and I'm left grasping at nothing but air—like every time I try to access my own damn memories. But it's never happened when I try to read someone else's.

Interesting.

I look down the road, trying to get another glimpse of the man—only to find myself dizzy and disoriented. Stumbling inside, I close my door and have a seat on the couch. The exertion it takes to really dig in—it's almost too much at times. Especially when the impressions are blocked.

Once the room stops spinning, I stand up and make my way slowly to the small kitchen. It's barely big enough to open the cupboard doors without smacking into the other side, but I sorta love the coziness of it. I open the refrigerator, clutch the chocolate bar I'd been saving for when I'm PMSing, and rip open the wrapper. I need to get my blood sugar back up and this is as good a way as any. Besides, it has caramel in it, so ya can't beat that.

I take a big bite and edge slowly along, clutching the gray countertop until I can take a seat at the breakfast bar. Before I even settle in, I have another bite of chocolate in my mouth, and my head thumps down onto the cold, hard Formica. Colors roll into one another as my system tries to reset.

After all this time, I still don't understand why some uses of my gifts will drain me this way. While others—the incessant, stupid cupid matches, for example—I could do for hours on end. It's annoying. Someone out there is laughing maniacally knowing they set me up this way.

There was a time when it wouldn't matter that I was helping people with their trivial problems. That was a loooong time ago. But good god almighty, it's getting old dealing with the same old boring questions day in and day out for as long as I have.

I'd give my left boob to finally be able to answer some of my own damn questions for a change. Today, I'd start with who the hell that guy is and why the hell was he in my house.

Then I'd track his sorry ass down and make him buy me a new shoe and fork up the cash for some cranial massage work because, damn, my head is killing me.

I suppose after that, I'd move on to the ones I've been trying to answer my whole known life.

The floorboard behind me squeaks a little too loudly— right as a sunburst flashes through my vision and the darkness consumes it.

Tap, tap, tap…

For some reason, my head lulls to the side as I try to place the sound. It's familiar but doesn't register in my brain. My eyelids are heavy, weighted down by the over-exertion of using my abilities—and something else. My forehead thumps, and I try to reach for it, only to find my arms as heavy as my eyelids.

My eyes flicker open, but I can't keep them that way.

They roll in my head and darkness beckons me in twinkling bursts.

After a few moments, I pry my eyes open again, raising my head to damn near upright.

"Good lord, took you long enough," a man says, from across the room. He's sprawled across my couch, one leg draped over the arm, as he leans back, placing an elbow on the cushion behind him. He has an oddly put-together air about him as his leather jacket falls gently open, revealing his sophisticated style not many straight men know how to pull off.

Arrogance rolls off him in waves. He knows he looks good and he's perfectly comfortable with it. Hell, I don't need to be psychic to pick up on any of that.

The guy drums his fingertips slowly across the single pane window behind him.

Tap, tap, tap…

"Who in the hell are you?" I finally spit out. "And why are you in my house?"

Finally removing his hand from my window, he spins around to face me head-on.

"Now, here I was thinking you should know all those details already," he says, as the corner of his mouth slides into an obnoxious smirk. The trimmed, dark goatee adorning his face accentuates his cheekbones and broad jaw. The deep brown, bordering on black from the top of his head, lacks the flashes of red his facial hair has pulled from his genetics.

I glare back at him.

Who the hell does this guy think he is?

His brown eyes twinkle mischievously, inciting the desire to want to punch him right in his smug little face. Instead, I sit up straighter and fight to keep my head upright.

"I said, who in the hell are you?" I repeat, but more slowly with the hopes he'll actually understand the friggin' question. "You have no idea who you're dealing with."

"Apparently, neither do you." He chuckles, shrugging his shoulders.

He's right. I get absolutely nothing from him. No name, no general motive. Not even the food he ate for lunch or the last time he took a piss.

I tilt my head to the side, trying to clear the fog from my brain.

"I tried to tell them you were likely a fake, but honestly, I didn't know it would be so easy," the man says, his eyebrows furrowed. "Kinda glad, considering the time constraints and all."

"How about speaking in English here, buddy? Because I'm lost," I mutter through clenched teeth.

Despite the complete zilch I'm able to read from him, there's a strange electricity in the room. Almost as though he's blocking me with a feedback loop, or some sort of electromagnetic something or other.

Damn, I really should pay more attention to the new-fangled science terminology.

"I don't need your damn help," he says, standing up from the couch in a single, graceful move. "Especially when you'd be wasting my time and their money."

He flings a manila packet across the room, which lands in my lap, and slowly crosses his arms.

Pressing my hands to the envelope, images of the little girl from this morning suddenly start rolling in—Esther. She's not alone; someone has moved her. Nearby is a false door of some kind; probably the one she was led through. She's not hurt, but I sense plans being made in the room adjacent to hers. She's scared shitless and she knows she's been gone too long. Her parents are going to be so worried... The truth is, she doesn't have much time. They're planning to move her again—sell her to someone who takes children for a living and prostitutes them. The man with the puppies—Brent—he's not the real man the cops should be looking for. He was a patsy, thanks in part to his naive nature.

Now that I'm away from Ted's guilt, I can see that.

There's a small home by the river—it's not one of those fancy new multi-million dollar builds, though. It's a well-kept 1980's style, complete with the original orange shag carpet and olive-green walls.

"Oh my god. She...she's not with the man with the puppies. He was the lure. They're looking in the wrong place," I say without being able to stop myself.

The smug man pulls up short, and for a brief moment, I fight the urge to be the one to smirk.

"What did you say?" he asks, his eyes wide.

"I don't have time for this. I have to get this information to the police," I say, unable to shake the vision of the carpet. There have been many kids who've been kept there over the years. Far too many.

The man rushes to my side, concern sweeping across his features.

"You'd better not be pulling my chain. How would you know all that?" he asks.

"I—I saw it when you threw the packet at me. Esther's in a cabin by the river. I need to get these details to Detective Radovich so we can locate it. She doesn't have much time. There's a man—someone the family's never seen—he's the one who—" I say, pulling up short, blinking back the surprise.

"Don't stop there, what else?" the man says, leaning in.

"Hang on, who are you?" I say. "I don't even know why the hell I'm telling you all of this. You could be part of the whole scheme, for all I know."

I clutch the packet and stand up. Backing away, I hold a hand out as he tries to follow.

"Back the hell off," I warn.

"Okay, okay," he says, holding his hands up, "My name's Blake Wilson. I'm Ted and Lacy Trundle's friend," he says. For a far too long and awkward moment, he holds my gaze.

"Friend? Since when do friends break into people's houses?" I say, narrowing my gaze.

"Well, I'm also a private investigator—"

I cast my gaze to the floor, absently consuming this new information.

"Why on earth are you wasting your time with me, then? Shouldn't you be out there doing your damn job?" I say, anger suddenly welling up.

"As a matter of fact, I am. I needed to know for sure you could be trusted," he says. "You may have convinced Ted with whatever parlor trick you had up your sleeve today, but I can't have someone working with me I can't trust. I needed to know for sure. Hell, I'm still not entirely convinced. You could be spouting off BS, for all I know."

"Trust for what?" I say, pressing the packet to my chest. "As far as I'm concerned, between the two of us, I'm a goddamn saint. I haven't accosted you or broken into your house. Besides, the one you really need to be concerned about is whoever took Esther."

"Ordinarily, I'd say you were right. But before your talk with them today, Ted was convinced you were a charlatan. He was concerned about you impeding the case with some wild goose chase, but Lacy has been hellbent on bringing you in. This is their daughter, we're talking about. Then something changed; whatever you said to him this morning had him confused, but he wanted me to confirm before I brought you in. I don't need some fake psychic screwing up my investigation. I gotta know you are what they say you are. Or what they think you are, anyway. It didn't seem, well until now, like you had anything special," he admits.

"Gee, thanks for your thorough analysis," I say, making a face and flipping him the bird.

"You know what I mean. Every interaction with you has yielded absolutely nothing. You didn't even know I'd come back into the home," Blake says, reaching for his cellphone.

"No offense, but it doesn't always work that way," I say, glaring at him. "Sometimes I actually have to push myself to see things. Other times, they come easy."

I let out a long sigh.

Why in the hell do I feel like I need to defend myself to this arrogant asshat?

"Fine. You'll have to tell me more on the ride," he says, pushing send on his phone.

"What?" I snort.

Holding up a finger, he walks a few steps away, waiting for someone on the other end to pick up. "Yeah, it's me. Might be something to this psychic chick, but we're gonna have to confirm. She thinks we're looking in the wrong place. According to Diana, we're gonna need to refocus the search along the river. I'm bringing her in to go over satellite images now to see if her hunch pans out. Be there in a few."

Blake ends the call and turns back to me.

"Ready to go?"

I fling the manilla packet back at him.

"Since the moment I got home, I've been assaulted by you twice, nearly passed out from using my abilities, not to mention knocked out by you—god, I probably have a lump on my forehead now, thanks by the way—and interrogated like a criminal. I think I need a minute to regroup."

Blake's deep brown eyes widen and his eyebrows tug in.

"I didn't knock you out. You passed out as I walked back in."

"Well, that's a relief," I say, rolling my eyes.

"Look, you said it yourself, we don't have much time. If Esther's with this man at the river, we have to get our asses moving. If things really are going down the way you say they are, then this should be super easy. I'm sure I don't need to tell you the statistics for missing kids and the chances of being found alive, but if I do—"

I hold up a hand. "No need. I'm well aware."

"Well, good. Then you know we need to figure out which house we're dealing with and we need to know now. If you're as real as you claim to be, I need you to come with me so we can corroborate your story."

"Story?" I say, my mouth popping open.

"You know what I mean," Blake says. "We gotta help her."

His eyes plead with mine and I can't help but be a little moved by it. I mean, here's a guy who has only a friendship connection to the family but he's genuinely concerned about finding her in one piece. It's written all over his face.

"Yeah, yeah okay. Let's go," I agree, walking over to him. "Don't get your panties in a bunch."

As soon as I move toward him, dizziness bubbles up, and I reach for the front of my head.

"You okay?" Blake asks. "I swear, I tapped you on the back to get your attention and you passed out. Your head slammed on the kitchen counter. I didn't expect you to pass out like that." He reaches for my arm, hoisting me up and helping me walk along with him.

"Yeah, well, I swear you knocked me out," I say, shaking my head.

"I don't know what kinda man you think I am, Diana, but I don't make a habit of knocking people out when I don't have to," he says snorting.

"Is that so?" I say, crinkling my face, and shaking my head.

Cobwebs and tendrils from passing out threaten to consume what's left of my consciousness.

"Just because I didn't knock you out doesn't mean I wasn't going to take advantage of the situation. There was information I needed, so I set ya on the chair and waited for you to come around," he says, reaching for the front door.

"Smooth. So you're a 'take advantage' kinda guy," I mutter.

"Lady, seriously, you ain't got the first clue about the kinda guy I am. Seems like you can't get a single fix on me at all—which is a bit questionable as a proclaimed psychic don't you think?" he growls.

Clearly, I touched a nerve. But he's also right.

"You know what, let's get moving. The sooner we're there, the sooner I can identify the property, and the sooner Esther can be found," I say.

And the sooner I can get the hell away from you and never have to see your sorry, perfect ass again.

3

*M*AYBE IT WAS STUPID to assume we were heading down to the police station. But that's exactly what I did. What a moron. I blame it on post-ability blackout or something.

We've left the safety of the city I know and love—only to enter a wooded area with winding dirt roads.

"Where in the hell are you taking me?" I ask when I reclaim my bearings.

Blake sighs deeply and shoots me a sideways glance.

"What? It's a reasonable question," I say, not even trying to mask my alarm.

"We're heading back to my place, Diana," he says, keeping his eyes on the road.

My fingertips fly to my forehead and I scratch at my eyebrow. The lump on my forehead itches.

Dammit, my abilities have certainly picked a fine time to go on hiatus. Never—not once have I ever been caught off guard quite so many times. Especially not in one day and sure as hell not by the same damn person. How do normal people go through life like this?

"Why exactly are we going there?" I say, squinting my eyes at him.

"I have all of my specialized equipment back there. If you think we're gonna get the details we need outta the Helena PD, you've sorrily overestimated the intelligence of their detectives. Why do you think I was brought in?" Blake says, a hint of amusement playing at his tone.

He clearly enjoys making me uneasy…as well as flashing his high regard for his own intelligence.

Narcissistic ass.

"You know, you could have been upfront to begin with," I say, my eyes flitting to the passing trees beyond the confines of his Range Rover.

"I coulda," he says, nodding in agreement. "But then again, you never asked."

"Ugh," I groan.

Taking a deep breath, I lean back, pressing hard into the headrest of the seat. More than anything, I want to find the little girl, make sure she's safe, and slide back to my ordinary, everlasting life. Not to mention, get away from this guy.

I take back everything I said about wanting more of a challenge than ordinary people and their mundane requests. I'd take all of it over this, any day.

Could my abilities be totally on the fritz now? Or worse… slipping away after the ritual last month, too?

Would that really be so bad? I mean, after all these years, it might actually be a blessing.

I sit up straighter in my seat, suddenly curious.

"What are you doin'?" Blake asks, his eyes flitting to me.

"What's it to you?" I say, casting a glance of indignation.

Oddly enough, he laughs. "Fair enough. We're almost there. You know, in case you're curious."

"Well, yippee skippy. If we were gonna take much longer I

woulda said there was no point in looking for the girl," I say, far snippier than I originally intended.

Still sitting upright, I close my eyes and focus on Esther.

Can I sense her if I try?

Instantly, flashes inundate my mind—moments of calm before the oncoming storm. She sits alone in a room, playing with a puppy; her insides are coiling with guilt and worry. She knows exactly how much trouble she could be in, but she's still trying to believe it will be okay. The sensations are odd—a juxtaposition of her innocence, and something much more malevolent lingering to the outskirts of her awareness. The man on the other side of the wall has horrible intentions, but she doesn't have the frame of reference for any of it.

Shuddering, I wrap my arms around myself.

Blake pulls the car up to a small Tudor home, partially hidden by the large oaks in his front yard. Light cascades from the oversized windows, illuminating the dormant grass and guiding the way to the front door.

I reach for the car handle, but Blake hits the locks and grabs my left hand, pulling me up short. His hand is warm—bordering on hot—and it makes me shiver in the chill of the cold night.

"Do me a favor. Let me do the talking, okay? You're here to guide us to which house we need to get into," he says, his eyes suddenly serious. Any previous hints of mischievousness fading away.

"No promises."

I'm not sure who the hell's inside he's so afraid I'm gonna talk to, but I hope it's a wife or something. I'd love to watch him squirm after the hell he's put me through today.

I tug my hand from his and exit the Rover. Without a glance back, I walk confidently up the stone steps to the entrance and wait for him to unlock the massive front door.

My strength is returning, and the crisp night air and moonlight continue to do me some good.

Blake walks up a few moments behind and simply pushes open the door—no keys required.

"You may enter," he says, smirking as he swings an arm out.

"Right," I mutter, ushering myself past him.

"Aiden, we're here," Blake calls out, his voice bouncing around the small, empty entryway.

I flit my eyes around. Despite the character and charm of the outside of the home, the inside is sparse.

"Ever think of decorating a bit?" I mutter.

"Why?" Blake says, raising an eyebrow.

A young man, no older than twenty bounds around the corner. His shaggy brown hair reminds me of a sheepdog, the way he has to toss his head to the side to see.

"Heya, Blake. I got all the specs pulled up," he says, grinning from ear to ear. "Ready when you are."

The young man's eyes bounce from Blake, to me, and back to Blake.

"Great," Blake says, walking out of the entryway and down the hall Aiden came from.

Aiden and I stand together in the entryway staring at each other for a long, awkward moment.

"Hi, I'm Aiden," the kid finally says, holding out a hand.

I look down at his outstretched limb and take a second to decide if I want to follow through with the mundane ritual. His blue eyes latch on me expectantly, so I take his hand in return.

"Diana," I say as our hands lock.

Before I can catch a breath, Aiden as a young child floods my consciousness. He's no more than eight himself, playing with a toy robot. In the room with him, adults talk in hushed whispers. They all think he's too young to be alone in this world. His parents are dead and there's no one left to take him. They need to find a solution, poor boy. Through Aiden's memories, I see Blake, without hesitation, offering up himself, his home, as he opens his life to an unexpected single-fatherhood, despite having only been in the special forces for a year and a half.

The vision is ripped from me as Aiden removes his hand.

I step back, surprised. Not only for the insight of Blake and Aiden's interesting dynamic but by the selflessness of Blake's actions. It doesn't jive at all with the man I've met thus far.

Aiden's eyebrows tug in as he watches me curiously.

"Uh, let's head this way," he says, putting his hands behind his back as he walks out after Blake.

Suddenly left alone in the entryway, I take a final glance around, then follow after. By the time I reach the hallway, both men have disappeared, so I follow the sound of their voices to pinpoint their location. Ordinarily, I'd have gotten far more details with my abilities by now. My gifts would have told me how long Blake has been here, why he did what he did for Aiden—hell, how often he brushes his teeth, works out, or has sex. But, just like the starkness of his home, nothing.

Everything is utterly, completely, blissfully, silent.

Even details surrounding Aiden seem to be short-lived and limited.

As I round the corner to where the men's voices are the loudest, I notice an open doorway—the only room adorned with things on the walls. Stopping for a moment to have a better look, I'm abruptly cut off as Blake rushes past me and closes the door right in my face.

"Er—that's private," he says, his eyes shifting from me to the door and back again. "We're this way."

Blake turns my shoulders to square up with the walkway and gently nudges me along.

"What are you hiding back in there?" I ask, curiosity getting the better of me.

"Nothing, it's just—nothing you have to worry about. Has nothing to do with the case," he says.

"Ah, so is it a sex dungeon, or your 'My Little Pony' collection?" I say, smirking.

Blake's left eyebrow quirks upward.

"Wouldn't you like to know?" he says, ushering me into the next room.

"I vote My Little Pony collection," Aiden chimes in.

Blake rolls his eyes.

I stop abruptly, surprised by the sheer amount of technology crammed into the twelve-foot-by-twelve-foot space.

"Wow," I say, my eyes opening wide.

"Yeah, ya see why we don't leave this kinda thing to the cops?" Blake says, the left side of his lips curving upward.

On the wall directly in front of me is a large monitor with a satellite view of the Mississippi River and each of the houses along the route flash brightly. Beside it are three more screens, all operating on their own, searching for something I wouldn't even have the first guess at.

"Okay, Diana, we need you to help us narrow down where along the river you think you're seeing Esther. Was there anything that stood out about the house?" Blake asks, his face serious, and his stance wide. "Right now, we have more than four hundred homes along the shore and there's no way in hell we're knocking door-to-door."

I take a step forward and nod.

"Uh, yeah, actually. It was an older home, but not so old you'd think the creep would be holding a little girl against her will in there. It was blue outside with white shutters—

and had an early eighties vibe inside. Orange shag carpet kinda stuff," I say, remembering back to the vision.

"Good start," Blake says, turning to Aiden.

"On it," Aiden mutters, turning to his keyboard. His fingers fly expertly and within seconds lights along the river go out. Another moment later, five homes load on the monitors in sequence, each showing the front face of a blue home with white shutters.

"Holy shit," I mutter under my breath.

That was fast. Like, blink and you'll miss it kinda fast.

The irony of how similar technology has become to my abilities is not lost on me. A shudder skitters down my spine. Technology creeps the hell outta me.

No wonder some people don't want to believe in psychics.

"Any of these?" Blake asks, intensity rolling off of him in waves as he points to the screens.

I take another step forward, peering at the monitors.

"Yep, that one," I say, raising my arm, and touching the one on the bottom left.

Aiden whimpers, "Please don't touch the screens." He gets up, grabbing a small black cloth, and wipes furiously.

I back away and stifle a small chuckle.

"You sure?" Blake says, his dark eyes monitoring my every movement.

"Dead sure," I say, returning his intensity.

Blake turns on his heel and heads out the door. "Stay here with Aiden," he calls out over his shoulder.

"Uh, what? Like hell I am," I say, rushing after him. "I'm coming with you."

Near the front door, Blake stops dead and squares up with me. "What kind of training do you have?"

His eyes are deep, dark pools of serious desperation. There's something hidden there—something buried deep and separate from this case. If my abilities were working with him I'd know instantly what he was trying to hide.

I blink back in surprise, "I, uh…"

"That's what I thought. Stay here and leave this to me. You've done your bit, assuming you're telling the truth. Aiden's already calling in backup. The last thing I need is you getting in the way—or worse, getting yourself into trouble. I'll have enough to worry about going in."

Suddenly, my brain kicks back in.

Who the hell does he think he is?

I'm freaking Diana Hawthorne.

I'm not some pretty face incapable of handling myself. I've seen more than this man will ever witness in all his years —and then some.

"Look, Blake, I may not have any specialized training I'm assuming you've undergone, but I've assisted on over a dozen cases in the past two years alone. All of them ended up with good results because I was with them. I don't need you to save me, or worry about me. I can handle myself. But Esther—I can help you locate her. I've seen where she's playing—where he's hiding her," I say, grabbing his arm. "What if you get there and it's not obvious? And I'm sure as hell you don't have a warrant to search the premises— unless you happen to have a cop in your back pocket. I can get the dude to invite us in and never even know what hit him."

Blake looks down at my white-knuckled grasp clutched across his forearm and sighs. "You're not gonna take no for an answer, are you?"

"Nope," I say, jutting out my chin.

"Fine," he concedes. "You can come with but you'll stay in the Rover until I need you. Got it?"

"Whatever you say." I grin, nodding and holding my hands up.

"Change of plans Aiden. She's coming with," Blake calls out as he opens the front door.

His eyes flit back to me and concern creeps across his features.

In the distance, Aiden calls back, "Got it."

Grinning, I march out the door and head back to the front seat of the Range Rover.

Blake slides in the driver's seat, turning the vehicle on, and plugging coordinates into his in-dash GPS. Within seconds, the vehicle is in motion—swerving along the curvy drive with ease. His focus reminds me of my own.

The confusion from earlier is waning and my senses heighten, as they always do when I'm helping with a case. Of course, I'll probably sleep for days after we're done—but it will be worth it if we can find the little girl before anything truly bad happens.

I can't imagine the kind of hell she'd have to deal with if we fail.

Turning to Blake, I whisper, "Who was it?"

"Excuse me?" he says, not taking his eyes off the road.

I watch his every move, trying to figure him out. It's curious—I've never had to read someone solely based on body language before. It's an interesting, almost refreshing twist.

He shifts in his seat.

"Who did you lose?" I ask.

Even though I got the details about Aiden's parents, I'm not certain that's the entirety of it.

Blake snorts. "What makes you think I lost anyone?"

He shoots me a sideways glance, but again his perfect little ass shifts in the seat.

"Hmmm," I mutter.

"Hmmm? What's hmmm?"

I shrug, casting my gaze out to the road in front of us.

Trees fly by far faster than they should, as he presses the limit on how quickly we should maneuver the bends.

"You're an odd one for me." I finally admit. "On one hand, I can't get a read on you. But on another, I get these impressions. Just calculated guesses really because they're not based on my insights—or gifts. Whatever you want to call it. Christ, is this how you have to go through your life? Watching for patterns and making guesses, hoping they'll pay off?"

"Huh, never thought of it that way before," he says.

"It's excruciating," I whisper.

"C'mon. You're telling me you've never had to make a calculated guess before?" he snorts. "I'm sure even self-proclaimed psychics have their moments."

I shake my head, letting the snide remark slide.

"No—never for the things that mattered. I've always been able to see the past, present, and future accurately."

Well, okay, that's a lie.

The only other blind spot has been my past, but we won't get into that.

"Never? Then why would I be so different?" he asks, glancing at me.

"No idea. To be honest, it's kinda annoying. I don't know if it's me—if my abilities are on the fritz, or if it's you. Just you. You know? Have you warded yourself?" I ask.

He throws a glance in my direction and snickers. "Like, with witchcraft and stuff?"

"Sure, if you wanna be an ass about it," I say, throwing my hands up in exasperation.

"Well, c'mon. Wards? Are you even using English?"

"It means using something to protect yourself from being read. Well, in the reference I'm using it, anyway. You can call it magic or witchcraft if you want. It's another form of energy work," I say, biting my lip.

"Nope. No warding happening here. Just me, in all my ordinary glory," he chuckles.

"So weird," I mutter, shaking my head.

"Well, so far, supposedly you've been able to see other stuff pretty well, right? Until it happens more frequently—don't worry. I'd consider it an isolated incident. Then again, that's just me," he shrugs.

The Rover swerves to the left and I have to put my hand out to avoid smacking into the door.

"Nearly there," Blake says, more for himself than me. Even without the GPS dictating our course, I can sense we're getting closer.

Such a weird sensation—it's a tingling playing at the back of my neck, like someone's there, breathing against my skin.

Perhaps Blake's right. Maybe it's a completely isolated event. It seems that way so far, at any rate.

All I know is, when this is all over, I'll need to do some heavy-duty chakra clearing.

A couple of blocks away from the eighties-style house—or maybe it's a cabin, Blake slows the vehicle down to a normal speed. His facial expressions flit back and forth, as he works out exactly how to go about things, I assume. I watch him, enthralled despite myself. Ordinarily, in this close proximity, I'd be hearing snippets of everything, the whole damn plan. Unless, of course, I specifically warded my own mind from the barrage.

Finally, he parks the car in the driveway and cuts the lights.

"You sure this's the place?" he asks, turning back to me.

In the light of the waxing moon, the house stands nearly silent. Only a single sign of life inside is evident; the television set in the living room as it flickers with the commotion of whatever the man's watching. He's on the edge of drifting off to sleep; cheap whiskey the culprit at this early hour. My eyes flit to the clock on the dash. It's just barely gone 9:00 p.m.

I nod, taking a deep breath.

"All right, stay here. Trust me, I've got this covered," Blake says. "It's not my first rodeo."

Before he can exit the Rover, glimpses of the Esther asleep inside the cabin flood in. She's clutching a tattered teddy bear—it's not hers, but it reminds her of home. The puppy is curled up beside her. The space is tiny but the sound of the TV creeps into the small enclosure in muffled bursts.

"Blake," I call out before the door closes.

"Yeah?" he says, twisting to look inside the vehicle.

"She's in there—in a small room. Maybe a closet?"

His lips press into a thin line, and he nods. "She's okay, though. Right? Alive?"

I nod.

With a tip of his head, Blake closes the door and saunters up to the front entry. Despite myself, I'm mesmerized by his walk.

Damn, those jeans definitely suit him.

I run my hands over my face and close my eyes.

Get a grip, Diana. This is the same jerk who pushed you into the puddle and stormed your house.

Blake knocks on the door, and after a moment, a light flicks on in the entryway. A second or two later, an older man—nearly seventy by the looks of it—opens the door. His grey hair is matted against his forehead, and he looks as though he hasn't changed his dirty grey shirt in days.

The man's got a gun stashed nearby and isn't too keen on strangers. Especially ones who knock on his door as night is falling. Especially pickup nights.

Reaching for the handle of the Rover, I pull up short. Something must have been said to appease the man's initial skepticism because he opens the door wider and lets Blake inside. He doesn't look back my way at all, just waltzes straight in.

The moment the front door is closed, mine is open, and I'm on my feet.

I don't care how much this Blake guy thinks he has this under control—I'm not about to sit this one out. A little girl's life depends on it.

4

OLLOWING MY INTERNAL GUIDANCE, I creep from the Range Rover to the back of the house. With Blake occupying the creep inside, I should be able to slip in and out with Esther relatively easily. In fact, I'd wager it'll be done way faster than Blake trying to fumble around in whatever manhandling kinda way he's used to.

Thanks to Blake's stunt earlier with his own front door, I check the handle on the back door of the house, finding it unlocked. Images of sleeping children with pillowcases placed over their heads barrage my mind, but I push past them and shut their assault down. There will be time to deal, and make this monster suffer. Just...*not yet.*

Holding my breath, I slip quietly inside.

After all of these years, one thing I've learned to do well is sneak about unnoticed. Call it another one of my gifts, if you want.

The stench of alcohol and decomposing food assaults my senses as I enter the kitchen. Certainly a stark contrast to the outside appearance. Pieces of the laminated floor are missing, and others are peeling up in large chunks. It doesn't look as though anything has been cleaned for years. Beyond the grungy kitchen, Blake and the man are discussing something in hushed voices.

I try to reach out, to get a better idea of his plan, as well as try to anticipate their next movements. Unfortunately, whatever block I have with Blake influences everything going on in the other room.

Talk about inconvenient.

Training my ears in their direction, my eyes flit from wall to wall as I search for the hidden doorway I saw in my vision. Rather than focusing on the men, I take a moment, training my senses on Esther—using her like a homing beacon; telling me whether or not I'm getting close.

I close my eyes and broaden my awareness so it blankets the house, searching each crevice and corner. It settles on the wall in the main hallway, separating the living room from the rest of the house with a large staircase. She's under the stairs. Of course, he's kept her close.

I tiptoe closer, scanning the wall on this side of the hallway for the hidden doorway but it's no use. I'm pretty sure it's on the other side—where, of course, the men are.

"There are a lot of crazies out this way, to be sure," Blake's voice filters to my ears. "Glad to hear you're staying safe."

"Yeah, I dunno about none o' that, but I 'preciate ya stomping—er, stopping in," the man says, his words garbled and slurred.

A small scuffle shudders through the hall as someone gets out of a chair in the other room.

"Mind if I use your bathroom quick? Gotta take a piss," Blake says.

I take a step closer. If the man shows him where the bathroom is, maybe—just maybe—I'll have access to the living room long enough to get Esther out.

"Do what ya gotta do. S'down the hall on the left," the man mumbles.

"Thanks," Blake says.

Before I have time to back away and hide, Blake turns the corner and nearly topples over me. His brown eyes blaze into mine.

"What in the fuck are you doing here?" he whispers through gritted teeth.

My eyes widen, but I don't say a word. All I can think to do is grin wildly and shrug.

Without another word, he grabs me by the scruff of my jacket and hauls me with him to the bathroom, and closes the door.

"I don't want to be in here when you're peeing," I say, grossed out.

"Are you trying to fuck this whole thing up?" Blake whispers furiously, his hands flying to the top of his head.

"Excuse me? You're the one chatting him up. What the hell are you doing to get Esther out?" I spit back.

"I've been waiting for the drug I slipped into his drink to kick in, dumbass," he says, throwing his hands up in exasperation.

I scrunch my face up, "Well…oh. What about backup? When are they supposed to arrive?"

Blake's hands fly up, looking as though he's about ready to strangle me—but he regains his composure and grits his teeth instead.

"Your nostrils are flaring," I mutter, pointing at his reddening face.

"Seriously, are you always this dense? I'm a private investigator. There *is no backup.*"

I scrunch my face, "But you said—"

"You were on my case. I wanted you to stay behind. Good

god, it's like dealing with a damn child." He runs a broad hand over his face.

"Normally I have a better read on what's going on. You're a freakin' blind spot, remember? I'm not used to handling that kinda thing," I whisper, enunciating each word with a stronger start than necessary.

"Well get a freakin' grip. You're about to screw this whole thing up," he says, pursing his lips.

I roll my eyes. "Please. Do you have any idea where he's keeping Esther? Or have you been too busy drinking it up with the bad guy?"

"Just a hunch, but under the stairs," he says without hesitation.

I flinch and try to recover as quickly as possible.

Figures he'd know without my help. Maybe he was right. Maybe he didn't need me for this.

"Yeah, but how do you get in?" I say, scrunching my face.

"Pretty sure there's a door somewhere," he says, raising an all-knowing eyebrow.

"Well, if you know everything, why did you even need me?" I mutter.

"As I recall, I didn't. You chose to come—and you promised to stay put unless I needed you," he says pointing out the obvious.

A loud rap on the other side of the door makes us both jump.

"E'rything okay in there?" the man of the house asks.

Blake places a hand firmly across my mouth and opens his brown eyes wide. His nostrils flare as he presses his lips into a thin line.

"Yeah, sorry. Takin' a little longer than I thought," he mutters.

"Somebody in there wit ya? Thought I heard talking."

"No, just me. I, er...was watching a YouTube clip on my phone," Blake answers back.

"Thar's magazines next to da pot."

We both look toward the toilet. Sure enough, a stack of magazines rests in various states of decay. Mostly old Penthouse issues, with a couple of Guns & Ammo thrown in for good measure.

I shudder.

Gross.

"So there is. Thanks," Blake says, casting me a sideways glance.

"You bet," the man slurs.

We stand absolutely still, listening to the sound of footsteps dragging their way back to the living room.

"Listen to me and listen closely. I want to you leave through whatever doorway, window, or crevasse you crawled in through, and get your ass back to the Rover. I want to get away clean, and without complication. I can't do that unless you're back where you're supposed to be," Blake says, grabbing hold of my arms. "Do you understand me?"

I lower my eyebrows and cock my head to the side. "Listen up, Blake. I don't know who you're used to dealing with, but I'm not your date and I'm not your employee. I'll do what I want, as long as it's what makes sense to me. Got it?"

The door to the bathroom slams open, making us both jump back. The man points a shotgun in our direction, his face scrunched like he ate a crate full of lemons.

Still clutched to my arms, Blake takes a step forward and shoves me behind him.

"Knew yer were lyin'. Who's da broad? What she doin' here?" the man says, swaying in the doorway. His eyes blink slowly, trying to stay focused and alert. His trigger finger rests precariously on the trigger—not to the side as I wish it would. Even I know better. All it would take is one drunken swagger and he'll set off the gun.

"Uh—sorry. My girlfriend was scared to come in. I let her in through the back door so she could use the restroom. Thought I'd try to sneak in a little risky sex before we headed out." Blake leans toward the man and whispers loud enough for both of us to hear, "Gets her hot, if you know what I mean?"

The man visibly relaxes a bit. After a moment, he tips the gun up and rests it on his shoulder.

Blake might not be psychic, but he certainly knows how to read people in his own way. Somehow, he knew exactly how to disarm him without ever raising a hand.

I exhale my held breath and allow my shoulders to relax slightly.

"Eh, likes the risky stuff, huh? Feel like sharing?"

The momentary relief washes away as terror replaces it.

Blake remains calm, keeping his tone cool as a cucumber as he says, "Nah, thanks, man. I gave her what she needed."

"If ya change yer mind, I wouldn't mind a piece," the man says, twisting to get a better view of me.

"Like hell," I blurt out. My hand flies to my mouth as soon as I realize what I've said.

The man's face turns sour again, and he braces himself on the door frame.

"Say tha' again," he demands.

Blake turns around, his eyes wide. He mouths to me, *'Keep your trap shut.'*

"What she means is," Blake counters, "she knows who her keeper is."

The man eyes Blake, then glances at me.

"Think it's best you two get yerselves gone."

Blake nods. "Yeah, think you're right. Sorry to be a bother."

He takes me by the hand, marching me through the house and to the front door. The man stumbles behind us, the shotgun still firmly clutched in his hand. Opening the door, Blake shoves me out into the porch and turns around.

Without hesitation, I keep walking to the Rover. I might be headstrong, but I sure as hell ain't stupid.

How the hell are we going to get Esther out now?

There's no chance the man's going to let us back in after all this.

I watch from the seat, wondering what Blake could possibly have to say to the man at this point.

A moment later, Blake takes a step onto the porch but turns back to the man—firmly swiping his elbow upside the man's head. Almost in slow motion, the man drops like a marionette whose strings have been cut.

Kicking the car door open, I rush up the stairs.

"What the?" I say, my voice higher pitched than it should be.

Blake turns back to me and shrugs. "Damn drug was taking too long to kick in."

"Holy shit, is he okay?"

Blake releases an absurd chuckle as he turns to me. "Does it really matter at this point?"

I glance down at the old man sprawled out on the orange shag carpet. He's actually not as old as I suspected originally. Without the panic of being shot lingering over me, I realize he's only in his mid-forties—fifties, tops. But all the years of alcohol abuse hasn't been kind to him.

"Not so much," I say, shaking my head.

"Good, then help me find Esther, and let's get the hell outta here," Blake says, rushing to the closet under the stairs.

"Shouldn't we—I don't know—tie him up or something?" I ask, pointing at the man's sprawled-out body on the floor.

"Nah, it will take hours for it to wear off. By then, he'll be locked up good and safe in his very own cell," Blake says, rushing to the closet door at the back of the stairs.

I take a final glance at the crumpled body of a wasted life.

How does anyone ever get to this point? Alcohol, drugs, sex addictions, money problems. Human beings can be so easily warped and twisted.

I don't know where to put the sorrow welling up. Not necessarily for the man, but for innocence lost. If I know anything about people, it's they don't start out this way. *They're made.*

"What the hell? There's nothing here. It's just a coat closet," Blake calls back, an air of panic playing at the edges of his rough exterior.

Shaking my head, I walk to the door frame and have a look inside. He's right. There's nothing. Flinging apart the drabs of old coats, flannel shirts, and overalls, I trace the back wall. There's no door—no buttons.

"Step aside," I say, pushing past Blake and heading back to the man.

"So help me, Diana…if I knocked out some poor old drunk dude for no reason—" Blake warns.

"It's him. I know it is. She's here."

Walking over to the man, I lean down and place my right hand over his.

"What are you doing?"

"Shhhh. Give me a minute," I tell him, as I close my eyes.

My mind is flooded with garbled images; thoughts and memories are all mashed together in a strange conglomeration of near incoherence. Dark holes, swimming doorways, a necklace swinging around his fingertips with something dangling at the end, laughter, and more drinks.

"Dammit," I mutter, standing up and having a look around the room. I walk to the other end of the room to get a different vantage point.

There has to be something here. Something to clue me in.

"What's going on?" Blake asks, following me. "Diana, talk to me. Where is Esther?"

"I don't know, Blake. I'm trying to read the room. Can you shut up and give me a minute, please?" I say, casting a back-the-eff-off glance his direction.

"Unbelievable. I knew it…" he says, walking away and reaching for his cellphone.

With him out of the room, colors, sensations, and impressions clear up. I home in on the ones related to Esther—because I can sense her here. Now and before. The echoes and impressions of when she first arrived are muddled with the excitement she was feeling about getting to finally cuddle the puppy she'd been promised. Yet, she also knew something wasn't quite right. She didn't like the smell of the house or the stench of the man's breath, and she knew she was too far and her parents were gonna freak.

All of my instincts and impressions are screaming she's close by—only the path to her is hard to see.

"Blake, can you step outside?" I call out.

He steps back in the room, covering the voice end of his cellphone, and makes a face. "Excuse me?"

"I need to get a clear read and you're getting in the way."

"Oh, so now this is my fault," he says, rolling his eyes. "Yeah, sure. I'll step outside while I'm trying to find a way to clean this mess up."

"Super," I say sharply.

As soon as he leaves the house, the back end of the room lights up like a Christmas tree. Red and green light surround the grungy back wall of the living room.

Standing up, I walk to the main entrance to the living room—the one leading to the stairs and the hallway, then back around to the closet and second entry on the other side.

There's way more space beneath the stairs than the

tiny closet uses. I place my hands along the walls and close my eyes. Esther suddenly floods my mind as she slams on the other side of the wall. It's mildly sound-proofed—but I can still hear her trying to get the attention of anyone on the other end. Pulling back, I search for how she got in there. Remnants of energy used to bring us to the here and now.

With my eyes closed, I continue to walk along, hands on the walls, until my palms abruptly burn. Flashes of the old tongue and groove wood wall shifting aside slides into my mind and I open my eyes. I'm back in the living room, back to the grungy wall where I started.

I search for a trigger—something that allows the wall to pop out or slide back. The man isn't that sophisticated, so it has to be something simple, something in plain—

A small knot in the wood has been cleaned out, revealing a simple, but open hole. It could be so easily missed or dismissed. Placing my right index finger inside, I grip the wood and pull. The facade easily pops off the wall and I nearly lose my balance as it lands on top of my feet. Throwing it to the side, I drop to my knees. Beneath the fake facade, set back half a foot or so, is a small insulated door, barely four feet tall.

Tugging on the handle, it doesn't budge.

"Shit. Of course, it's locked," I mutter under my breath.

Luckily for those incoherent images from earlier—I know exactly where the key is.

Scrambling to my feet, I rush over to the man sprawled out on the shag carpet. Dropping to my knees, I push him over so he's on his back.

"What the hell are you doing now?" Blake says, walking back into the house. His eyes are wide with surprise and he steps forward with his hands splayed open.

"Shut up and go take a look at the wall. She's in there. I

need to find the key," I say, mentally preparing myself to search the man for the necklace with the key.

Taking a deep breath, I thrust my hand under his shirt in search of the necklace. Nothing's there but an overly hairy chest.

Flashes of him twirling the necklace and shoving it in his pocket come to mind. I shudder, pulling my hand back.

"Ugh, you've gotta be kidding me."

"Christ, how'd you find this?" Blake says from the living room.

"How the hell do you think? Psychic, remember? Just because you don't believe it, doesn't make it less so."Taking a deep breath, I plunge my hand into the man's right pocket and pull out the key.

Blake's jaw drops open, but thankfully he doesn't say another stupid statement. Instead, he backs away and makes space for me as I scramble back over to the little doorway.

Placing the key inside, the satisfying click of the lock pulling back is like nothing I've ever heard. I yank the door open and inside, Esther falls back on her butt, tears streaming from her red face. With her inside is the little puppy that lured her here, a small cloth for a blanket, and the ugly orange shag carpet.

"C'mon, let's get you outta here," I tell her, extending my arms to her.

Esther's eyes widen, and she clutches the puppy to her body.

"It's okay, Esther. We gotta go," I urge.

She shakes her head. "Where's my mom?"

Blake pulls me back, taking my place.

"Hey, sweetie. Do you remember me? My name's Blake and your mom and dad are both very worried. They've sent us here to come get you. Will you come with us?" His voice is low and soft—the kind of tone I suspect a good dad uses when they're trying to get their kid to bed.

"Mom's gonna be so mad at me," Esther says, fresh tears streaming from her eyes.

Blake shakes his head. "Nobody's mad. We all want to see you get home safe and sound. Will you come with us?"

He offers his arm out to her and she nods. "Okay, but can I keep the puppy?"

"Sure, Esther. Bring her along, too." He nods, pulling both of them in close.

"It's a boy. See?" Esther lifts the puppy by its front paws revealing its gender.

"So it is." Blake chuckles. "C'mon, let's go."

Blake takes a step back, helping Esther out of the little room.

"Where the hell ya'll think yer going with her? She's mine, ya hear," the man slurs from the floor.

5

E BOTH SPIN AROUND surprised to see the man of the house rousing and reaching again for his shotgun. His gestures are slow, and sluggish as he struggles to get to his knees.

"Told you we should have tied him up," I blurt out, my voice nearly a screech.

Esther screams and flings herself back inside the little room.

Blake pushes past me, rushing forward, and kicking the shotgun out of the man's reach. He follows the movement immediately by landing his steel-toed boot squarely upside the man's head. For the second time tonight, he slumps to the floor.

"Oh my god, tie the man up, would you?" I say, my eyes blazing into Blake's before turning back to Esther. "It's okay, sweetie. It's safe now."

Reaching for my hand, hers shake as she bends down and exits the small enclosure. Her eyes widen at the sight of her captor on the floor, and she hugs the puppy tighter—who in turn squeals and tries to break free from her grasp.

Without a word, Blake sets to work, hoisting the man up into a small armchair, and tying him up with whatever ropes and cords he finds available. He secures him expertly, tying knots I haven't seen in years.

"Boy Scout, were ya?" I say, pulling Esther close, unable to take my eyes off him.

"Something like that," Blake mutters, not breaking his focus.

When he's satisfied with his handiwork, he finally pushes up to a stand and lets out a sigh of contentment.

For a moment, his dark brown eyes lock with mine. Something plays at their creases but it's more than simply relief. Curiosity, maybe? Borderline appreciation? All of it? In those brief seconds, I wish like hell I knew what was going on in his mind. What I wouldn't give to know what he was actually thinking.

Such a strange sensation, when your whole life, you've never not known the ins and outs of someone else's mind. Hell, half the time I understand most people better than they know themselves. Makes for awkward, and usually irritating romantic entanglements, that's for sure.

Blake pulls out his cellphone again and points to the front door. "Diana, can you get Esther out to the Rover? I'm gonna call this in to the authorities so they can come collect this monster," he says, turning his gaze back to the man. If looks could kill, I'm pretty sure the man's limp body was blazing in the seventh circle of hell for the eleventh time.

Turning to Esther, I wrap my arm around her shoulders and usher her past Blake and her captor and toward the front door. Her little body tucks easily beside my own, as she continues to quake from the bizarre experience she's just lived through. Her feelings begin to emerge—muddied at first, but clearer the further from Blake we are.

She's afraid of how her parents are going to react when

they find out what she did. But at the same time, she's so happy to be out of the scary closet and happy she's still got her puppy. Her mind plays at other memories—ones she doesn't want to rehash but still flash through her. Groping hands and violent slurs...

"Come on, Esther. Let's get you home," I say, more than a little appreciative that we were able to save her from any more darkness.

I open the back door to the black Range Rover and she slides inside.

"Do you need help with your seatbelt?" I ask, reaching for the buckle.

She instantly scoffs and makes a face. "I'm not four," she says, reaching for the belt and aptly clicking it into place.

"Right," I say, nodding to myself.

Clearly, my years of avoiding most human contact have left me pretty clueless on the capabilities of an eight-year-old, compared to those younger.

As I close the door, headlights flash in the distance and I instantly get the impression of two men coming to collect the girl. They're talking about how pleased their boss will be because they've been trying to move on her for ages.

A shiver creeps down my spine and I immediately race back to the house. "Blake—Blake, we have to leave," I say, clutching the arm of his leather jacket and tugging him toward the door, "—now."

"Diana—I'm on a call with the PD. What in the hell are you—?"

"See those headlights?" I say, pointing to the distance. "They're significantly closer and if we don't leave now, we're gonna have a hell of a lot more trouble on our hands."

"Yeah, so?" he says, shaking his head.

"They're here for Esther," I say, yanking him out the door. "Hang up the phone and let's GO."

Blake doesn't second guess me, *thank god*. He crams the cellphone into his coat pocket and we race together back to the Rover. As we slide into our seats, Blake starts up the vehicle in record time. The nondescript van pulls up beside us as we screech into reverse.

It takes a moment for the new arrivals to realize what's happening. As we hit the street, Blake spins the Rover around —slamming both myself and Esther against our doors as he makes his getaway. Shots are fired and flare off the backend of the vehicle. One bullet hits its target, shattering the back windshield into thousands of pieces.

Esther's high pitch screams flood the vehicle, as she grabs her head and tucks down. The puppy jumps at the opportunity to get free and scrambles off her lap to cower in the footwell.

"Stay down," I say to her, reaching around and holding her hand.

She grabs on tight but does as she's told.

"Hang on," Blake says again, turning a corner faster than he should. Up ahead, flashing lights can be seen, and Blake noticeably relaxes. "About goddamn time. Christ, what would we do if we really needed them? It's been nearly five minutes since my damn call."

He drops his speed to a more manageable level and eases back into his seat.

"Are you going to flag them? Let them know it's us?" I ask.

"Hell no." Blake snickers. "They have bigger fish to fry."

"What about Esther?"

"We'll get her back to her parents. From there, we'll let Ted and Lacy decide what happens next," he says, releasing a sigh.

Blake takes a moment to call Ted and Lacy, filling them in that we're on our way, and asking them to call the police to meet us.

I look back at Esther. She hasn't moved since the glass shattered, but her left hand has begun to search for the puppy's fur to stroke.

"How are you holding up, Esther? I'm sure this has to be quite the night for you," I say, trying to put on an air of indifference. I mean, honestly, do we need to freak her out any more than she already is?

Her huge eyes meet mine, but she doesn't respond.

"How are *you* doing?" I ask, turning to Blake.

His hands are firmly gripped around the steering wheel, but the hyper-focus he had going on is starting to dissipate.

"I'll be feeling a helluva lot better once those assho—sorry—*jerks* are apprehended," he says, looking over his shoulder at the little girl.

"Me too. Do you think they have them yet?" I ask.

"Sure as hell hope so. I mean, we practically handed them all over on a silver platter," Blake says, turning left toward town. The city lights begin to emerge and even I can't help but relax a little bit.

I release Esther's hand and she picks up the puppy and clutches him close again. Twisting around in my seat, I look out the front windshield and let my gaze soften. The passing lights begin to blur as my own body and senses begin to come back down from their heightened use.

"Hope so, too," I mutter.

"What about you?" Blake asks.

I twist around to him. "What about me?"

"Are you okay?" he says, giving me a side eye.

"Yeah, I'm okay. A bit drained now."

"Well, good work back there," he says, shrugging his right shoulder.

I turn for a second time to look at him. "Did you just give me a compliment?"

He shrugs again.

"I give credit where credit is due," he says.

"Wow. Well, thanks, I guess," I say, rolling my eyes. Despite myself, I can't help but crack a smile.

"No, seriously. I don't know how you found that secret door, but I'm glad you did."

"You know how I found her. You just don't believe it's possible."

We enter the full throes of the city, and I can't help but wonder how things will change for Esther. What will Ted and Lacy do to keep her safe now? Will they go overboard and be overprotective? Or will they carry on with life as normal now that she's back?

"It's not that I don't believe, per se. It's just—I find it highly improbable. Not to mention, a bit freaky," he says, throwing me a sideways glance.

"Freaky? Why? Do you have things to hide Blake?" I say, raising an eyebrow.

"Don't we all?" he snorts.

I lean back in my seat. "Yeah, I guess."

"If you're for real, doesn't it get, I don't know—weird or something? I mean, knowing things all the time, or whatever. How does it work, anyway?"

I open my mouth to respond, but Esther leans forward and points to a house. "That one's mine," she says.

"Yup. Been here before," Blake says, winking over his shoulder as he maneuvers to Esther's driveway.

For a moment, none of us move. We sorta sit in the knowing we're out of harm's way and we did a good thing tonight. Behind us, the puppy yips.

"What are you going to name her?" I ask.

"Him. It's a him, remember?" Esther says.

I bite my lip and make a face. "Oh, right. Him."

"I don't know yet. I was thinking maybe Fluffy. Or Spot," she says.

"Way to get creative, kid." I chuckle.

Before we have time to open our car doors, Lacy throws open the front door and races down the steps of their small two-story rambler. Ted follows close behind.

Without hesitation, Esther opens the back door of the Range Rover and drops into their open arms. Fluffy, or Spot, or whatever she's gonna call the dog, because you know damn well they're gonna let her keep him now, is squished between them. Both Blake and I follow but stand further back so the family can focus on Esther.

Lacy wraps her arms around Esther, sobbing uncontrollably. Ted drops to his knees beside them.

A squad car pulls up, its lights flashing, but siren turned off. Two officers step out, walking directly toward us. After what feels like forever filling them in—they're finally satisfied enough to let us be on our way.

"Ted, Lacy—we're gonna let the three of you get settled for the night. I'll be back in touch with you tomorrow to discuss everything. I'm sure the police will want to follow up and talk with you more tonight, anyway," Blake says. "Sounds like they plan on keeping at least one officer here for the night, too."

Ted turns to the two of us and walks over. "Blake, Diana. I don't know how to thank you enough. We would never have found her this quickly—*or at all*—if it wasn't for you."

He holds his hand out in appreciation. Blake takes it first, shaking his hand vigorously and patting his shoulder.

"Don't mention it. We're just glad she's home," Blake says.

Ted turns to me and I fight the urge to leave his hand there. I quickly reach out, shaking it as well, and trying to avoid the feedback it might invoke. Instead, I get snippets of relief and joy—mixed with gratitude for having Aiden in his college English course. It's how he and Blake became friends.

"Glad things turned out the way they did," I admit.

"Yeah, makes two of us," Blake agrees.

Walking around the front of the vehicle, he opens his door. For a moment, he hovers there, one hand resting against the frame. Curiosity plays at my mind as I watch his eyes lingering on the front room window, half grinning to himself.

Why do I suddenly wish my gifts were working on him? My whole known life I've wished I could shut it off, but now...

"Ready?" I say, breaking the line of thought.

"Yeah." He nods, taking a seat.

I open my door and slide inside. This whole day has been a weird juxtaposition of discombobulating circumstances since the moment I ran into Blake—*literally*. Not only did I start off on the wrong foot, but I've gone through a more unusual day than I can ever remember having. In part, thanks to him.

"You did a good thing," I say, turning my gaze back to the passing street lamps as he heads out.

"No," he says, shaking his head, "*we* did a good thing. As much as it pains me to admit it, there might be something to your psychic abilities."

"Oooh, is the skeptic turning?" I chuckle.

He raises a hand. "No, I wouldn't go quite that far...but I'm not willing to completely dismiss it yet, either."

"I feel so special," I say, bringing my fists together and placing them beneath my chin.

"You know what I mean. If you were in my position, would you believe you?"

I lean forward, considering.

Part of me would love to say hell yes, I'd believe me. Then again, I can't trust most people on their best days, let alone if they were talking about something completely out of the box. Most people are lying, obnoxiously self-centered jerks.

"I see your point," I admit.

"It would be negligence to simply believe in something without proof. It's my job to question everything. I've found sometimes the smallest, most insignificant details can lead to the path of discovery. For myself. For my clients," he says.

"I take it you're not a god-fearing kinda man, then." I chuckle.

"What makes you say that?" he asks, his eyebrows tugging in as he turns in my direction.

My mouth drops open slightly, and I scratch the top of my head. "Your skepticism I guess. What you said about believing something without proof," I say. "Am I wrong? Guess it wouldn't be the first time today."

"Yes and no." he admits.

"You confuse me."

"I take it you don't easily confuse?" Blake turns the Rover down my street, and instinctively, I place my hand on the handle of the door.

I chuckle. It's like a weird ritual of round-robin. Tit for tat.

"What makes you say that," I say, playing the part.

"Well, if you are what you say—then confusion probably doesn't land squarely in your court a whole lot. Then again, you could be really good at educated guesses." He shrugs.

"The world may never know." I shoot him a mischievous grin.

Blake pulls the vehicle into my single car driveway and I automatically open the door as we come to a stop.

"Well, Blake, I wish I could say it was nice to meet you... but it's been an odd day at best. Good luck getting the back windshield fixed. Thanks for the ride home."

Before he can say anything, I close the door and cross the front lawn. I'm halfway up the front steps when I'm pulled up short.

"Hey—I, uh—have a good night," Blake says, as I turn around. "I appreciate your help."

"You said that already," I say, my eyebrow quirking.

"Did I? Oh, well, in that case... Night," he says, stepping back and waving awkwardly goodbye.

I stand on my front steps, watching him turn around and walk away. Even at this late hour—even after getting to know him a tiny bit—he still has a great ass.

I sigh to myself and turn to the front door. With my keys in hand, the lock clicks open, and I walk inside; closing the door behind me.

I'm not sure what it is about Blake but he makes me question myself.

No—that's not true. He makes me question my previous assumptions about people. It's pretty obvious he's a good guy —at least his heart's in the right place. He's still a jerk in his own way, though. Deliberately running into me, breaking into my house.

Mental note: I gotta figure out how he did that. Kinda creepy.

Probably should have asked him...

I roll my eyes at myself.

Flicking my keys onto the table in the entryway, I make my way to the refrigerator and grab the Mexican leftovers from last night's meal. Until this moment, I didn't realize how incredibly hungry I am. I suppose being damn near kidnapped the moment you get home will do that to a person.

With lights low, I sit down at my dining room table and eat. My mind races through the evening's events; through all that happened and all that coulda went wrong. I avoid any stress—or forcing my abilities to go anywhere they don't want to go. As it is, my body is already heavy and ready for rest.

If I didn't have such an aversion to technology, this is

where I'd pull out a smartphone or something and text Renaldo to have him cancel tomorrow's appointments for me. If I'm up before noon, I'll be surprised. Unfortunately, I don't have one and likely never will.

I reach for the ordinary landline wall phone that's probably as old as this house. Dialing his number, I glance at the clock on the stove. 1:47am.

I cringe.

Brody's gonna kill me.

Fortunately, his voicemail picks up, and I leave a quick message. "Hey Ren. It's me—sorry to call so late, or early depending on how you look at it. Anyway, I'm not gonna be able to make it to work today. I'll explain later. If you can reschedule my list, I'd appreciate it. Talk to you in the morning. Bye."

With that said and done, I finish up eating, and place my dishes beside the sink. Then I go through my nightly routine —pee, floss, brush teeth, rinse and spit, slip outta the day's clothes, and into my tank top.

I don't bother with my lights, instead opting to wander the halls in darkness. Sliding into bed, I take a final breath, resting back into my pillow, and squirming around enough to get comfy. My eyes close and almost instantly, I'm drifting into the peaceful bliss of sleep.

Before I can enjoy any of it, I'm pulled back to the Range Rover—to being shot at. Glass shattering.

As our vehicle speeds off, the two men haul ass inside. After seeing Ralph—the man who was holding Esther, as it turns out—tied up to the chair, they race to the hidden room and find it raided. They know their time is limited, so they shoot him in the head and vacate the premises.

My eyes pop open.

Shit, they never got caught.

6

ESPITE THE REVELATION of the men getting away, I close my eyes and try to slip back into sleep. There's nothing I can do about it, anyway—and besides, the cops should know by now. They were coming in right as we left. I'm sure they're already on the hunt, trying to locate and apprehend them. The best thing I can do is stay out of their way before someone freaks out at my gifts again.

Darkness consumes me, and I give in to its beckoning. For the longest time, I drift, quietly and peacefully through a multicolored mist—reenergizing; reconnecting to the source of all. After a while, the energy shifts, molding into something familiar, but distant—as though it's a dream I've walked once before but have never recalled.

Torches burn along the walls of a cavern. It leads somewhere important, but I can't place why. My heart thumps against my chest because I already know the outcome isn't good. Somewhere within my soul, the awareness seeps in.

He's gone. Someone's taken his energy and displaced it. Even though he means something to me—I don't know who he is. Or why. All I know is I need to make this right—

As I reach the end of the tunnel, light floods into the walkway from inside. Torches along the wall smoke and flicker, but within the chamber, is utter silence. Before I can cross the threshold into the main chamber, I notice a symbol along the wall. It looks like a cross between the more modern male and female symbols I'm used to —but not.

I reach out to touch the symbol, drawn to the power emanating from it. As soon as my fingertips touch it, I'm thrust from the cavern and back into my bed.

Knock, knock, knock, knock.

My eyes flicker open, and I take in the streaming daylight cascading in from my bedroom windows. By the looks of things, it's mid-afternoon.

Knock, knock, knock.

I sit up in bed, trying to place the sound until I realize it's someone knocking on my front door. Sliding out of the sheets, I reach for my robe and gingerly walk to the front door. Every muscle is sluggish, but light at the same time. As though I got enough sleep but fought in a world championship boxing fight the day before.

The cold floor seeps into my feet, making my entire body frigid. Before I even reach the door, I know who's waiting for me: Detective Radovich.

I unlock the deadbolt and swing the door open.

"Come on in, Dan," I say, stepping back and swinging my hand out to offer up my living room.

The detective's stance is wide, but timid at the same time; clearly conflicted with why he's here. His blonde eyebrows raise high above his dark blue eyes, and he lets out a relieved sigh.

"Hi Diana, sorry to bother you this way. I've been trying to call you this morning, but you haven't answered. Your employee was getting nervous," he says, stepping inside.

"Huh?" I say, shooting him a confused look.

"Renaldo, I think his name is."

"Yeah, that's him. What do you mean he's getting nervous? I called and left a message for him last night saying I wouldn't be in."

I walk over to my recliner and take a seat. The detective does the same, opposite me on the couch.

"Diana, that was four days ago," Dan says. "I listened to the message myself. He's been here knocking at your door several times, but you've never answered. He got worried."

My eyes widen, "What? You have to be kidding me?"

"No joke. Wish it was," he says, his eyebrows flicking up to his head.

The impressions of his own surprise are palpable. He's always been an advocate for my abilities, but he's still shocked I wasn't aware of how long I've been MIA.

"Everything okay?" he asks, glancing around the room.

Stifling back a yawn, I take a quick assessment of how I feel. Tired, but overall starting to regain most of my faculties.

"I'm okay. I think I over-used my abilities. Needed to take a beat to catch up on rest," I admit.

Dan takes a moment to consider, then nods his head.

"You were awfully busy. In fact, we've been having a helluva time with the case you and that PI were working on, too. Coulda used some help these past few days," he says.

"I know," I say, remembering the vision I had before I passed out.

"You do?"

"Yeah, the men got away, right?" I say, leaning back in the chair and tucking the bottom of my robe around my legs.

Dan nods. "Yeah, sure did," he says, pressing his fingertips together. "One guy's dead—"

"Well, I'm sure you'll be able to find them. At least Esther's safe now."

"Very true. From the way your PI friend tells it, her rescue was damn near your sole accomplishment," he says.

My lips spread downward in surprise. "He actually said that?"

"Pretty much. Said you were *instrumental* in getting her outta there," Dan says, smirking.

I didn't expect Blake to lie, per se, but I've gotta admit, I'm surprised he gave me as much credit as he did. I mean, he's right—I was the one to figure out where she was and get her outta there. Not to mention, warn him about the others. But still…

"Well, I won't keep you any longer," Dan says, glancing at my robe. "Looks like you need to get dressed."

I smile uneasily.

"Yes, I guess I do. Thanks for stopping by, Dan. I'll give Ren a call now so he can stop worrying."

"You do that," he says, standing up.

"Good luck on the case. I'm sure you'll find the other bad guys. They didn't seem like overly criminal masterminds, if you know what I mean. Mostly arrogant assholes who thought they could get away with anything," I say, remembering the impressions I got from the other two.

"Thanks. Sure do hope you're right. Anyway, talk soon," he says, opening the front door and stepping outside.

As he closes the door behind him, I walk up to it and lock the deadbolt into place.

"Looks like I have some explaining to do," I mutter to myself.

"You're telling me some strange guy broke into your house and you decided, 'Oh, what the hell? I'll go with him?' And all this time you were *sleeping*? Like, actual *sleep*, sleeping?" Ren says for the second time, his eyebrows edging toward his hairline. As if it didn't compute the first time around.

"Yes, for the love of all that's holy. *I was sleeping,*" I say, annunciating slowly. "Why is that so hard to fathom?"

Christ, what in the hell else would I be doing for four goddamn days? I'm not that kinky. Sheesh.

I shake my head in disbelief.

"What a waste of four days. You coulda at least lied and said you took an impromptu road trip to Cancun with the PI who broke into your house because you fell wildly, madly, *deeply* in love, and wanted to live it up for a few days. That I coulda believed and at least admired," he says, slumping in his seat across from me, "But this?" He sighs indignantly.

"Sorry to disappoint you, Ren. No wild, mad love here. In fact, he was kinda frustrating more than anything else."

"Aren't they all?" he says, flippantly.

"Uh-oh. Trouble in paradise?" I say, raising a knowing eyebrow, and leaning back in my chair.

I don't even have to be psychic to know Ren's feeling

neglected again. He and Brody have had an on-again, off-again romance which can be best described as true love. They annoy the hell outta each other so much, there's no explanation for it. They're made for each other, truly.

"Oh my God, *please*, Diana. I don't want to talk about Mr. 'let's drop my skivvies anywhere but the hamper.' I need something happy. Tell me something happy," he says, pressing his hands together in mock prayer.

"After four days MIA, you now know I'm alive," I say, grinning and doing jazz hands. "Yay."

Ren sighs, leaning back in his chair and crossing his arms. "You suck at this."

I can't help but chuckle.

The bell to our little shop door dings and Renaldo sits up straight. "Gotta go. Duty calls."

"Geez, that boss of yours is a slave driver," I say, giving him a sideways smirk.

"Don't I know it, sister," he says, jostling his head back and forth, and snapping in mid-air in true, stereotypical fashion. He blows me a kiss and walks out.

I shake my head, reaching for my Tarot card deck to pull today's cards. I'm curious what messages I'll receive today. Even if I can't get any psychic impressions for myself, I've found the cards to be helpful in at least discovering trends.

"She in here?" a man's voice filters in from the shop.

"Diana doesn't take walk-ins without a referral," Ren replies.

"I'm not a walk-in. I just need to talk to her for a minute," the man says.

"Honey, don't they all? Look, how about you tell me your —Hey!" Ren says as the door to my reading room bursts all the way open.

"Diana," Blake says, a bright smile beaming across his face.

"Blake," I reply, setting my cards aside and standing up. "What are you doing here?"

Renaldo quirks an eyebrow and gives Blake the once-over from behind his back.

'Nice ass,' he mouths at me, pointing.

I widen my eyes and shoo him with my hands. He, of course, closes the door only part-way so he can stand outside and eavesdrop.

Sighing to myself, I return my gaze to Blake.

"I feel like we got off to a bit of a rocky start," Blake says, shoving aside my large amethyst cluster and rose quartz to place his perfect ass on the opposite side of my glass table.

"Oh, yeah?" I say, raising an eyebrow.

"Well, I, uh—yeah, a little," he says, rubbing the back of his neck.

"Okay," I say, waiting.

"Granted, we did find Esther. I mean, what could be better than that? Overall, I'd say we made a pretty good team," he grins, the hint of a dimple emerging beside the edges of his goatee.

My hand slides up over my face.

Christ, he has dimples. How did I not notice this before?

"Yeah, we did. Which is why I'd say our partnership has officially come to a close," I mutter, shoving him off the desk. "So, pretty sure you can go on your merry little way and I'll go on mine."

"Well, see…there's a problem," he continues, "the perps—"

"Got away," I finish for him.

"So, you've heard?" he says, leaning forward and placing his hands on the table instead of his ass.

I glance at his hands, then back to his face. "Something like that," I say.

"Well, aren't you the least bit interested in helping get these guys behind bars? I mean, if your abilities are really a

69

thing, you could be the one to crack this open quickly," he says.

"Blake, you might be getting paid to go hunting for these guys, but the last time I checked, I wasn't employed by the police department, or you, for that matter. I have a business to run, and clients I need to contend with. I can't go on a wild goose chase just because you want to—what? Get the credit?" I say, sitting back down.

"Who the hell says I'm getting paid?" Blake says, his dark eyebrows coming together.

"Oh, I guess I assumed—"

"Your *abilities* are still off with me, I see," he says, doing air quotes when he says the word, 'abilities.'

It's true, as much as I hate to admit it. I'm just throwing in the dark when it comes to my observations and assumptions.

"Well, that doesn't change anything—" I say, swiping my hand through the air dismissively, "There are plenty of assholes like those guys out in the world. I can't go hunting down every last one just because I have abilities beyond what others do. Besides, I don't know if I could take dealing with it day after day."

"Yeah, but if you could put just one of these bad guys away so they can't hurt another kid, isn't it worth it? I mean, sure—you have a point. There are lots of assholes out there. But they're faceless assholes. These sick ones shot up my damn Rover and were taking part in child trafficking."

I shudder. "I'm sorry, Blake. The answer is no. So, perhaps it's time for you to leave."

He holds his ground, still hunching forward on my glass table. "Okay, look. I respect your decision. I do. So, maybe we could, I dunno, go out for coffee or something instead?"

My eyes widen at the audacity. He's been nothing but a thorn in my side from the moment he bumped into me on the street and he wants to go out for coffee?

"She'd *looooove* to," Renaldo says from the doorway.

My eyes flash from Blake to the doorway. In the small crack, Renaldo peers inside, tipping his right shoulder and grinning like a Cheshire Cat.

"Butt the hell out, Ren," I spit back.

"C'mon, Diana. It's just coffee," Blake reiterates. "I promise, no shop talk."

Turning to Renaldo, I say through gritted teeth, "I'll deal with you in a moment."

I hold up my pointer finger, trying to decide whether or not to turn it into a fist. Instead, I press it against my lips. Hard.

Part of me—an annoying part—is sorta thrilled he's asking me. Don't get me wrong, he's nice to look at. As stupid as it is, it's been a while since I went out on a date. It's damn hard to make a real connection with anyone when you can hear their every thought. The other part of me is too smart for my own good. Of course, his request is meant to soften me up so I'll eventually say yes to helping him track down the bad guys. C'mon.

The more I think about it, the more it pisses me off. I mean, do I have 'dumbass' stamped across my forehead or something?

I take a deep, cleansing breath, trying to center myself before I completely lose my shit.

Squaring off with Blake, nostrils flaring like a raging bull, I stare deeply into his eyes. I need him to understand I'm deadly serious and if he won't listen to my words, perhaps he'll get the freakin' idea another way. I refuse to move my gaze, or even blink until he squirms uncomfortably.

"Look, I appreciate the offer, but as I said, our partnership is over," I say in a low, controlled voice. "Now, if you'd be so kind as to find the nearest exit, I'd like to get back to work."

"Honey, your next client isn't due for another hour," Renaldo chimes in from the other room.

"See?" Blake says, pointing and nodding at Ren. "Plenty of time for a quick cup."

"Are you deaf and stupid? I've tried to be nice, but get the hell out," I say, my voice elevated to the point of cracking.

Blake chuckles. It's a deep, boisterous laugh bordering on infectious if the timing were right—which it definitely is not.

"What in the hell are you laughing at?" I spit.

"You. Anyone ever tell ya, you try too hard?" Blake says, smirking.

I snort, double-taking at the comment. After a moment, I shrug. "Okay, I'll bite. Try too hard at what?"

He leans in close, his dark eyes pulling my gaze into them, and the heat of his breath sending an odd chill through me. His cologne—the one more suited to him, and not whatever nonsense he used the day we met—wafts around us. It's a heady aroma, and despite myself, my heart flutters traitorously.

"At being a hard ass. It's all an act. You know it. I know it," he whispers, tucking a strand of my pink bangs behind my ear. "The question I wanna know is, why are you so desperate to push people away?"

I swallow hard.

His touch, as simple a gesture as it is, stirs something I'd rather leave unstirred. Especially when he's so close to hitting the nail on the head.

"It's not complicated. People are stupid and rarely worth my time," I say, making a face.

"Says the woman who spends her days helping people," Blake fires back, still holding my gaze.

"I've said the same thing," Renaldo calls from the storefront.

I sigh, exasperated.

"Would you please, mind your own damn business?" I call to him.

"Are you kidding? Honey, this is better than daytime TV right now," Ren calls back. "I need some popcorn."

Blake licks his lower lip, a hint of a smile threatening to emerge.

"Blake, I'm asking you one final time… Please leave," I say as nicely as I can without walking around my desk to knee him in the groin.

"All right, all right. I'll go," he says, finally standing up straight and holding his hands in the air.

"Hallelujah," I mutter under my breath.

"But I'll be back," he says, shooting me a grin. "I'll get you to say yes."

"Don't friggin' bet on it," I snort.

"I don't have to. I can already *foresee* it," Blake says, as he turns around and saunters out.

My eyes shift to his backside as he walks past Renaldo, tipping his head in acknowledgment of him. Then he disappears through the front door without another word.

For the first time in as long as I can remember, regret unfurls from inside my stomach, stretching and making room for full-on panic.

He's right. I don't even need to use my own abilities to know he'll eventually win if he's persistent enough.

Dammit.

7

"*D*ID YOU SEE THE ASS on that man?" Renaldo says, once the door swings shut. He fans himself furiously. "Mmmm, Mmmm, Mmmm."

I bury my face in my hands.

The last time I allowed myself even a glimpse of an opening for a relationship it ended up in flames. We're not talking little candle-type flame, either. We're talking apocalypse, end of the world kinda flames. It took me half a century to get over it.

"I mean, seriously," he continues, "if I wasn't taken, I'd have coffee with him. Then drag him back to my place for some—"

I hold up a hand. "Whatever you were planning on saying, please stop there."

"Lord woman, your bits are gonna shrivel up and die from lack of use. What excuse could you possibly have to say no to that?" Ren counters.

"First of all, how shallow do you think I am? Great ass or not, I gotta have more than looks. Secondly, you've seen my track record, Ren. How long have we been working together now? Ten, twelve years? Relationships and me are unmixy things. Always have been, always will be," I say, straightening the items on my table, and putting them back where they belong.

"First of all, it's been thirteen years, six months, and sixteen days. And honey, all the past relationships not working out are all meant to lead you to the path where it will," he says, raising an eyebrow.

"Seriously, you have to stop eavesdropping in on my sessions with clients," I say.

"How else am I gonna get relationship advice?" he says, leaning on the door frame. "Besides, it's good advice."

"I know it is, which is why I use it. But I dunno, I'm different. Those rules don't apply to me," I say, scratching my head. "I wish they did, though."

Renaldo rolls his eyes. "Right, I forgot. 'Ms. Diana, the one cursed to walk alone.' Please," he says, swiping a hand in the air. "You're more melodramatic than I am."

"No, it's accurate."

In all honesty, he has no idea. It's been thirteen years—but he's never, not once, asked why I look the same. Why I never seem to age. Why I tell everyone I'm in my twenties and have been the entire time we've been working together.

If I told any of them my real age—at least the age I know from when I started counting—they'd flip their ever-loving shit.

"If you ask me, you need to get your scrawny butt back into the world. Mr. Cute Ass might be just the ticket. Doesn't have to be anything more than a date. I mean, you only gotta commit to a cup of coffee—not lifelong servitude, for crying out loud," he says.

"I totally didn't ask you for your advice. So, how about we drop this and move on with the rest of our day?" I say, batting my eyelashes.

75

Ren's eyes widen, and he holds his hands up, backing away.

The doorbell dings again as someone enters the shop.

"Whatever you say, Ms. Grumpy Pants," he mutters as he leaves the room, closing the door behind him.

Grabbing my coat, I walk out the back door to get some air. The small garden behind the cottage is pretty minuscule, but the gorgeous flowers do wonders for lifting my spirits. The array of colors are pretty awesome, too. I love how my landlord Sebastian didn't go with a single color choice but instead opted for as many as he could stand. He's a good guy.

Pacing the garden like a labyrinth, my mind circles the conversation with Blake.

Was I too hard on him? Should I have said yes? What would come of it? What's the worst that could happen?

I cringe.

I know all too well the worst. I could become attached. Ultimately, that leads to having to let him go. Who in their right mind would want to be with someone who never ages and lives…well, as far as I know…*forever*?

It's not often I think about my immortality anymore. It's best left to the side; ignored. But it certainly pops up from time to time—days like this. If only I knew why…maybe then I'd be able to counteract it. Or understand it. But every time I try, the results are disastrous. Like, land people in the hospital, disastrous.

"Your next client is here. Want me to tell them you need a minute?" Ren asks, poking his head outside.

"No, why would you say that?"

"Because you're doing that walking thing you do," Ren says, circling his finger around.

"I'm thinking," I say, heading back.

"Oh really?" he says, grinning. "Did something I say resonate?"

I shove him aside as I step in. "Give me five minutes to prep, then send them in, would you?"

"Knew it." he grins triumphantly.

"Just do it," I say, spinning him around and pushing him out of the reading room.

My god, his ego would explode if I told him I actually was mulling it over.

Taking a few moments to center myself, I breathe deep and close my eyes. I inhale the scents of frankincense and myrrh, allowing them to transport me into a calmer mental space. One where I can be more present for my clients, and less focused on myself.

I flip the switch on my desk, signaling Renaldo I'm ready. I dim the lights and relight the candles around the room. After a couple of moments, a small, meager man walks in. His timid stature is immediately disarming, but he's hiding something—or trying to conceal it, anyway. His name is Lenny and he steals from his boss. He then uses the money to go to the strip club on Fridays.

"Please, have a seat," I say, pointing to the chair opposite my reading table.

"Thanks," he mumbles, grabbing the chair and taking a seat.

I take my position opposite him, quietly setting out the table before use. I place my Tarot to one side, a couple of crystals to the other. His eyes widen, but he says nothing.

"There's a lot we need to cover," I begin, "so I'm going to get straight to it. I wouldn't worry so much about your boss and instead, start worrying about the coworker who's been watching you."

Lenny's eyes widen, and he bites the side of his cheek.

"But that's not why you're really here," I say, staring deeply into his green eyes. They'd be pretty if he weren't so mousy-looking and unkempt. His dishwater blonde hair has been over-combed across the top of his head, and his outfit is disheveled. Almost as if he'd been roughed up in the parking lot but I already know it's because he doesn't pay attention to such things. The concept of dressing nicely is pretty much lost on him. It's part of why his addiction continues to circle around.

Lenny shakes his head.

"No, I—*er*—I don't know what to do. It's sorta been a—"

A man with short, curly red hair flashes into my mind. His smile is infectious—as is his silly, infectious laugh. There's something special about the man, and Lenny knows it. That's why he's fallen in love with him.

"Oh, right," I say, nodding.

This sort of thing doesn't happen often in our small town, but with Ren in my circle, it happens more than you might think.

"So you're wondering if he's noticed you, too?" I say.

Lenny's green eyes go as round as saucers, but he bites his lip and nods.

Part of him is ashamed. He doesn't understand how the feelings were aroused for this man—he's always been heterosexual, or at least he thought he was. But now, it's thrown everything he's known into chaos. He can't sleep. He's tied up in knots as he tries to reconcile his feelings.

"The first thing I need you to do is find someone safe you can talk to. Being attracted to another man—there's nothing wrong with it and I'm guessing you have years of programming you'll need to unlearn before those knots in your stomach unclench. Do you have anyone you could turn to?" I ask.

"D-do you count?" he asks, making a face.

I shake my head. "No, and yes. I mean you need to get into depth with someone. Perhaps a therapist to help you work through your feelings. This anxiety isn't doing you any good."

"But, how do I get him to notice me? Or—how would I even know if he's interested?" he asks, his voice reduced to a hushed whisper.

"You'll know, Lenny. Trust me," I say holding out my hands, palm side up.

He reaches out, tentatively placing his hands in mine. I close my eyes, trying to get a better feel for the orange-haired man. He's about the same age as Lenny, but much more outgoing. He's spent time with Lenny—yet the situations are odd. Like it's a weird cross between a working relationship and something more. There's a definite energy pull, but the other man's confused, too. He's not sure whether or not to try to reach out to Lenny. He's noticed how he's gone downhill lately, and it's concerning him. He—*Andrew*—his name is Andrew—he doesn't want to see anything bad happen to Lenny.

"I'm not sure where his feelings are for you right now, but he certainly knows you exist. I'm picking up on a lot of platonic love and friendship, but at the present time, that's all," I say, opening my eyes.

Lenny smiles, tears on the verge of welling over. "He knows I exist?"

"Yes, he really does," I say nodding.

"Thank you, Diana. Thank you. That's really all I needed," he says, smiling. Creases form in the corners of his eyes, brightening his face.

"Now, if you can kick the—*eh-hem*—bad habit at work, you'll be in a better place. I feel if you continue down that path, you'll lose your chance with Andrew. And for sure your job."

His eyes widen.

"Whoa. You picked up on his name? Please—please don't tell the police," he says.

"Everything here is confidential. I wouldn't dream of intervening for something like this. It's not my job," I say, trying to reassure him.

"But you're—you're the one who helped find that little girl recently, right?" he says.

"I am, but that was a different type of situation. I was pulled in on the case. And your situation hardly requires me to step in for police interaction," I say, cocking an eyebrow. "Even if it's totally not cool."

Lenny nods vigorously. "I'm—I'll stop. I'm done. I want my shot with Andrew."

He stands up, brushing off his legs as he gets up, trying to decrease the wrinkles. It doesn't help.

"Great. You'll come back and keep me posted, right?"

"Sure—sure, I'd love to," he says, reaching for my hand again.

I take it, placing my other hand over his.

A much happier future for him opens up. As if the pathway he was on was leading him down the destructive path to heartache, but in the past instant, he's made a new decision—a life-altering decision. These are the types of interactions that are the reason I continue to do this. When you can see a life shift from destruction, to something far more pleasant.

It's so strange how simple—and how difficult that is. *Choice.*

We're always one choice away from a completely different life.

Smiling at him, I let go of his hand and walk him out of the reading room and into the main part of the shop.

Renaldo looks up from the gossip magazine he was reading and feigns surprise—it's written all over his face.

He's surprised I left my reading room "cave" to enter the real world of the store. When I can help it, I generally avoid the front because you never know who might see me and want to attempt to weasel their way into a free reading.

I roll my eyes and smirk.

"Okay, Lenny—Renaldo here will get you all squared away," I say.

As soon as I look at Lenny, a cord of energy bursts from his chest, linking to Ren's.

"You know what," I say, looking between them, "Ren, I think you may be a good person to talk to Lenny. He doesn't have many people he can turn to, but for some reason, I get a good vibe about you two."

Renaldo's eyebrows flick upward but he's known me long enough to know when I say something like that, to go with it.

"Hmmm, okay, I'm intrigued," Ren says, putting his magazine down and walking over to Lenny. His flamboyant attitude is so similar to Andrew's—at least from what I can tell—and it instantly puts Lenny at ease.

"I'm Renaldo, Diana's boss—" he says, shooting me a coy grin.

"You wish," I say, chuckling and heading back toward my reading room.

I leave the two of them alone, allowing them some space to have the conversation they need to have. It's so interesting how this universe works sometimes. It all takes place in whatever orchestra it's meant to—like every string is so carefully pulled so the timing is perfect.

I stop walking, surprised at my own train of thought. It's almost as if all of this is happening not just for Lenny, but for me as well. The color green floods my entire perception and I know it's true. I've hunted for so long for clues of my past, but this is a mixed message—like it's made with invisible ink and if I look at it too long, it will all melt away.

But what exactly is meant to be?

Am I supposed to be making the choice to be happy? To help Blake on this case? To… *Ugh*—give love a chance?

Again, green lights up. But not just for the last thought—for them all.

Dammit.

Fear unfurls from my stomach again—twisting and turning. Being hard is easy. Having a protective shell is pretty much my thing. But learning to let go of all that? Can I even handle it?

No—I'm not ready. Not yet.

As much as I want to move forward, there's still so much from my past I need to have answered. I can't let it go and become something new until I know what I was. Who I was. Why I'm here and stuck this way.

"Oh honey, I can totally help you with that," Renaldo says to Lenny. His words pull me from my own thoughts.

"Really, you'd help me?" Lenny says, surprise painted in his tone.

"Are you kidding me? Taking on a project like you is a dream come true. We can go shopping—get this hair cut and —oh my god, a manicure. When was the last time you had your hands done?" Ren says, gasping.

I have to laugh to myself. If there's one person who can whip Lenny into shape, it's certainly Ren. And if he's the one guiding him to Andrew—it'll be perfect.

Sitting down at my desk, I reach for my phone.

Maybe I should call Blake. I don't have to commit to anything but coffee, right?

I pick up the old-fashioned, corded receiver, then set it back down.

I don't even have his number.

Placing my hand over my face, I chuckle to myself. What on earth am I thinking? It was like I was going to call him for the hundredth time—and I don't even have his number.

Come on Diana, where is your head at?

"Thanks so much, Renaldo. I'll definitely give you a call later tonight. I really do appreciate you being willing to teach me," Lenny says.

"My pleasure, Len. You got this," Renaldo says.

The doorbell to the shop dings as Lenny exits.

A moment later, Renaldo bounds into my reading room.

"What a beautiful soul," he says, holding his hand to his chest.

"So, you decided to help him?" I say, already knowing the answer.

"Of course. Did you see him? He's hopeless. Lord, if someone doesn't show him the ropes, ain't no one gonna notice how beautiful his eyes are," he says, dropping into the chair across from me.

"Good, you both had a pretty strong cord. He'll be around for a while. Maybe this is an answer to your prayers, too," I say.

"What do you mean? I'm not leaving Brody for—"

I wave my hand dismissively, "No, not that. I mean, maybe once he and Andrew are together—if they continue on that trajectory—because it's not certain yet, I could see you all hanging out together. It would lighten Brody's load to keep you entertained."

Renaldo gasps. "I'm not that much of a diva, Diana. What are you saying?"

"You know you're a piece of work, and damn lucky to have found Brody."

"Hmph," he says, crossing his arms.

"But at least it looks like you'll be on the upswing," I say, shrugging.

"Well, as long as someone lets me dress them, it's a start,"

Ren says, his eyes distant as he no-doubt mentally rearranges Lenny's wardrobe. "Now, what are we going to do with you?"

"Nothing. I'm going to go about my day as usual. In fact, when's my next client due?" I ask, glancing at my wrist.

Ren's lips tug into a straight line, but he says, "Any minute, I suppose."

"Good. I'm gonna go sit outside and enjoy the fresh air while I wait," I say, standing up and heading once again to the back door.

"You can't survive on fresh air alone. Do you want me to call down to the cafe for lunch again?" he asks, making his way to the front.

"No," I say, shaking my head. "I think I'll go out today, instead."

Ren's jaw slacks open, "Are you feeling okay? You haven't been out since—"

"Good god, I'm fine. Now, go wait for the next client, would you?" I say, shooing him with my hands.

"You can run, Ms. Thang, but you can't hide," he says. "One of these days, all this running will catch up with you."

"Yeah, yeah. Going now," I say slamming the door behind me.

8

*T*HE NEXT FEW DAYS drag by. I'm talking the pace a grandma snail would be proud of. My mind keeps toying with the idea of finding Blake—or maybe finding a way to call him. Of course, I always think better of it.

I mean, who am I kidding? Even if I went for coffee or offered to help on the case, having him around hinders my abilities anyway. Besides, it's not like he isn't capable on his own.

"Daydreaming again?" Renaldo says, breaking my concentration, and causing me to jump.

"Christ, don't sneak up on a person like that," I squeak.

"Ooooohhh, musta been a good one, too. Were you dreaming about tall, dark, and tight ass?" he says, rushing in.

"Would you drop it, Ren? I'm not even dating the man. He wanted help on a case," I say, rubbing my cheeks.

"True, but as I recall, he also asked you out to coffee, did he not?"

"He did, but it was so he could try to talk me into helping him. Nothing more," I say.

"And how do you know?"

The doorbell rings and Ren holds up a finger. "Hold that thought. I'll be right back. Should give you plenty of time to come up with something."

I shake my head. Leave it to Ren to turn an acquaintance into a full-blown love interest.

But I have to admit, Blake's a hard nut to crack. What is it that makes him impossible to read? Could he be tied to me somehow? Or am I leaning on some bizarre wishful thinking? Possibly both?

Ren bounds back in, a spring in his step and a box in his hands.

"The box of Valentine's goodies is here," he says, a chipper tone in his voice. He's always loved Valentine's Day. It's the one time of the year when he can pretty much guarantee the attention he generally hopes for from Brody.

"You know these items are meant for customers, right? *Paying* customers," I say, leaning back in my chair.

"What exactly are you insinuating, Ms. Diana?" he says, feigning surprise.

"Exactly that. Unless you're a paying customer, it stays here."

"I wouldn't dream of stealing from you. Though, if you paid me more, I'd be able to afford more…" he shoots me a knowing look.

"A vicious cycle, I'm afraid," I say, chuckling.

He pulls out a whip that looks more like a feather duster than something to spank anything with. His eyebrows practically bury themselves in his hairline. "Mmmm. *Roar*," he says. "I'm thinking you should take one of these."

"*Paying* customers," I reiterate. "Since I'm not paying, nor a customer, I think not," I say, shaking my head. "Besides, what the hell would I do with it, except whip my dust bunnies into shape?"

"You're such a party pooper," Ren says, frowning. "There's so many drool-worthy goodies in here."

I shake my head and pick up the box. I place it squarely in his outstretched hands. "Take this to the front and do your magic, please."

Sighing heavily, he takes the box and turns on his heel, throwing a dramatic head spin in for good measure.

The doorbell dings again, and I take my spot at my reading table. The room is ready; candles lit and incense burning.

"Hey, got a sec?" Blake pops his head inside the room.

My mouth drops open, and I stand up, nearly knocking over the table.

"I—uh, no. I don't actually. I have a client who'll turn up any minute now," I say, trying to overcome my surprise. I scramble to keep my rose quartz crystal ball from rolling to the floor.

He watches me flounder for a moment, edging further into the room and crossing his arms.

"Kinda klutzy, aren't we?" A lopsided smile emerges, sending shockwaves through my veins.

Good lord, how old am I?

"What do you want, Blake?" I ask, firmer this time.

The last thing I need is for him to know he's getting to me.

"So, I was thinking about what you were saying before," he says, taking another step into the room.

"You'll need to be more specific," I mutter, trying to center myself. I feel heady—and off. Like there's not enough oxygen in the room and I'm desperately trying to breathe.

"You said people are stupid and rarely worth your time. It got me thinking about my own situation and I still think we'd make a good team."

My breathe catches and I force an exhale. "Why is that?"

"Because I think you're wrong. People are generally flawed—*yes*. Plenty of them have issues, as you saw the other day. But I've also witnessed some pretty amazing people in my time. For whatever reason, I feel like you're missing out if you're not witnessing that side of people, too," he says, taking a last stride forward and leaning on the back of the chair opposite me.

"I seriously doubt you've had enough experience with people, if this is your take," I say, leaning back.

"Come on, let me show you. Let's do coffee—and maybe, if you want, we can work together on this case and I'll help you see the world a little differently," he says, grinning.

"You're not going to take no for an answer, are you?" I say, irritation welling up.

Who does this guy think he is?

Seriously, I've been around a while. I highly doubt his thirty some odd years—*maybe forty*—have gifted him more people experience than all of mine.

"So, is that a yes?" Blake says, his eyes flashing mischievously.

"Screw you," I sputter, suddenly unable to contain myself. After all, he's done this past week, I can't believe I'd actually considered calling him.

"Could be fun, but I don't generally make a habit of it on the first date." He smirks.

I roll my eyes.

Wonderful, we have a comedian in our midst telling Dad jokes already. *Swell.*

"Let me make this abundantly clear to you," I begin, folding my hands across the table. "I will, in no way, shape, or form ever—EVER go on a date with you. There will be no screwing for that matter, as I'm not even sure you'd pull your head outta your well-shaped ass long enough to entertain the thought of someone else's pleasure…"

"As a matter of fact, I've been told by many women I'm very attentive," he says, cutting me off with an eyebrow quirking smugly.

An absurd shiver squiggles down my spine and I instantly get unwanted flashes of intimate moments he's had with women. Of course, they're all from my imagination as it springs into action, instead of any sort of reading from him. But they're unwanted, just the same.

"Gah—" I cry, throwing my hands to the sides of my head to try to ignore my mind as it plays tricks. "That's—it's not the point. The point is, it will never, ever happen with us. So the sooner you can get it through your thick skull, the better off we'll both be."

Blake takes a step around the table toward me, his dark eyes penetrating mine in the most intimate way. I can't explain it—it's like he strips me down to my bare essence. Not the naked me, but the *soul level* me. The corner creases of his eyes deepen as he takes me in, and his lips tilt ever so slightly upward.

Reaching his right hand out, he cups the side of my face without a word. Warmth radiates from the palm of his hand, making me shiver again, despite myself. My body suddenly craves to lean into it.

"Give me time," he finally whispers, winking.

I glare at him, knowing full well my traitorous insides want desperately to give into anything he wants.

Dammit.

Leaning away, I pull my face from his hand.

"Listen, I don't know about you, but where I'm from, touching someone without consent can be considered assault," I warn.

My skin blazes, tingling from his touch.

Blake chuckles, his dark eyebrows rising in a high arc.

"Oh, is that so? Well, I'll keep that under advisement," he

says, tipping his head. "It was good to see you again, Diana. Think about it." Without another word, he turns on his heel and walks out the door.

My eyes stray, mesmerized by the way he walks.

"Mmmm mmmm," Renaldo mutters, appearing in the doorway. "Honey, I don't know what the dealio is, but damn, that man has a fine stride."

"Go away, Ren," I say, my eyes flicking to his from beneath my eyebrows.

I don't know what kind of magic this guy has, but I'm not about to be his bitch. I've been around the block long enough to know when to stay the hell away. Everything about Blake screams RUN—even if half of me is in direct disagreement.

"I'm just saying… How long's it been since you…" he wiggles his eyebrows, "…ya know?"

I stare at him unblinking.

Four years, eight months, and 12 days. But who's counting?

"It wouldn't hurt ya to use him to get a little somethin' somethin' and ignore the rest—if that's what floats your boat. I mean, your nether region is gonna atrophy, if you're not careful. What I wouldn't give to have your kinda freedom," he says, his eyes going distant, and a giddy smile stretching across his lips.

"Oh please," I say. "You and Brody are perfect for each other and you know it. Even if you were able, you'd still be chasing him around like a lost pup."

Renaldo snaps his fingers in the air. "Oh no you don't, woman. Take it back. If anything, the lost puppy would be him."

I chuckle and walk to the doorway. "Sure, if you say so. Let me know when my next client is here," I mutter, ushering Ren out and slowly closing the door to my reading room, so I can seal myself off.

Walking to the window overlooking the garden, I stare out into the sea of color. If it were up to me, none of these flowers would exist, and I'd have nothing to appreciate as I stand here. Thank god for Sebastian and his green thumb. He's the first landlord I've ever had who couldn't stay away from gardening. I can't even count the number of times I've spent walking the garden, pulling in their potent fragrance and allowing it to wash the day's energy from my aura.

I stare out at the hydrangeas, watching as they buzz with activity from the bees roaming the garden.

How does Blake get under my skin so easily?

It's not like there's anything special about him—*not really*. Sure, great ass. But as much as I can appreciate his physique, it's not what's annoying the crap outta me. Maybe it's the fact he's right. Something is sparking between us, despite my best efforts to ignore it. For the first time I can remember, I'm not in control of how it's gonna play out and that scares the hell outta me. Something's sweeping me away and I'm powerless to stop it.

Honestly, I'm not sure whether to be intrigued or pissed off.

Suddenly, flashes of a possible future consume my vision and I stumble backward. They flit back and forth: caught in Blake's embrace, white dresses, birds flying, and music playing. The emotions come through clearly—bliss, love, light. Green lights twinkling.

I shake away the vision, surprised.

Green means go.

The thought repeats in my head—the same words I tell my clients all the time.

The only difference, this is for me.

I've been at this for centuries—of that, I'm certain. I've kept my journals dating back to when I realized I wasn't aging. But this—this is the first time I've ever seen anything of my own possible future or gotten any specific info or details. And believe me, I've tried. It's even put Demetri in the hospital.

What in the hell?

A knock on the door makes me jump.

"Everything okay in here?" Ren asks, leaning in.

"Yeah, I uh—yeah, why?" I say, blinking away the last tendrils of the vision.

"Because I've been buzzing you for the last ten minutes and you haven't responded, weirdo," he says.

I walk over to my reading table, "Sorry, I was—send them in please," I say, taking a seat.

Ren shoots me a sideways glance, and turns to the woman beside him. "Diana will see you now."

He does his typical flourish with his hand as he sweeps it out to allow her entry.

"Thank you," the Asian woman says, ushering past him and walking to the seat opposite me.

"Hello, Tina," I say, picking up on her name immediately. It was loud and clear—as if it was the one thing she wanted me to know before anything else. A test, most likely.

"Hi. Hi, Diana," she says, taken aback, but recovering quickly. "I—do you need me to tell you why I'm here?"

"Why don't you take a seat and we'll get to all that," I say, sweeping my hand toward the chair.

She circles the chair and sits down quickly, placing her hands in her lap and facing me tentatively, fidgeting with the ends of her long hair.

Her nervous energy gives way—sending over details. Light and dark—life and death.

"Did you lose someone?" I finally say.

Tears well up in her eyes and she nods.

I nod to myself, tilting my head slightly as I wait for more details. After a moment, I reach my hands out across the small round table. "Can I have your hands for a moment?"

Tina holds out her hands and places them face down over my own. Her hands are cold and clammy but our contact relays who she's thinking of. She's recently lost her boyfriend, Trevor, to a car accident.

"Okay, I think I see. You're wondering about Trevor. About whether or not you'll ever see him again," I say, opening my eyes. "Am I right?"

She nods, large droplets falling from her eyelashes to her lap. "Is there—I need to know if there's anything after this life. Will we ever be together again?" she asks, her lip quivering. "Will he be...*reincarnated*?"

This is one area where I honestly have no idea. The universe has never relayed information one way or the other about it. I can't say in all the time I've been alive, I've ever stumbled upon anything conclusive. At least, as far as I'm aware of. And with my lifespan as it's been, I would have thought if it were a thing, I'd know.

"Physics dictates all energy created can never be destroyed. Whether or not you'll join Trevor in the recognizable form as you are now—I honestly can't say, nor can I promise. The universe hasn't given me that kind of insight. However, I do know he's around you now. Part of his energy and essence will always be with you," I say, trying to carefully tread the line between honesty and hopefulness.

Her eyes widen. "He's here? Now?" She looks over her shoulder.

"No, not like that. He's not a ghost or anything. I just mean, part of his energy—his atoms if you will—are with you. They'll stay with you until the end. Does that make sense?" I ask, watching her.

"I miss him so much. I don't know what I'm supposed to

do now. Do I wait? Do I try to move on?" she whispers, dropping her eyes back to her clasped hands resting in her lap.

"If there's one thing I know for sure, it's Trevor wants you to go on living. He may not be here, but he doesn't want you to stop living your life. He wants you to embrace all this world has to offer. Run at it headlong and don't ever look back."

The words *'keep trucking'* pop into my head.

"Keep trucking," I say, before I can consciously think otherwise. "He wants you to *keep trucking*—if that makes sense."

Tina's head jerks up. "He—he used to say that all the time," she gasps.

It's a clear sign to her. I see it in her eyes.

"Thank you, Diana. Thank you," Tina says, standing up.

She rushes around the table and leans down, embracing me in an awkward, tight hug.

"Don't mention it," I say, patting her arm.

"Thank you, thank you," she gushes. She then quickly releases me and walks to the door.

Whatever I said was clearly what she was looking for. I lean back in my seat.

It's so strange the way humans love—even after a loss. We're all so willing to run headlong into it. At least, the first few times. But after a while, losing those you're close to wears on you. It makes you bitter. I should know.

It's not often I'm asked about the afterlife—or reincarnation. That was more Demetri's jam. But it always makes me pause when it does come up. The universe is a good many things, but an open book is certainly not one of them.

When I hear the ding of the doorbell, I pop my head into the storefront. "I'm gonna head down to the coffee shop. Want anything?" I ask.

"Ooooh, you're a lifesaver. I'm dying for a mint mocha

latte. A splash of skim milk, no whip. Heavy on the mint," Ren says, his eyes lighting up.

"Got it," I say, knowing he'll be lucky if I even remember the mint part.

I grab my jacket and head out the front door, hands in pockets, and hood up.

The midday sun hangs slightly lower than it does during summer, casting deep shadows across the pavement as I walk the concrete sidewalk toward the coffee shop up the road. *Ruby Moon.* I'm not sure where the name came from, but I've always loved it. It's a fitting nomenclature for the type of place I'd like to gift my money to.

Besides, they make a helluva good cup of coffee.

I listen to the birds in the trees flitting around, chirping and trilling away and can't help but smile. It's not quite spring yet, but twitterpation is certainly in the air.

Walking up the front steps, I swing the door open and waltz to the counter. The owner, Maxwell, is stationed behind the register, and a young barista leans against the counter, picking at her nails. Only one other customer graces their presence, as he rests belly up to the bar.

"Hey Diana, the usual?" Max asks.

"That'd be—" I begin, glancing at the man at the counter beside me. I double-take.

"Ah, right on time," Blake says, twisting on his pedestal seat and facing me. "Told ya I'd get you to have coffee with me one way or another."

9

*M*Y MOUTH DROPS OPEN and I'm at a loss for something to say. I've been to this coffee shop hundreds—scratch that—*thousands* of times, and I've never, not once, seen him here.

"What are you doing here?" I ask indignantly, unable to help myself.

"Having…coffee," he says, cocking his head. "You?"

"I uh—" I step back, glancing from Maxwell to Blake, then the barista, who looks just as bored now as she was before. "Getting coffee for Renaldo."

"Isn't that sorta his job?" Blake says, raising an eyebrow. "I mean, to get coffee for you?"

It's true. Ordinarily, he'd be the one doing the running, but I wanted the fresh air for a change. Especially after everything going on.

"That's kinda sexist," I blurt out.

"Has nothing to do with sex," Blake says, his eyes twinkling mischievously.

My body warms at the way he says it. Like he's deliberately taunting me and he wants me to know it.

Turning from Blake, I square up to Max. "Yes, the usual for me, please. And a mocha latte thingy for Ren."

"His usual?" Max asks, grabbing a paper cup and writing something along its side.

"Possibly?" I say, dropping my chin and shaking my head with uncertainty. It's never occurred to me to pay attention to what Ren's usual is. How terrible is that?

"See, you don't even know what the hell he's meant to drink." Blake laughs.

"I do, too. It's a long, complicated order," I scoff.

"Shouldn't a psychic be able to pick up on what it was without a notepad to remind her?" Blake taunts.

Maxwell's eyebrows skirt up to his hairline, but he doesn't say a word. He passes the order on to his barista who sets to work, her expression never changing. The only thing that could make her more cliche is if she were snapping gum, but she's not.

"We've been over this, Blake. It doesn't work like that," I say. "I'm not omnipotent. Still human, here."

Granted, if I really wanted to, I could probably pull up a mental recall...

He sets down his drink.

"Hmmm, seems I have something to learn about you and being psychic. Care to join me at a booth? Chat with me a bit?" he grins, pointing at the booth near the window. "I've got some time to kill and I could use a lesson."

"I can't. I have to bring Ren's coffee back to him, remember?" I say, shaking my head and pointing to the coffee being made.

"I can have Amy bring it down to him, if you'd like Diana," Max says, a hint of a smirk spreading across his lips. He doesn't look up from what he's doing—a sure sign he wants me to take him up on the offer. Seems like everyone is trying to hook me up.

"See?" Blake says nodding and pointing at Amy. "Amy will do your bidding. So, it's a date, then?"

"It's soooo not a date," I say, trying to control the drumming of my pulse. It kinda feels like a date. An impromptu—*'Where the hell did this come from?'*—date.

But a date nonetheless.

"It could be if you wanted, though. Right?" he says. "It's all about mindset." His dimples deepen beside his goatee, and I sigh. His authentic smile just about rivals his physique.

Would it be so bad to sit down for a cup of coffee?

"Fine," I say, grabbing my cup of coffee from the bored barista. "I'll sit with you for a minute. But it's not a date."

Blake throws up his hands. "Whatever you say."

Turning to the nearest booth along the bank of windows, I slide into my seat and take a deep sip of my coffee. The foam on top makes my lip tickle, and I set the cup down. Sliding into the spot right beside me, he forces me to shift over and effectively locks me between him and the window.

"You know, there's another seat on the other side of the table. Makes for an easier way to have a conversation," I say, pointing to the empty bench.

"Eh, where's the fun in that?" He grins.

There's a strange playfulness in his energy, if I can call it that. I can't read his aura, but I still feel it somehow. Plus, the smirk on his face broadens the longer he sits beside me.

Amy shoots me a strange—*'Aren't you a little old to be so awkward?'*—kinda look as she heads out the door with Ren's cup in hand.

"So, what exactly did you want to talk about? I doubt world peace and I already said no to helping you on your case," I say, returning my gaze to him, and feeling the need to throw that in there.

Blake shifts closer; the scent of aftershave or cologne

wafting around us. It's a heady kind of smell, making me want to lean into him and take a better whiff.

Before he answers, he grins again, then takes a slow, deliberate sip of his own coffee. "What exactly is Diana's usual?" he finally asks, pointing to my coffee cup and ignoring my question completely.

"It's the campfire mocha," I say, raising an eyebrow. "Why?"

"Normal variation or your own special blend?"

I shift in my seat, twisting a bit to look him in the eye. "White chocolate, not milk chocolate," I say, a slow grin spreading across my lips.

"Interesting," he says, nodding in approval. "I happen to like my coffee black as my soul, but if I did add chocolate, it would be of the white variation."

"Ewww. Black coffee. Really?" I say, sticking out my tongue and making a face.

"What's so wrong with that?" he chuckles. "Nice look for you, by the way."

I shove him.

"Oh shut up. Black coffee is wrong on so many levels," I say, shivering.

"Enlighten me," he says, tipping his head and taking another swig.

"The only reason to drink coffee is for the sugar and caffeine. When you take away the sugar, you only have the caffeine—and I can get the same effect drinking tea, or a shot of an energy boost drink. So, no." I shake my head and lift my own cup to my lips.

"Good to know," he says, nodding. He takes another sip of his coffee and waits.

"Gross," I mutter, unable to hide my grin.

"You get used to it. Besides, too much sugar isn't good for you," he adds.

"Oh boy, you're not one of those crazy health nuts, are you?" I laugh.

"If I were, I wouldn't be drinking coffee. Caffeine is just as bad," he says.

"Really?" I say, unable to stop the raising eyebrow. "And how would you know that if you weren't one of those crazy health nuts?"

"Because I had a friend who blew out her adrenal glands with a coffee addiction," he says nonchalantly.

"Yikes. Sounds brutal," I say, glancing at my cup of coffee. "How much does one need to drink for it to be considered an addiction?"

"Way more than a cup." He laughs.

"I figured," I say, rolling my eyes.

"Hey, you asked." His eyes fall to his cup while his fingertips fondle the handle. I can't stop staring at his dark eyelashes. He has the kind most women would kill for, but they definitely suit him.

"So, have you always lived here in Helena?" I ask.

"The outskirts, technically," Blake points out.

"Yeah, yeah. You know what I mean," I say, shaking my head.

"Well, no actually. I used to live in Minnesota, if you can believe it," he says, shifting in his seat.

"Eeewww. Really? Isn't it, I dunno—freakin' cold there?"

My mind traces back to my short stint in that direction. I don't remember the winters fondly, that's for sure.

Blake laughs a hardy, deep laugh. "That's an understatement."

"Then why?"

"Family, I guess. I grew up there. But, my folks passed away and I had no other ties to Minnesota. So, I decided to come down here," he says, biting his lower lip, and eyeing his cup.

"Oh, I'm so sorry. I didn't mean to—"

"Nah, it's no big deal. It's been a few years," he says.

"Do you mind if I ask, how?" I say, leaning in and suddenly curious.

"Mom passed when I was younger—breast cancer runs in the family. A heart attack got Dad, though," he says, his voice low.

Reaching out, I place a hand on his leg closest to me. "I'm sorry Blake. I'm sure losing your parents was so hard."

His eyes widen as he looks from me to my hand. He shifts his eyes slightly, but nods. "It was, especially at first," he clears his throat, "So, what about you? Are your parent's still around?"

There it is, the dreaded questions about me and my life— the ones I hate answering because they can unravel so quickly into a complete cluster.

I shake my head. "No, they're gone."

It's the truth—though I don't remember them at all. For the amount of time I've been alive, there's no way they've managed to survive. Unless they've passed down this insane longevity to me, but they've never come looking, if they did.

"Sorry, this has, ah—taken a turn," Blake says, scratching the back of his head.

"It's okay, it was a long time ago for me, too."

"I suppose it's what drove you to helping people, huh?" Blake says, watching me closely.

I pause for a moment, considering. For the most part, it transpired gradually. My gifts have always been around and not adhering to them didn't feel right.

"I suppose in a sense it did. But I don't think I really had a choice. When you know things, hear things—*see things*— ignoring them and going on with your own life isn't always an option. As you know," I say, pointing to him.

Blake's eyebrows flutter upward in surprise. "I do?"

"Well, yeah, once I could see things more clearly with Esther, I couldn't not get involved at that point. You know?"

"Oh right. You're still talking about you. Got it," he says, shaking his head.

I chuckle and scrunch my nose. "What did you think I meant?"

"I thought—I thought you meant me. That when I see things, ignoring them isn't an option."

"Well, I suppose that's right too. Isn't it?" I say, grinning.

"Yeah, yeah, I guess it is."

"Sooooo," I say, trying to fill the awkward silence surrounding us. "What's the deal with you and Aiden?"

Blake shoots me a sideways glance. "What do you mean?"

"Well, I got something off of him when we first met. You've known him a long time, right?"

"I thought you couldn't read stuff about me?" Blake says, his voice a bit tighter than before.

"I can't, but when I shook Aiden's hand, I got snippets. He must have been thinking about it," I say.

"What kind of snippets?" Blake asks, his eyes wide.

I blink fast, trying to recall.

"Uh, something about him being little. He lost his parents, too, right? A car accident—but you stepped in even though you were trying to work your way up the Special Forces ranks," I say, biting my lip.

He narrows his eyes, giving me a once-over.

"You're shitting me, right? This is some sort of a joke?" he says, shifting back a bit.

"No," I say, shaking my head. "Why would you think that?"

"Did he put you up to this?"

"You asked me to sit down with you, remember? How the hell would Aiden put me up to anything?" I say, suspicion rising.

Blake's lips press into a thin line as he shifts a few inches away from me, facing the other side of the booth instead of looking at me. His face flits back and forth through myriad expressions until he finally stops and twists back around to me. "You're telling me you picked all that up from shaking his hand?"

I roll my eyes. "Duh. Psychic, remember?" I say, pointing at my head for effect.

"You know, I—I gotta go. Thanks for the talk, Diana. I'll see you around," he says, shifting out of the booth and out of the door before I even have time to process what's happening.

Shifting in my seat, I press my back into the booth.

What in the hell just happened?

"Sure know how to freak a guy out, eh?" Max says, wandering over to the booth. He grabs Blake's cup and wipes up his spot with a wet rag.

I turn and glare at him. Something in his smug grin makes me snap. "Your girlfriend's cheating on you with the mailman," I blurt out, downing the rest of my mocha.

I've known for ages, but it's none of my damn business. I guess now I don't care.

Max steps back, eyes wide with panic.

I push past him and walk out the door before the backlash of questions can hit. Glancing up and down the street, Blake is nowhere to be seen, so I walk back to the shop on my own.

Why would it matter if I knew about Aiden's parents or the way he gave up his military life? And besides, why is it a shock to Blake? It's not like I hide being psychic. What in the hell gives?

Opening the door, the ding of the bell pisses me right off.

"Who the hell installed that stupid bell?" I say, glaring at Ren as I walk in the door.

Ren's face goes from borderline bored to *'oh-shit'* in under a second.

"Uh-oh. Things not go so good with Mr. Tight Pants?" he asks, trying to be both playful and delicate at the same time.

It doesn't work.

"Ugh. Shut up, would you? And do something about that damn bell."

I head straight into my reading room and slam the door.

"What the fuck?" I groan, walking to the back door. I place my head on the window with a thud.

I'm so stupid. Honestly, it's not like I haven't learned in all these years but something about Blake let me relax a bit and open up. And why? To be bitten in the ass again?

Stupid, Diana. What a naive, idiotic move.

Ren knocks on the door. As it opens, he waves a white handkerchief from the crack.

I roll my eyes and take a deep breath.

"What do you want, Ren?" I say, walking to my desk and sitting down.

"Wanna tell me what happened?" he says, walking into the room like there are eggshells all over the floor.

"If I knew, I'd tell you. I honestly have no idea."

Renaldo grabs the chair from my reading table, dragging it over to my desk.

"He didn't try anything funny, did he?" Ren says, crossing his arms over his chest and going all protective.

"In a coffee shop?" I shoot him a look from under my eyebrows.

He shrugs. "You never know. Stranger things have happened."

"True."

I bite my lip, trying to keep myself from combusting. For a moment, a simple, strange, beautiful moment—I felt like I was connecting with someone. Not through my gifts, not with the knowledge they placed in my head—but in the normal, ordinary, blissfully human way. Person to person.

"I thought—I actually thought things were going okay."

I drop my head to my hands, raking my fingertips through my hair as it falls forward.

"So, what then?" Ren asks. "Did you piss him off? I mean, not that you would. Okay, maybe you would, but—"

"I told him about something I picked up at his house. An impression about him through his adopted son, Aiden. That was all. I mean, it's not like he—"

"So ya wigged him the eff out, huh?" Renaldo raises his eyebrows, casting a knowing look my way.

"How? I mean, it's not like I haven't been upfront about the whole thing from the start. For godsakes, it's how we got put in each other's way in the first place. He needed my help."

"Did he really?"

"Oh, would you stop with the cryptic? Just spit out what you want to say," I say, frowning.

"Well, mkay. Here's the thing, and you know this better than anyone, but I'm guessing your emotions are starting to muddy the waters. You freaked him out because he wants to believe you. It's pretty damn obviously there's a vibe going between the two of you and if ya wanted, it might go flammable. But my guess is, as much as he wants to believe you, he sorta doesn't either. Am I right?"

I bite the inside of my cheek. "My abilities—they don't work right when I'm around him."

Ren shifts in his chair, his mouth popping open. "And you're only telling me now? When did you first learn this?"

"I don't know. The first night, I guess. I didn't know what to make of it. It's never happened before."

"Well, no wonder. The man didn't really give ya much credit, because you didn't give him much to go on." Ren shakes his head and shrugs.

"So this is my fault?"

"Hell no. Serves him right. You don't get to be as renowned as you are by telling bullshit," he says, batting the thought away like it was nothing.

My eyes widen and I smirk. "I'm renowned?"

Ren flicks his hand in the air absently. "As if you didn't know. Pu-leeze. Well, if you ask me, you have two choices."

"I do, do I? And what are they exactly?" I cross my arms over my chest and wait.

"You have to decide—does it matter he thought you were full of rainbow farts, or doesn't it? If it does—and I'm pretty sure it does—then you need to go out there and show that man who's boss. I mean, you're Diana friggin' Hawthorne, dammit. He'd do well to remember it." He nods his head in final punctuation to his declaration.

"I think he's already acquainted. It's what freaked him out, remember?"

"Then show him why it matters. Find those men, close the loop on the case you both worked on. I can handle the fort here."

"And how do you plan on doing that?" My lips flatten into a thin line, and I can't help but envision Ren throwing a party —frat-style—while I'm away.

"Duh. I'll have a massive sale with all the goodies we just got in. And I'll raffle you off on a date," he says, grinning.

"Deal. With everything but the date," I say, standing up and pushing away from my desk.

"Where are you going?" Ren spins around in his chair as I make for my coat.

"Following your advice. I'm going to show Blake who's boss."

OR THE LIFE OF ME, I can't remember the way to Blake's house. I wasn't paying enough attention when he was driving, and God knows I can't use my abilities to locate him. I try tapping into Aiden instead, but the damn kid is in town. All signs are pointing to the college, so that's a whole helluva lot of no help.

"C'mon, Diana. There has to be another way," I mutter to myself, my hands sliding down my face.

My eyes widen, and I could smack myself in the face for the stupidity. You don't realize how much you rely on your abilities until they go on the fritz like this. Deductive reasoning goes out the window when it's easy to just know something.

I pick up the green, corded phone in my kitchen and call the store. After a few moments, Ren picks up.

"Inner Sanctum Books and Gifts, Renaldo speaking. What can I do for you?" he says with his signature lilt in his voice.

"It's me. Can you do me a favor?"

Dropping his 'shop' pretenses, he says, "Of course. Have you found Mr. Tall, Dark, and Handsome yet?"

"Er—yeah, not yet," I say, shaking my head. "That's why I need your help. Do you have a number for Ted and Lacy?"

"Yeah, I think so. Hang on," he says, setting the phone down with a thud. A scrambling sound erupts on the other end, then a small thump before he picks up. "Okay, got it. Ya got a pen or something?"

"Sure, go ahead," I say, getting my pen and notepad ready.

"Alrighty. It's 273-3593. Hopefully, they'll be able to getcha hooked up."

The double entendre in his voice doesn't go unnoticed, but I let it slide all the same.

"Thanks, Ren. I appreciate it. Now, get back to work."

"Of course, slave driver. There's oh, so many people here to contend with now that you're gone."

I can practically hear him roll his eyes.

"Well, then it's your job to drive more people into the shop, isn't it? Get those MyFace ads up and running, would you?"

Ren's sigh is thick. "Facebook, dear. *Facebook*."

"Whichever. Pull more people into the store, kay?"

"Yeah, yeah. Gonna be harder now without our illustrious psychic in the shop. But I'll do my best. Ciao." He hangs up before I even get the chance to say goodbye.

Shaking my head, I immediately dial-up Ted and Lacy's number before I lose my nerve.

"Hello?"

"Is this Lacy?" I ask.

"Yes. Who's this?"

"This is Diana Hawthorne."

"Oh—oh. Hi, Diana. What can I do for you?" Lacy says, her voice instantly perking up at the sound of my name.

"Well, a couple of things actually. First, how's Esther doing? She okay now that she's been back home?"

"So far. We've been dealing with nightmares, but nothing we can't handle, thanks to you and Mr. Wilson."

I breathe a sigh of relief. I can only imagine how difficult it was for her.

"Great, that's what I was hoping to hear. I mean, not that she's having nightmares, but that she's adjusting after such a traumatic ordeal. I hope she continues to get better."

"I'm sure she will. We have a great psychiatrist working with all of us."

"Good. I'm sure there's a lot you all need to talk about. Say, the other thing I was wondering about. Do you happen to have Blake Wilson's address or phone number handy? I'd like to get in touch with him, but I don't seem to have any of his contact details here."

"Sure, let me have a quick look. I'm pretty sure it's in my phone. Can I put you down for a second?"

"Absolutely, take your time," I say, tapping the end of the pen on the notepad in front of me.

After what feels like an eternity, Lacy comes back to the phone.

"Okay, I have both. His number is 273-4414, and his address is 22341 Wild Rebel Road."

I snicker to myself at the street name. It suits him. "Thanks, Lacy. I appreciate it."

"Don't mention it. It's the least I can do. Is—is everything okay? With the case, I mean…"

"Oh yeah. Everything's fine. I just have some questions for him. Don't worry. It's nothing to do with you or Esther."

"Oh, thank goodness." Lacy's sigh of relief is palpable.

"Well, thanks again. Talk to you soon," I say, hanging up the phone.

I stare at the details on the page.

Do I call? Or do I show up unannounced?

The social anxiety in me says to call and be done with it.

The psychic in me wants to see his reactions and get a better read on him and the situation.

"Dammit."

I rip the piece of paper off the notepad and grab my car keys. Walking out the back door, I head to my tiny garage. My itty-bitty Prius has sat dormant for months, resting inside the barely wide enough space. Seriously, whoever built garages in the early 1900s didn't expect people to be able to open car doors once they were finally inside.

Sliding behind the wheel, the car still fires up on the first try. No problems whatsoever.

I rub the steering wheel, giving a little silent praise before shifting into reverse. It isn't until I've left the confines of my back alley that it occurs to me, I have no clue where this Wild Rebel Road actually is. And without the creepy assistance from a cellphone with a navigation thingy, I need to do things the old-fashioned way—with a map. Especially with my intuition on the super fritz when it comes to him.

Pulling into the nearest gas station, I fill up on gas and yank the map of Helena out of the glove box. It takes ages to finally pinpoint the street on the map, but thankfully, the course is relatively simple. In fact, now I can see why alarm bells didn't go off right away. We drive right by the Helena PD on the way to his place.

Taking a deep breath, I lay the map out on the passenger seat and climb back inside.

"Okay, Diana. Let's do this," I whisper under my breath as I put the car in gear.

The roads look different during the day. Far more relaxing as I leave the confines of the city for a more open layout. It doesn't do much to chill out my nerves, unfortunately.

I take a deep breath and roll my eyes. "For Godsake,

you're not asking the man to marry you, Diana. Would you get a grip?"

I twist my fingertips around the steering wheel and concentrate on the road. The drive there is fairly easy, now that I have a clear direction, thank goodness. Before I know it, I'm already turning down his twisting, long driveway.

The Tudor-style home still looks impressive in the daylight and the massive trees in the front are probably gorgeous, come summertime.

Putting the car in park, I open my door and walk to the front entry before I can talk myself out of it.

I rap on the door hard, then step back and wait. Crossing my hands behind my back, I pace the front stoop for a moment before deciding it's been long enough and try again.

When still no one answers, I try the handle, hoping for an easy win. Unfortunately, the door's locked.

Dammit.

Had my gifts been working, I would have known not to drive all the way out here.

I should have called first.

Leaning toward the narrow window beside the front door, I place my head on the glass, trying to get a good look inside. Unfortunately, the narrow access only grants a view of the entryway wall.

"Now what, Diana? Wait around like a lost puppy? Or go home and give him a call like you should have done to begin with?"

I start walking down the steps when a dark red, beat-up pickup drives up. It comes to a halt beside the garage door.

"Hey, whatcha doing here?" Aiden asks, throwing open the driver's side door. "Was Blake expecting you?"

I shake my head. "No, kind of an impromptu meeting. Is —is he home?" Tipping my head toward the house, I keep my eyes trained on Aiden.

111

"Dunno. I'm here with you." He smirks. "One way to find out. C'mon." Aiden grabs a backpack and unravels his keyring in search of the front door key.

"Are you sure? I mean, I don't mean to intrude or anything."

"Are you kidding? You're *saving* me." Aiden chuckles as he twists the handle and swings the door open wide.

"Oh?"

"Yeah. I'd have to do trig homework if you go." He laughs.

"Well, I can't let you die of knowledge, now can I?" I chuckle.

"Exactly." He winks, throwing an easy smile. "You hungry?"

My eyebrows tug in. I really only had one purpose—to put Blake in his place. Not raid his kitchen.

"I'm okay," I say.

"You sure? I'm gonna whip up some nachos quick. I'd be more than willing to share."

Aiden nods to the kitchen, urging me to follow along.

"No, really. I'm good."

"You'll miss out. I'll even put avocados on it," he says, as we enter the broad expanse of a kitchen.

It's still as sparsely decorated as the rest of the house, but you can tell a lot more care and consideration has gone into this space. Things are laid out very precisely, and the stainless-steel appliances are meticulously clean.

"Oh, and there's coffee to be had," he adds.

"All right, you twisted my arm. Coffee would be lovely."

I take a seat and belly up to the breakfast bar the way I would at home. Aiden's energy is very easygoing and relaxed. Surprisingly, he sets me at ease right away and dispels some of the anxiety I was feeling about coming here.

Aiden sets to work, maneuvering the kitchen like a true

pro. Grabbing pans, and fresh ingredients from the refrigerator.

"So, you said you were here for Blake, right?"

"Yeah, I need to talk to him about some stuff. We kinda got off on the wrong foot last time we were together," I say, leaning forward.

"Yeah, he has a way of putting people off at first, but once you get to know him, he's really a big teddy bear."

I smile, getting impressions immediately from Aiden of all the good times he's had with Blake. Christmases, surprises, special treats, and birthday parties over the years. The images flash by quickly. So quickly, in fact, he probably doesn't even realize he's conjured them with such potency.

"You've known him a long time, huh?"

"Yeah, guess you could say that." He nods, stirring some sort of black bean mixture and adding cheese to another pan to start melting.

"How did you first meet?" I already know the answer to how they got thrown in this situation together, but not how they initially met.

"I don't know. He's always sorta just been in my life. He was best friends with my birth parents, so he was kinda like big Uncle Blake from the time I could walk and talk."

"And your parents—they're not with us anymore?"

"Nope. They died when I was pretty young. Eight, I think."

"I'm so sorry, Aiden. That must have been hard for you."

"Yeah, it was. A lot of people weren't sure this was the right path. Going with Blake, you know? Right away I knew my life was never gonna be the same. But Blake, man, he made sure things stayed as stable and recognizable as possible for me. I don't know what I'd do without him. He's really given up a lot over the years."

"He sounds like a good guy," I say, flicking my eyebrows

in recognition.

"The best. I know it sounds all cliche and stuff, but he's my best friend."

"Blake was saying you lived in Minnesota before you came here. Was that weird for you?"

"Nah, it was pretty awesome. I wanted to go to the University here, and Blake up and moved us so I could make it happen."

"Do you miss Minnesota?"

"Not even a little bit. It's damn cold there." He chuckles.

"I suppose it would be. I mean, it's practically the North Pole."

"You're not wrong."

I shake my head. I lived in Minnesota once. Pretty lakes. But seven months of cold is enough to drive a person batty. One thing you learn when you've been around as long as I have—don't live where the air hurts your face. Gorgeous lakes or not.

"Blake should be back soon. He usually runs errands while I'm in school, but tries to be back about the same time I am," Aiden says, dumping coffee beans into the coffee maker and flipping the switch on.

The room fills with the sounds of beans grinding, then subsides to the percolating noises I'm used to.

"I gotta get me one of those fancy coffee pots. I still grind my beans by hand," I say, chuckling.

"Hardcore."

"Yeah, compared to that crazy thing," I say, pointing.

The room begins to fill with the smells of coffee, warmth, and kindred spirits. I'd forgotten how easy it can be to talk with people sometimes. Not everyone is as laid back as Aiden and Blake.

"So, you go to school around here?" Aiden asks.

"Me?"

My hand flies to my chest as I try to digest the question. I forget sometimes how young I still look—despite my super-advanced age.

"Yeah, you're what? Twenty-five or something? I suppose you don't need to, with your line of work. No offense."

I run my hand along the back of my neck. "Uh, yeah. No college necessary."

He nods, handing me the first cup of coffee. "You take cream or sugar or anything?"

"All of the above." I nod.

I grab hold of the handle, pulling it in tight to me so I can inhale the aroma even more. There's something magical about the scent of coffee. Even after all this time, I don't quite know what it is. Sure, the caffeine buzz is nice, but it's deeper than that.

Aiden takes out the milk and sugar and hands them over to me, along with a spoon. The front door creaks open, and my heart kicks things up a notch.

"We're in here," Aiden calls out, continuing to work on his nachos.

There's some scuttling in the hallway, but Blake calls back, "Who's we?"

He enters the kitchen, bags in hand from a grocery shopping excursion. The smile on his face fades as his lips form an 'o.'

"Diana—" he says, recovering.

I flit my eyes from him to Aiden and back again. Aiden continues to cook, oblivious to the awkwardness permeating the room.

"Hey Blake," I say, trying to force my lips into a genuine smile.

"What—I mean, not that it's not great to see you, but what are you doing here?"

"I didn't like the way things ended last time, so I came to

talk to you. Do you have a second?" I say, hopping off the bar stool.

Blake strides quickly to the counter, placing the bags down. "Aiden, would you mind putting this stuff away when you get a second?" he asks.

"Sure thing."

"Great. Uh—Diana, do you want to follow me to the study?"

I nod, sweeping my hand out to suggest he lead the way.

Blake bites his lower lip and takes the lead.

We walk down the narrow hallway, past the room with all the computers and gadgets, and into a large study on the opposite end. Books adorn the walls in floor-to-ceiling shelves spanning the entire room. By far, it's the most decorated room I've seen in this house.

I walk up to the shelves, my fingertips grazing the spines.

"You like books, huh?"

Blake nods, his eyebrows raising up quickly. "You could say that, I guess."

"Hmmm."

"Hmmm?" he asks, standing in the doorway.

"Look, I didn't mean to upset you. I forget sometimes to dial down what I know. I guess, I thought you could handle more than you could," I say, leaving the books and walking back to him.

Blake's face flashes between expressions quickly, as if he's fighting internally with himself. "Look, you just caught me off guard. I've had some time to work through it now, though. So don't worry."

I let out a sigh of relief. "Oh, good."

"I mean, once I realized you and I aren't all that different, it all made sense."

I blink, confused. "I'm not following."

"You did your homework, right? After you met me and

Aiden, you what—used Detective Radish or whatever his name is to pull our records?"

"No—first of all, I'd never invade your privacy like that," I say, my indignation rising. I take a step forward, invading his personal space a bit instead.

"Come on. You can't possibly expect me to believe you're *really* psychic," he says, making a face.

"No, not at all. I expect you to know it. Where the hell were you when we got Esther out? Did you think it was just an educated guess?"

"Educated, perhaps. Mostly, I figure it was more a lucky guess. It happens sometimes."

"Oh my God, please." I roll my eyes and lick my lips.

How on earth can someone be so dense? The evidence is right there in front of him, but he's oblivious to seeing it.

Blake keeps his intense brown eyes trained on me.

"You're a moron, you know that?" I spit, pacing back and forth like a caged animal with him hovering in the doorway.

"Excuse me?"

"You heard me. You're dense if you think it's all lucky guesses and wool pulled-over eyes. What about the warning I gave about the other car? And why bother asking me to help you find the men who got away? I mean, what the hell?"

Honestly, I have no idea why it bothers me so much that he doesn't believe me. It's his prerogative, I guess. It wouldn't be the first time. But for some reason, his rejection stings more than most.

Blake doesn't say anything. He simply watches me like a hawk as he crosses his arms over his chest.

I stop pacing and turn to face him head-on, widening my stance and refusing to look away. Suddenly, I know what I have to do to convince him once and for all.

"What are you doing?" he finally asks.

After a long pause, I say, "Fine, I'm in."

*B*LAKE TAKES A STEP BACK. His eyes narrow, and his mouth twitches.

"What? Like, now?" He releases his arms and scratches the back of his head. "This wasn't a ploy to get you to say yes, you know."

I shrug.

"Even if it was, now I have something to prove and I can't remember the last time I felt like that."

"What if I've decided to let it go?" Blake says, shaking his head.

"You wouldn't do that."

"Oh, let me guess, another premonition, right?" He makes a face, but for the first time, he enters the room. He walks to the big picture window on the far end of the space and stares out into the late afternoon.

"No, educated guess, moron," I spit back, walking over to him.

Blake snickers. "Right, you still can't get a '*read*' on me."

I fight back the urge to punch him after he air quotes.

"See, that sarcastic tone in your voice is why I'm doing

this. I'm looking forward to wiping the smug look completely off your face when it finally occurs to you there's more to me than smoke and mirrors."

"No, you're not," he says over his shoulder. He doesn't look my direction, but there's a hint of something—wonder perhaps—starting to blossom in his tone. He probably wouldn't admit it but I've been around long enough to hear it.

"No, I'm not, what?"

Blake turns around, leaning back as he rests his hands behind him on the window seal. "You're not doing this because you have anything to prove. At least, not when it comes to your psychic skills—*mojo*—whatever. I mean, what's one person who thinks you might not be who you say you are? You have a reputation around here, even if I don't entirely believe you. And you're not doing it for an 'I told you so' either."

"Okay, smart ass. Enlighten me. What am I really doing it for?"

Now it's my turn to cross my arms and take a step back.

"Like I said before, *you try too hard*."

"Ugh, not that again…" I roll my eyes and loll my head.

I take another step back and start to walk toward the door.

"It's true. You want people to see this, I don't know—hard shell. But it's bullshit. You do all that because you've been hurt by caring too much. I'd wager my life on it. But every once in a while, the real you slips through. You want to care. You want to do good in this messed up world, but you don't want anyone to know it's the real you."

My eyes widen, but I don't dare say a word.

He takes a step forward. "But I see it," he says, his tone hushed.

"Well, thanks a ton for your assessment, Dr. Phil. Now,

are we gonna get to work, or are you gonna psychotherapy my ass all day?" I say, shuddering away from the goosebumps his words invoked.

Blake crosses his arms. "I know I'm right."

"Then it looks like we both have something to prove."

"Guess so." He nods.

"Super. Now, where do you wanna get started?"

"I uh—I don't know. I kinda got blind-sided by all this. Mind if I take a day to regroup? I need to talk with Aiden and see where he left off, I suppose."

"Sure, do what you need to do. Take all the time you need," I say, laying the sweet on thick.

Blake's shoulders ease up a bit.

"But I sure hope that extra day doesn't mean another girl —*or ten*—being kidnapped," I add, heading for the door.

With an exasperated sigh, Blake's chin drops to his chest.

"What? Honesty? Gotta love it," I say.

"Fine. What do you propose?" he says, raising his head enough to glare at me from under his eyebrows.

"Well, sounds like you had something in play. Why not go chat with Aiden right now and see where we go from there? I mean, he is here. And we're here. Why wait?"

"Yeah, I guess. Let's go."

Blake ushers me out of the study room and back to the kitchen. Aiden's at the breakfast bar, snarfing up the last of his nachos as only a college kid can but looks up long enough to do a double-take.

"Something you need?" he says through a mouthful.

Nodding, Blake scratches at the back of his neck. "Yeah, you got some time this evening to go over some of the stuff we found on the pedophile ring? Diana here would like to join us after all."

"I thought we decided to table the whole thing—"

"I know what we decided. But I think Diana wants to

check things over herself and maybe we can go from there," Blakes says.

The two of them exchange odd glances, but Aiden shoves the last bite into his mouth and stands up. "Let's do it," he says, walking to the dishwasher and tossing his plate and fork inside.

Blake leads the way back to the super-techie room, with me following close on his heels, and Aiden just behind me.

"Hang on, I need to grab something," Blake says, opening the door on the right, just before we get there.

The last time I was here, Blake ushered me out rather quickly and I'd give my left foot to know what he's hiding.

"What's this room for?" I ask, peering around the door.

The lights remain off as he walks into the space.

"Nothing, just go with Aiden. I'll be there in a minute," he says, quickly walking back to me and pulling the door in tight.

"You know, it would probably help you find whatever you're looking for if you turned on the lights," I say, slipping under his arm before he can close the door any further. I flip on the light switch and gasp.

Blake twists around, immediately flipping the light switch back off.

"You need to go. Now," he practically growls, grabbing hold of my arm. "This is private."

Light may be sparse through the one large window, but I certainly caught an eyeful.

Every inch of the walls are covered in drawings. Some in pencil, some charcoal. Big, little, massive—they're like a collage put together in an attempt to transform the room into a cavern or something. Some drawings look like rocky walls, others are macro impressions of rocks, knives, blood. The blood is the only thing done in color. It's all got a very macabre vibe.

"What is all of this?"

Blake's lips are pressed into a thin line—his eyes wide. "I said follow Aiden," he practically shrieks, grabbing for my wrist. "Are you hard of hearing?"

Sidestepping his clutches, I take another step into the room. A handful of drawings catch my attention. They have the strange symbol on them, the one from my...dream? Premonition?

Stepping over to them, I can't help but stare.

"Do you know what this symbol means? Why—why have you drawn this? I mean, these drawings are yours, right? You've created these?" I say, my eyes widening as I touch the largest version with my pointer finger.

Taking a deep breath, Blake walks to his desk, opening a drawer and slapping a folder on top of the desk.

"Yes, I drew them. I don't know what the symbol means— not really. The closest I can figure is it's Greek. I keep seeing it in my dreams and it—well, all of this has freaked me out ever since I was a kid. My therapist—yeah, yeah, I had a therapist—she encouraged me to start drawing it all when it bothered me. I guess I just kept going. It helps me keep track of how often the dreams come about."

"Fascinating," I say, mesmerized by the sea of pictures.

If I had to draw every time I had a premonition, or a strange dream, I'd need a mansion the size of Detroit.

Despite the low light from the windows, I walk from one drawing to the next, unable to take my eyes off of them. There's something eerily familiar in the decor—the cavernesque quality, as well as the overall vibe.

"The other night—well, I suppose it's been over a week now—I had a dream. It was the night I came home after we met—and saved Esther. Anyway, I saw this symbol, too. I wasn't sure if it was a dream or a premonition. Sometimes they can get all jumbled together and hard to decipher. But this—this tells me it was no ordinary dream. It was obviously tied to you in some way."

"Yeah, well, I wouldn't bet on it. You can't read me, so don't pretend to start now."

"Not fair," I say, shaking my head. "I'm telling you the truth."

Aiden pokes his head into the room after a few minutes. "Hey, guys... you coming? I have everything up and ready."

"Yeah, we were just leaving," Blake says, grabbing the manilla folder and taking me by the arm.

Still stunned by the imagery in the small office, I allow Blake to lead me down the hallway to the tech room where Aiden has all of his computer stuff set up.

Even though I've been through the evolution and very inklings of computers and technology, there's something about it I simply don't trust. Not that I'm not grateful for those who can wield it, though.

Aiden watches us enter the room and gives us a moment to get situated on the chairs opposite his. The monitors behind him each have their own thing going on—some are static, others display constant movement. Truth be told, it's rather distracting.

"Alright, so here's where I think we should start," Aiden begins. "I've tracked the pedophile ring to a group operating out of Europe. Based on the images from the Range Rover's cameras, I was able to track the guys who shot at you and pulled up some of their aliases. The good news is, I got faces to go along with the false names. But the problem I've run into is my facial recognition software caught a glimpse of them at the airport."

"Isn't that a good thing? I mean, did you let the police know?" I say, leaning forward and placing my elbows on my knees.

"In theory, that would have been smart, had I been

keeping a watch on it. Unfortunately, Blake had already decided to let things go. I literally just got this info as I was waiting for the two of you."

"So how long ago were they at the airport?" Blake interjects.

"A day and a bit." Aiden shrugs.

"So they could be anywhere by now," I sigh, leaning back in my chair and glaring at the ceiling.

"Well, not anywhere. I mean, I was able to track the flight. I have a general idea—but I don't know where within the vicinity without a little more research."

"Where were they headed?" Blake says, mimicking my movement and leaning forward.

"Italy," he says, making a face.

"So?" I say.

"Tickets to Rome run between $1500 and $2400. Per person," Aiden says. "That's not including rental cars, hotels, and other stuff."

"So?" I repeat, eyeing them both.

Blake scoffs. "It'll take me a few days to pull together that kinda cash for that big of a withdrawal on my debit card. My bank has a waiting policy," he says leaning back. "Unfortunately, I can't magic it out of nowhere. And before you ask, no, I don't have credit cards. They're shit. They're just corporate control meant to keep people down."

I shoot him a sideways glance.

"I'll pay," I say, shrugging. "My bank has no problem letting money leave my account."

Aiden's eyes widen, as he looks from me to Blake.

Blake's eyebrows scrunch, along with his face. "That's the most ridiculous thing I've heard yet. I wasn't trying to get you to pay."

I roll my eyes. "Oh come on. You're not one of those

macho guys who feel emasculated when a woman pays, are you?"

Blake shifts in his chair. "It's—it's not that. I just don't think it's fair, is all."

"Do you want to find these guys, or not?" I say, standing up and crossing my arms.

"Well, sure. But—"

"Good, then it's settled. Aiden," I say, turning to him, "can you pull up those ticket details for me? Let's get tickets booked."

"Holy shit, this is all happening a little fast. Don't you think?" Blake says, standing up and walking to my side.

"No, I don't. These guys are on the run and the only way we're gonna track them down is to get our asses on a plane. I know the area, I spent a few—er, a year in Italy. Their trail will run dry, and even with my gifts, I won't be able to locate them. Which defeats damn near the entire purpose of this."

"If this is all about showing me you really are psychic, you don't have to do this. I mean, that's a ridiculous amount of money to put on the line just to prove me wrong," Blake says.

"Then I better be right," I say, cocking my head to the side. "Besides, if it really freaks you out, you can pay me back."

Aiden's blue eyes flit back and forth between me and Blake like a ping pong ball before he shakes his head, the shaggy hair flopping from side to side, as he finally turns around to face the computers.

"You'll see. We'll get the bad guys and they won't be able to hurt anyone else," I say.

"Ugh, that's so cliche," Blake says, a hint of a smile causing the dimple on his left cheek to emerge.

I run my hand along the side of my neck, taking a small step back. I don't know what it is about his smile, but it coils inside my gut.

"Yeah, well, it's still the truth. And lucky me, I'll get to show you I'm not just a charlatan."

Blake takes a breath and exhales deeply. "I don't know if proof will make me feel better or worse," he says.

"Only one way to find out, I guess," I say, smirking.

"Okay, I have a couple of flight options, but it doesn't look like there are any direct flights happening in the next week," Aiden says.

"What are the options?" I ask, turning to him.

"Do you want cheapest? Or fastest?"

"Fastest," I say with a nod.

"Cheapest," Blake says at the same time.

"Fastest," I repeat, punctuating the end of the word and eyeing him from beneath my eyebrows.

"Yes, ma'am," Aiden says, twisting back to the screen. "The fastest has two stops. One in Atlanta, then another in Paris. You're looking at nearly a sixteen-hour flight time with the layovers."

"Okay, let's do it. What do you need from me?"

"Just your card," Aiden says, making a face.

"Sure, let me grab my purse from the car."

I walk out, past Blake, whose face is as pale as the entryway walls.

Trotting to my car, I grab my purse and head back inside. Part of me is excited for this adventure. It's been years since I was in Europe, let alone Italy or the area near there.

When I get back to the room, I take a seat and open my purse.

"Here you go," I say, handing Aiden my debit card.

If there's one thing that matters least to me, it's money. With thousands of years of accumulation, I have far more than any one person ever needs. Even an immortal one.

Aiden takes the card, eyeing it suspiciously.

"You know this is your debit card, right?"

I raise an eyebrow and stare at him unblinkingly.

"Mkay," he says, turning back to the screens.

Blake crosses his arms and starts pacing the room.

With incredible ease, Aiden's fingertips fly across the keyboard.

"Okay, last chance to back out," he says, his pointer finger hovering over the enter button.

"I'm good," I say, shrugging.

"You both have passports, right?"

"Yes," we say in unison.

"Good," Aiden says. His finger taps down, effectively booking our flight. "Your flight leaves tomorrow at eleven, but you need to be at the airport by nine."

"Aiden, use my card to book the hotel and car, would you?" Blake says, reaching for the back of Aiden's chair.

"Where do you want to stay?"

"Anyplace centrally located. Find the ring's last known location—or track any potential haunts. If we need to move around, we will—but it will be nice to have a hub to start with."

"Got it," Aiden says, nodding and handing me back my card.

I put it back into my wallet, just as Blake taps my arm.

"Can I speak with you for a moment?" he says, tipping his head to the door.

"Sure."

"We'll be right back," Blake calls out.

Aiden lifts his hand, giving a thumbs up.

"Oh, and you'll want to let Interpol know about the men," I say, speaking over my shoulder at Aiden. "They'll want to know what's going down—especially if they can help. More than likely, they have a team on the case already, so we wouldn't want to step on any toes."

Aiden nods. "Sure thing."

"How do you know so much about Interpol?" Blake asks as we enter the hallway.

"Uh—watched a lot of movies?" I say, grinning.

He shakes his head. "All right, so we don't have much time. I'm going to get packed and swing by Ted and Lacy's house to see if they've been able to glean any more information from Esther—and check in on them. I'll pick you up tomorrow about 8:30 a.m. Sound good?"

"Are you trying to get rid of me?" I say, cocking my head to the side.

"Not at all. I just figured you'll want to talk to your assistant about your absence and get packed yourself."

Ugh. I totally hadn't given any thought to how this would affect Ren. He's going to flip a lid. I'm sure he had no idea helping on this case would actually mean leaving the country.

"Yeah, okay. Good point." I nod. "Good luck with Ted and Lacy."

"Thanks," he says, his eyes searching mine for a moment. He opens his mouth, then closes it again. His tongue briefly sweeps across his lower lip. It's a somewhat distracting motion and I have to look away to break free from its intensity.

"Hey Aiden," I call into the openness of the hallway, "Thanks for your help. See you when we get back."

Aiden's head pops out of the door. He eyes the two of us, standing less than a foot apart, then extends his arm into the hall. My purse dangles from his wrist.

"Don't forget your purse. And no problem, Diana. Wish I could go, too, but I don't think my professors would understand. Or my bank account." He chuckles.

"At least you have our backs from here, right?" I say, smiling at him as I run back to grab my purse.

"Always," he says, with a single nod of agreement.

*R*ENALDO'S JAW slacks open. "You're going where?"

"Italy," I say for the fourth time.

"And why is that again?" His eyebrow arcs.

"Oh, for godsake, you already know why. Hell, you're the one who practically pushed me into it."

Ren feigns surprise, his hand pressing delicately against his chest. "I most certainly did not. I said to show the man what you can do and help him with the case. But I most certainly didn't say run halfway around the world with him. I mean, what am I meant to tell your clientele? A couple of days, I can handle. Sure. No problem. But an open-ended question mark without their favorite psychic? They're gonna freak the fuck right out. Oh my god, what about Mrs. Kaminski?" His eyes widen and he fans himself.

"What about her?" I chuckle under my breath.

"Don't you give me that, Diana Hawthorne. You know damn well if that woman doesn't find a way to connect with her cat every week she'll be haunting my stoop daily until she can. She smells like kitty litter and dawn dish soap. This is not a position I want to be put in."

"I'm sorry, Ren. I don't know what to say. Unless we can find these guys quickly—and I'm hoping we can—we could end up being there a while. I don't want to lie and say it will be quick. We're not going all that way only to turn around empty-handed. Who knows where they are right now. It's going to take us at least a day just to get our bearings. By that point, they could be in a different country, for all I know."

Renaldo shifts to his other foot and crosses his arms.

I sigh. "Okay, look. If Mrs. Kaminski gives you any trouble, let me know. I can see if Blake will help me set up one of those computer telecommunication program thingies. What's the one called? Snipe?"

"Skype," Ren says, running his hand over his face.

"Yeah, yeah, that's what I meant. That way, I can still do a reading for her if she gets out of control. Sound good?"

"Oh my god, *yes*. Bless you," Ren says, breathlessly as he drops his hands and grabs hold of both my arms.

My back goes rigid and I glance down at his hands. Too many images of him arguing with Brody flood my mind, mixed with long nights holding hands and making up.

He smiles awkwardly, then pretends to brush something off my sleeve, before letting go altogether.

"Great. Now that's settled. I do have to discuss the matter of payroll…" I begin.

"Oh, here we go," Renaldo says, taking a step back.

"Don't worry. It's no big deal. I'm going to be shooting you cash while I'm gone. But since I'm not here to look over timecards and whatnot, you'll have to take what you get. It'll be comparable to what your typical week is, though. We can work out any overages or shortfalls when I get back."

Heaving a big sigh, Renaldo nods. "Works for me. For a

moment there, I thought you were going to expect me to do all this from the goodness of my little black heart."

"No, but I do expect you to be on time. Every day. We have to keep up the shop. Especially with me gone. So, step up your game and make this place a hub for... what did you call them? Lust bunnies?"

I can't help but chuckle. Renaldo does come up with the best names. He really does.

"Can you remind me what you consider *on time*?" Ren asks, shooting me a sheepish glance.

"C'mon, man. We've been over this a bazillion times. 8 a.m. Sharp. You need time to prep the shop before you open at nine. Feel free to open the doors early, if you're ready."

"Really? Eight in the morning? Has it always been that early?" he says, scrunching his nose.

"Yes. For the love of god, *yes*." I reach up, tugging at the roots of my hair.

This is my ultimate battle. All the crazy people, the nonsense with my own life and amnesia from way back in the day—whatever, I'll take it. But this... One day, I swear, I'll get back at the universe for this.

"Huh. Wouldn't it make more sense if I showed up at 8:30?"

I glare at him, knowing anything I say is pretty much wasted breath.

"Whatever," I mumble, dropping my hands and reaching for my purse. "I gotta go pack."

"Ooooh—oooh. It just occurred to me. Where are you staying? Are you guys, like, staying in a hotel together?" Ren's eyes are wide and his lips curve upward.

I widen my stance, taking my best pot-head approach. "No, I figure we'll hit the streets. Wander aimlessly. Maybe sleep in the piazza when we get tired." I can't help but roll my eyes. "Of course, we'll be in a hotel together. But no—before you get excited—not in the same room. We each have our own spaces, thank you very much."

Ren's face falls slightly. "Pity. I was about to break out the pom-poms and send you off with a good luck cheer. Maybe even give you one of these."

Ren grabs a beginner BDSM kit and clutches it to his chest.

"On that note…" I say, taking a deep breath. "I gotta go. Thank you for all of your help, Ren. Take good care of everything—like I know you will. I'll call in as much as I can. I'm sure Blake will let me use his cellphone."

I walk to the front door and reach for the handle. An odd sensation rushes over me—like for some reason, this hunt for the pedophile ring—the way everything is playing out means more than I can completely fathom right now. When I get those types of feelings, I know to stop and take a beat because they're significant. It might not make sense now, but I have no doubt it will.

Turning back around, I pause and take everything in. The way the small shop is laid out—the lighting, the bookshelves, the herbs, crystals, and Renaldo's Valentine's Day merchandise. Ren's eyebrows tug in, but he doesn't say anything. He just watches me as I tune in.

The pungent smell of frankincense permeates the air, mixing with lavender and sage. I've become so accustomed to those smells, I hardly even notice them anymore. But now, it all seems significant somehow.

"Everything okay?" Ren finally says, breaking the silence.

"Yeah, I just—I don't know. Something made me pause," I say, shaking my head.

"What was it?"

"Not sure. Just a feeling, I guess. This trip is going to be significant. Perhaps life-changing, I just don't know how yet."

"Maybe you and Private Eye Tightpants will end up in one hotel room," Ren says, shooting me a devilish grin.

I chuckle. "Don't count on it. But whatever it is, I wanted to take a mental inventory of things. So I know what's changed when I come back. It may be nothing. Or it could be everything. Who knows?"

"You better take care of yourself, Diana. Be safe, for the love of all that's holy. Don't put yourself in any unnecessary danger or anything. Yes, I know you—Ms. Run and Jump Before She Looks."

Renaldo rarely goes all paternal on me, but when he does, it's because I've spooked him.

I walk over to him, putting my arms around him. He stiffens up, patting me on the back softly.

"I'll be safe. You better be, too. You hear me? Don't piss off Mrs. Kaminski. Or Brody, for that matter."

"I hear you. And I'll try not to."

"Good."

With that, I pat him on the shoulder and turn on my heel. I don't stop as I fling the door open and I don't turn around as I walk out onto the sidewalk and down the street. Instead, I make my way deliberately forward, knowing full well when I return, things will be very different.

When I'm back at my house, the strange sensations of significance hasn't subsided. If anything, it's gotten more powerful. Shivering away the energy, I instinctively flit my eyes to my calendar. One day to the full moon. Perhaps that's all it is?

Glancing at the clock as I set down my purse and keys, I take a deep breath. It's only gone 5:30 p.m.

I need to call Demetri.

There's still plenty of time to pack and if for some reason anything goes wrong, I need to say my apology out loud.

Walking to the corded phone on my wall, I pluck it from its holder and dial his number.

"Hello?" A woman's voice on the other end answers.

For a moment, my heart skips a beat, then plummets into my stomach. Demetri and I never were a thing—not like that —but he's always had a special place in my heart. He's helped me through so many rough patches over the years. If he has a new woman in his life and he didn't tell me—things are worse than I thought.

"Uh—hi," I say, recovering. "Is Demetri there?"

"Sure," the woman's upbeat voice responds. "Can I tell him who's calling?"

"It's Diana," I say.

"Oh," is the response. Not the upbeat, *'gotcha'* kind of 'oh,' either. More the *'holy shit, it's her'* kind.

I wince.

After a bit of scuffling and voices muttering under a muffled receiver, the call clears up.

"Hi, Diana. What did you need?" Demetri's rough voice answers from the other end.

"Hey, Demetri. You doing okay?"

Silence greets me on the other end and I wince again.

"Look, I know things didn't go so well last month—"

"That's an understatement," he says, his voice clipped.

I take a deep breath and bite my lip. "I know," I whisper, clutching the phone.

An awkward pause descends, as I search for the words I really want to say to him.

"Okay, I know I suck. I never should have pushed you to try the ritual with me. I figured since we were already working with the Violet Flame for Morgan and Gabe—well, I thought it would help me, too. It was stupid and reckless."

"Yeah, and it just about killed me, Diana. Stupid and reckless don't even cover it."

My fingertips graze my forehead as I nod gingerly. He's right. God, he's so right.

"I don't know what came over me. It's just been so long since I felt like doors might open. It was a long shot, I get that, but..." I take a deep breath, "I can't keep living like this and you were the only one who I trusted. You're the only one who understands my predicament."

Demetri blows out a puff of air. "I get your desperation. I really do. And I know it wasn't your fault. It's my fault, too. I'm the one who brought up the Violet Flame in the first place. I mean, how the hell were you meant to know how powerful the magic is surrounding Morgan's request, let alone your memory?"

"Well, I should have guessed. Morgan has power— more power than I've felt roll off a single person in years. And with me... I mean, it's been a helluva long time and I've never even gotten a glimpse of insight. Not even an inkling as to my life before I woke up that day. I've tried everything. Literally, *everything* I can think of. But I thought... I dunno, for whatever reason I thought that night was different. That the ritual we were doing together would be different." I mutter, frowning to myself.

"You were right about that, I suppose. It was different— just not in the way you expected."

"True."

"Look, Diana, we're friends and we'll always be friends. But I just can't get involved in that side of things anymore. I don't have the energy. Whatever magic I had—or whatever you wanna call it—it was obliterated in that ritual. I can't even summon spirits anymore, let alone locator spells. I don't know what my clientele is going to do when they figure out I'm totally BSing it all."

"I'm so sorry, Demetri. I didn't mean for any—"

"For fucksake, I know," he snaps. "I'm not looking for a pity party here."

"Is there anything I can do to—"

"What? Make it better? Bring it back?"

"Any of it. All of it. What can I do?" I say, tears threatening at the brim of my eyes.

"Live a good life, Diana. God knows it's a long one, but for the love, make the most of it, would you? You have power and magic and something incredibly special about you. But you waste it all pretending you're—I don't know... ordinary, I suppose. I won't try to wager why you do it. I have my guesses. Hell, maybe I'd do it too, if I was as old as you and seen everything you've seen."

"You've been a good friend, Demetri. I want you to know that," I whisper.

"Oh, don't go getting all emotional on me now."

I lick my bottom lip, trying to keep it from trembling. "Something—something big is happening and I don't quite know what it is. Maybe it's the full moon energy. Maybe it's nothing. I don't know. But I wanted you to know I'm sorry before I go," I say.

"Go? Where are you going? Are you leaving Helena for good?" he says, his voice suddenly airing on concern.

"No, nothing like that. At least, not yet. I'm helping a—private investigator," I say, gingerly. "We're going overseas to track down a pedophile ring."

"How in the hell did you get roped into that kinda mess?" he snorts.

Of all the things we've been through, this is certainly one of the stranger ones.

"It's a long story."

"Sounds it. Christ, I'm outta your life for a fortnight and you're working pedophile cases. What's the world coming to?"

I chuckle. Now that's more like the Demetri I know and love.

"I know, right? I don't understand it either. I just know it's something I gotta do."

I should tell him about Blake—about the weird feeling I'm having. But I don't want to bring him down or make him feel useless. Or worse yet, feel as though he should be helping, even though he can't. Besides, the last thing he'll want to hear about is how I'm waging my abilities and trying to get Blake to admit I'm psychic.

"Well, take care of yourself, okay. Be careful and all that touchy-feely shit."

"Yeah, I know. I will. I've got—" I stop myself, knowing where it could lead.

"This PI…" Demetri starts.

I take a deep breath. It's going there anyway.

"Yeah?" I say.

"It a he?"

"Yeah."

"Does he know what he's getting into with you?"

I suck in a breath.

There's so much I wish I could share with Blake, even though I'm not sure why. It's a strange sensation and one I'm not used to. Not even Demetri was able to lure it out of me so quickly. It was a decade or more before I let him in.

"Doubt it," I reply.

"Good. Keep it that way."

A pang of regret slices through my abdomen. Most people, especially completely normal people, simply can't fathom my life in the least. I was lucky to find Demetri. At least he shared some of my abilities and understood what it was like to really be gifted.

And I stripped all of that from him.

God, I suck so much.

"I'll try. Anyway, I suppose I better go. Gotta pack and all that."

"Okay," Demetri says, holding on to a few second's pause before he finally utters, "be safe."

"You, too. I really am—"

"If you say sorry one more time, woman, I'm gonna off myself and come back so I can prove to you there's an afterlife."

"Yeah, yeah…"

Demetri lets out a deep, heavy sigh.

"If I can find a way to help or bring it back, I will," I mutter.

"Don't make promises you can't keep, Diana. Ain't anyone taught you that in all these years?"

"For what it's worth, I'd gladly trade places with you."

"Helluva lot a good that does me now." He chuckles.

"I know, but it's true."

"Well, for what it's worth—*thanks.*"

"What about you? The lady who answered—is she treating you okay?"

"She's a friend, but yes. It's been nice having her around."

"Good. That's… good."

"It is," he says.

"Good," I repeat. "Well, bye, Demetri."

"Bye, Diana."

The click of the receiver echoes in my ear. The sound is all too much like a final ending of sorts and it does nothing to alleviate the tension building inside me.

Big changes are coming. And they're just getting started.

HE KNOCK ON THE DOOR tells me it's time to get a move on. Luckily, I have all the stuff I need—passport, cash, cards, clothes. You know, the essentials. The rest I can figure out while we're on the go. Besides, the last thing I need is to get held up by the TSA for having too much makeup or shampoo, for godsake. Added bonus, at least there's less to lose, should my suitcase go missing.

Trust me, stranger things have happened.

I smooth out the creases in my trousers one more time and stop briefly by the full-length mirror in the hall. Everything's in place—hair could use a good trim, but whatever. I don't have time for that kind of nonsense now.

On the way to answer the front door, I grab my purse from the kitchen counter, along with my keys. I glance at the green phone hanging on the wall, acknowledging the pang of guilt over Demetri, but at least feeling better that we spoke.

I flip my eyes to the stovetop and all the knobs—you know, just to be sure.

When I reach the entryway, I tug on the bottom of my top one more time and adjust my shoulders so I look more confident than I feel at the moment. I clutch my keys in my hand and swing the door open.

"All set?" I say, clutching on to my suitcase.

Blake turns around, his dark hair glistening in the early morning light. It pulls out the reds hidden in their depths. Smiling broadly, his dimples shine brightly—easily.

My stomach flutters. Such a stupid, childish feeling, but inescapable nonetheless.

I exhale slowly, shaking away the sensation as I lock the front door and slide my keys into my purse.

He adjusts his leather jacket and nods. "Yup, sure am. How about you?"

Reaching again for my suitcase handle, I pick it up, along with my small carry-on bag. "As ready as I'll ever be."

"Wow. That's it? Where's the rest of it? Your suitcase is smaller than mine," Blake says, pointing.

"I don't need much. I'd rather travel light," I say, shrugging my shoulders. Mostly, it comes from years on the go, moving from place to place before anyone realizes how I'm not aging. I find it's easier to just… walk away and start over.

"Marry me," Blake says, his eyebrows raised.

My eyes widen in surprise. "Uh—excuse me?"

"I mean, I've never in all my life seen a woman travel so light. You're an enigma," he says, flushing. He reaches behind his head, rubbing his neck.

"Oh, right. Well, occupational hazard. Enigma is practically my middle name," I chuckle. "Let's—let's go."I clutch the handle of the suitcase tighter, trying to steady my heartbeat and relinquish some of my surprise.

Blake steps off the front entry and walks toward his Rover. In the daylight, its dark exterior looks smooth—like the kind of car our local state senator would drive or something. He opens the back, extending his hand out. I roll my suitcase to him. Ridiculously fast, he collapses the handle and places my luggage inside. I flip the carry-on off my shoulder and rest it beside the suitcases.

Blake wasn't kidding. His suitcase is massive. It's one of those hard cases that looks like they're really a mobile armory instead of a place to put your underwear.

"What on earth did you fill that thing with?" I say, pointing at the massive case and chuckling. "A body?"

He shoots me a sideways glance but doesn't say anything. Instead, he flat out ignores my humor and walks to the front of the Rover to take his seat. However, the rosy color in his cheeks tells me it's a touchy topic. So of course, there's no way I'm gonna let it rest.

I quirk an eyebrow, nodding to myself.

Oh, it's on.

"I mean, did you fold Aiden up like origami so you could smuggle him over the border?" I say, as I take my seat beside him and reaching for my seatbelt. "Oh—oh, you're actually really embarrassed because you brought every outfit in your closet, just in case. I'm right, aren't I?"

Blake rolls his eyes and starts the Rover.

"Ooooooo, it's loaded with whips and chains," I say, before thinking through the words before they tumble outta my mouth.

He turns his head, his eyes wide, and cheeks beet red.

My jaw slacks open. "Oh my god, it is. There are whips and chains in there?" I scramble around to look at the case again, but of course, the back seat is in the way.

"It's not like that," Blake says smirking, his right cheek's dimple showing. He shifts the vehicle into reverse and gets us going a little too quickly.

"What is it like then?" I ask, cocking my head.

"Well, if we find the men involved, we need a way to apprehend them, don't we? I have my gear with me. Maybe for a psychic, you don't require much, but I have *my things*."

"Oh, right. Your things," I say, nodding slowly. "Like whips and chains."

I burst out into a full, deep laugh. God, it's been years—like, we're talking a decade or more since I laughed so hard. Of all the things for him to be nervous over—or try to keep to himself. It's ludicrous.

But kinda sexy—no, wait not sexy. Cute? Rugged?

Shit.

I shake my head.

Don't you dare start falling for Blake, Diana Hawthorne. Don't you effing dare.

My laughter peters out, but I steal another glance at him. His eyes are creased—dimples digging softly into his cheeks, but he refuses to look my direction. Instead, he deliberately chooses to keep his eyes forward and take the high road.

I inhale deeply, trying to center myself.

I'm so screwed.

Of all the times to start developing feelings for someone. Of all the people... Blake shouldn't be it. And it definitely shouldn't be now. I mean, he looks like he could almost be my father, for crying out loud. I've been trapped in this twenty-four-year-old body forever and he's gotta be at least forty. As if the people in this small, godforsaken town don't already think I'm weird, do I really want to add that to the mix?

I suppose I've managed to convince people I'm going on twenty-seven, but their complacency isn't gonna last long.

They'll start asking questions soon, like they always do. 'Wow, Diana hasn't aged a day. Isn't that weird?'

Then I'll have to find an excuse as to why I need to go. Sick grandma... Mom died. Best friend's husband left her, and I need to help her raise her three kids. Whatever you can think of, I've used it.

"Whatcha thinking about?" Blake asks, crashing through my train of thought.

"Uhm, nothing much," I say, breathlessly. I bite my lower lip and look out the passenger side window.

"Are you blushing?"

My hand instinctively flies upward. "No, of course not. Why would they be?"

Blake laughs. "You tell me."

"Don't be ridiculous." I snort, shaking my head.

"Oh, so now *I'm* the ridiculous one."

I smile. "You're always the ridiculous one."

"So says the self-proclaimed psychic."

"Indeed. So, I should know better."

"How in the hell does that work?"

"Uh, because I said so."

"Ah, so woman logic."

"No, just logic-logic, you chauvinistic pig," I say, laughing.

He shoots me another glance, his lips curving upward in the most easy-going way. The flecks of green and gold in his dark brown eyes sparkle—and I swear for a moment, his gaze could stop time.

How in the hell am I going to make this work? I mean, we're not on a date or about to go on holiday. We're hunting for pedophiles and hoping to put them out of commission. This is serious business.

Sitting up a bit straighter, I put on my best professional mojo.

"Blake, why do you think the men chose to go to Italy? Do you think there's something special about that country? Or do you think there's some other reason?" I say, trying to bring the subject back to the matter at hand.

Blake's smile fades and he shakes his head. "I'm not sure. We just need to follow the leads and let the story unravel itself."

I bite my lip. "Do you think they have any other girls with them?"

Taking a deep sigh, Blake's shoulders sag. "At this point, I'd say it's pretty likely. They got out of the country pretty damn quick. My guess is they have different rings around the world. Probably bailed on the US ring to avoid apprehension."

"Ugh. I hate to think of other kids being taken. You know nothing good can come of it. I just can't fathom—" I turn away, shuddering from the thoughts. Even after all these years, I still don't get it.

Unfortunately, I totally can fathom.

Men haven't changed a whole helluva lot over the centuries.

"The good news is, we're on to these assholes. If they do have others, at least there's that. We can save them the way we saved Esther."

"I sure as hell hope so," I whisper.

"See, there it is."

"There what is?" I say, turning to face him.

"The real you," he says.

"Oh, shut up."

He grins a lop-sided, goofy grin.

I roll my eyes and sigh.

Adjusting in my seat, I bite my lip and look out the window. Trees and houses flicker past, each blending into the next until suburbia is overrun with the urban landscape of the big city.

We sit in silence until we reach the airport jungle of a parking lot. Blake pulls us into the long-term parking area and I reach for my purse.

"Ready for this?" Blake says, shutting off the Rover and unbuckling his seat belt.

"Yup. Let's get some bad guys," I say, nodding.

It's been ages since I last took an international flight, but I can tell you one thing—things have certainly changed over the years. For starters, they serve alcohol in-flight, there's wifi, and tiny TVs on the headrest in front of you.

Talk about small miracles.

In some strange way, it feels like I'm returning home. I don't really know where my place of origin truly is, but overseas was certainly where I started my journey. At least the part I can remember.

After trying for years to uncover my past, or remember who I was, or why I can't remember anything, I finally had to give up and start living my life. I figured, if I have eternity, there was no point in standing still.

Blake shifts in his seat, though clearly at ease on a plane. Something tells me his past as ex-military has something to do with it.

I, on the other hand, am on my third drink and feeling nice and loopy.

Technology and I aren't overly on speaking terms. It doesn't matter if it's planes, cellphones, or even cars. I'm still pissed my 1968 Camaro died a decade ago and I had to upgrade to my Prius.

Human concepts are fallible and through the years, I've just learned to avoid common pitfalls by not joining in when I can. In some ways, it's stupid though. It's not as if I can die. But yet, the process of not dying when you should totally sucks.

"Would you like another?" the stewardess asks, pointing to my empty plastic cup.

"Yes, please," I say without hesitation, handing her the empty cup.

Blake chuckles. "Not a big fan of flying, are you?"

I twist uncomfortably in my seat. "Not overly."

"I can tell," he says, pointing to the full cup being handed back to me.

"If you'd seen as much as I have, you'd be nervous, too." I take another deep swig, letting the cool, bubbly texture flood my senses.

"Right, all those psychic premonitions flooding your mind," he says, nodding.

"Actually, that wasn't what I was meaning—but sure, that too." A small hiccup escapes my lips and I cover them with my middle and pointer finger.

Blake raises his eyebrows and shakes his head.

I fight the sudden, overwhelming urge to tell him everything—the immortality, the years and years of experiences. *Everything.*

But somewhere in the back of my mind, I know it's only the alcohol talking, and I'd regret it if I did.

"What's our first plan of action when we get to Italy?" I ask, swishing around the contents in the cup.

"I suppose get set up in the hotel, check-in with Aiden to see if he has any new leads, and… I don't know, see if you get any sorta read on things."

I nod, keeping my eyes fixed on my drink.

Yeah, a certain amount of sense in all that.

I blank out for a moment, considering his words. I cock my head to the side, making a face. I haven't had a single read on things since we got on the plane. Not one.

Usually, I get snippets here and there—but this time —nada.

Casting my gaze to the aisle, I sit up straighter.

"Everything okay? You're not going to be sick are you?" Blake asks, suddenly serious.

"No," I shake my head. "At least, I don't think so. No, it's just—I'm not picking up anything on the plane. In fact, I haven't gotten anything since we got on board. Hell, I don't remember the last time I got a reading on much of anything."

"You know, if you're just trying to cop out so you can't prove me wrong, you can just say so." He smirks.

"Shut up. It's not that," I say, smacking his shoulder with the back of my left hand.

He shifts slightly in his seat. "Look, there's been a lot going on. A lot to digest and take in. Maybe your senses—or whatever you want to call 'em are on overload."

"Maybe."

"Give it until we're settled in at the hotel. Then, if things are still not working out, you can freak."

"Gee, thanks for the vote of confidence," I say, taking another sip of my drink.

"Well, you are on your fifth drink," Blake says, his eyes twinkling.

"This is my fourth, thank you very much," I say, holding my chin up higher. "I still know how to count."

Blake squints, shaking his head and pursing his lips.

My mouth drops open. "Five? Really?"

"Yup."

"Oh, well. Bottoms up," I say, downing the contents.

"Wake up, sleeping beauty. Time to get off the plane."

My eyes fly open and I instinctively wipe at my mouth. "Holy shit. Where are we?" I say, shaking away the cobwebs. Instantly, I regret it. My brain thuds against my skull, making the world spin.

"Ugh."

I close my eyes, raising my hands to either side of my head.

Blake chuckles, patting me on the shoulder.

"We landed a couple of minutes ago and we're just waiting for the seatbelt light to turn off," Blake says.

"Oh my god, why did you let me drink so much?" I mumble.

"I don't think it was a matter of '*let*,' Diana. You're a big girl." He casts a knowing look my direction. "Who apparently can't handle her alcohol."

I groan. "I don't remember the last time I had a drink. It's been... years."

"Well, that would explain the lack of control."

I pop one eye open and glare at him. "What's that supposed to mean?"

The seatbelt light clicks off and a loud dinging broadcasts over the speakers.

"Welcome to Rome. The weather outside is 46 degrees and sunny. You're now free to unbuckle your seatbelts and make your way to the front exit," the perky flight attendant announces.

"Saved by the bell," I say shooting Blake a sideways glance.

He quickly unbuckles his seatbelt and leans over me to open the overhead compartment. I shift back in my seat, all too aware of how close his torso and nether regions are to my face. The thought makes me squirm in my seat.

"You know, I could have gotten our stuff," I say, clearing my throat.

Blake looks down with a crooked eyebrow. "Have you stood up yet?"

"Don't be a dumbass. You know I haven't."

"Well, I figured I'd save you the uncoordinated attempt as you try to get your land legs back."

He drops my carry-on in my lap and throws his over his shoulder.

"Thanks," I mumble.

I feel like I'm swimming in space and time. Light from the

cabin meshes around me in strange swirls and I close my eyes again.

It was a bad idea to drink.

After a few minutes, the doors open and a mad dash exodus occurs. I stay in my seat, refusing to budge until the last person has been herded from the innards.

"I think it's safe to go now," Blake says, gently reaching under my arm and lifting me to stand.

He's right. Standing is worse than sitting and I rock slightly from side to side, trying to awkwardly stay vertical.

I hate that he's right. This whole standing thing sucks.

Stumbling down the aisle with Blake dragging me along, I can't help but long for somewhere flat to rest.

"She'll be okay. She's with me," I hear him say.

"Yeah, I'm okay. Hate flying," I say, trying to sound more aware than I feel.

"Welcome to Rome," the flight attendant says, shaking her head.

A coffee pot whirs to life as it grinds beans somewhere nearby.

My eyes fly open and I bolt upright.

The blankets fall to my lap, revealing my torso in all its undergarmented glory.

"Why am I in my underwear? Where are the rest of my clothes?" I screech, clutching the blankets and pulling them close to my chest.

"The maid service has them," Blake says unfazed, as he stirs sugar into a coffee cup.

"Why—?"

"Because you threw up on them in the taxi and I figured

you wouldn't appreciate sleeping in regurgitated stomach acid."

My eyebrows tug in and I make a face.

Great impression, Diana.

"Oh," I sigh. "Well, ah—thanks."

"Don't worry. I didn't look. Much." He grins, walking to me and handing the cup over.

"Wonderful." I glare back, taking the offering.

"They should be back here soon," he says.

"Where's our luggage? I could just change—"

Blake shakes his head.

"It didn't make it. The airline's looking for our stuff. Guess you had the right idea."

"See? See—this is why I pack light," I say, flipping my hand up.

"Just as well, anyway. Once we got through Customs— thanks for holding it together until then at least—you pretty much turned into a jellyfish. I didn't know how the hell I was gonna get you back here and have to deal with the luggage on top of it."

I clutch the hair on the side of my head. "God, I'm so sorry. I don't know what came over me. I just—I don't do well with flying, or cars. It all makes me really anxious."

"Funnily enough, I did catch onto that."

I run my hand over my face.

What a mess.

"How long was I out?" I ask.

"Not super long. Long enough to sleep it off, though, I'm hoping."

"Okay, Mr. Cryptic. Wanna be more specific?"

"Well, it took some time to finagle you to a taxi. You weren't entirely with it. You know? So, I suppose, thirteen hours. Give or take."

"Holy shit. What?," I say, my eyeballs nearly falling out of my head. "First of all, why the hell would you let me sleep that long? Second of all, how freaking slow are the maids at this place?"

"It took us a couple hours to get here. I had to get you—uh, situated—then I checked in with Aiden. I slept for about five hours and now, here we are. Aiden's just gotten a lead, so I figured it was time to get you up and moving."

"Shit," I mutter, sipping my coffee tentatively to test its temperature. The sugar content and milk are almost perfect.

I blink up at him, surprised he can make a cup of coffee this good.

"Don't worry, it's not as bad as it sounds."

"I'm such a dunce. I'm so sorry, Blake. I never should have put you in that position," I say, biting my lip.

"It's no big deal. Really. We'd just be getting going now, anyway."

I close my eyes and ignore the thumping at the back of my head. "You said—you mentioned Aiden has a lead?"

"Yeah, if it pans out, we won't be staying here long."

"Why's that?" I ask, taking another sip of coffee. My senses and wits are slowly returning to me after the idiotic booze haze.

"His facial recognition system caught something in Greece. One or more of the men are there and it looks as though they're getting comfortable. They must have bailed on the U.S. girls to move a different group here. I suppose it makes sense if they were worried about being apprehended. If we're careful, we might be able to move in on them where they feel safe."

"That's—that's great news," I say, my eyes widening slightly.

Greece.

A knock at the door makes me jump.

"Room service," the voice says on the other side.

"Ah, drat. Must be your clothes," Blake says with a mock frown. He shoots me a quick wink before walking to the door. He opens it just wide enough for his body to block the doorway.

"Thank you. Much appreciated," he says, handing the woman on the other side some money before he closes the door.

He turns around, smiling triumphantly. "Just in the nick of time," he grins, clutching my clothes to his body.

"Wonderful," I say, holding my left arm out for them.

"Uh-uh," he says, quirking an eyebrow.

"Blake," I warn, "don't be a creeper. Give me my clothes."

"Oh, I will. But first, I have some questions."

I roll my eyes.

Leave it to a man to blackmail a woman with her own clothing.

$\mathcal{B}$LAKE STANDS FEET from me, holding my clothes just outside of lunging distance.

I consider reaching for them anyway. It's not like he hasn't seen the goods already. And honestly, after all these years, the last thing I have is an over-abundance of pride for human nakedness.

"What questions?" I say, letting curiosity get the better of me.

Blake narrows his eyes and chews gently on the side of his lip.

I cock an eyebrow and sigh loudly as I place my coffee down on the nightstand.

"Okay, okay. I'm trying to—I don't know. I need to trust you and I just—I waffle back and forth."

"You sound like a breakfast food. Would you just spit out what you want to say?"

"Fine," he says, nodding. "Truth—how did you really know about my relationship with Aiden. He told you, right?"

I shake my head. Until I have the chance to really show him what I can do, he's not going to believe me.

Why would he, I suppose? I wouldn't either.

"Look Blake, I get this doesn't fit in your world view, but I am exactly who I say I am. I pick things up. I always have and probably always will. Don't ask me why I don't get a read off you because I don't know. You are literally the first person this has ever happened with. The first. *The only.* In my whole life. At first, I thought it was nice—a breath of fresh air after having to constantly ward myself. But now, hell, I wish I did pick up on your shit because it's driving me a little bit nuts."

Blake's eyes widen, then narrow. "Can you—I dunno how this stuff works, but can you shut it off when you want?" he asks.

"Did you hear me when I said the warding bit?" I say. "I know we talked about that when we first met, so don't tell me you don't remember."

"What happens when you're around a ton of people? Like the airplane. Would you have normally been flooded with their bullshit? Or can you focus in on what you really need to —or not, I guess?" The tone in his voice tells me this line of questioning is still all hypothetical to him but he's playing along for the sake of it.

I sigh again, trying to decide if I should quit while I'm ahead, or keep going until I feel like bashing my head in.

"Depends," I shrug. "Most of the time, it's like turning down the volume, but it's technically always there. Things stream in and out all the time. But when I'm not focused on it, it's like being in a crowded room. You can hear all the chatter, but unless you stop to totally listen, only bits and pieces of it sticks."

Blake considers for a moment, then nods. "So, you're saying most of the time, if you really wanted, you can't shut it down."

"Are you asking me to try not to pick stuff up about you? We're alone and I can't read you. What more do you want?

What do you have to hide, Blake?" I ask, letting frustration get the better of me.

"Nothing—it's not like that. But I don't know. I don't like the idea of all my stuff just out there. You know? Would you like it if someone could tap into all that you are or have ever been without your permission?"

I hold his gaze for a moment, trying simultaneously to choose an answer and figure him out. Is it the military in him that makes him so secretive? Or is there something more? Maybe he's just a knowledge hoarder. Who the hell knows? I know I sure don't.

"I've had a long time to think about that," I say, biting my lip before I say something I'll regret.

Blake chuckles. "I can imagine the twenty-some-odd years has been rough."

"Oh, *you have no idea*," I say, casting my gaze to his feet. "Honestly, at this point, I don't think I'd mind if someone could tap into my shit. But that's just me. It would be a helluva lot easier than trying to explain my life at this point."

If I could pass on this curse of mine or share it with someone else so they can see all I've seen, I'd do it in a heartbeat.

I actually envy Demetri a little. Even though I know I shouldn't. He'd tell me I was a damned fool.

Kicking off my blanket, I stand up. I've had enough of this cat and mouse game. The only way for Blake to understand would be to walk in my shoes—and that's never gonna happen. Even if I tried to explain or walk him through what my life has been like, he'd have me committed. If he sees it in action, that'll be another thing. But who knows if that will ever come if he's constantly blocking my signal.

Stomping over to him, I thrust out my right hand. "Clothes, please."

Blake's eyebrows raise in surprise, but he hangs onto

them for a beat longer than he should have. His eyes follow the length of my body before I snatch the clothes out of his grasp.

"I uh—" he says, clearing his throat.

"Yeah, yeah," I say, tugging on my jeans and zipping them up.

He stands like a statue—not moving from where I left him. He also doesn't turn around or shield his eyes.

I pop an eyebrow. "So, Greece, huh?" I say, lowering my eyebrows. "It's been a long time since I was…"

I stop myself from saying too much. Instead, I scrunch up my shirt and throw it over my head.

"You've been to Greece?" Blake says, surprise lingering in his voice.

"Yeah," I say, trying to sound casual.

Blake takes a step back, his expression bordering on awe. "Huh, you don't strike me as a worldly type."

I snicker. "Wow. That hurts, man." I clutch at my chest the way Ren would have.

"C'mon. You know what I mean."

"No, I actually don't. What do you mean?" I say, placing a hand on my hip.

Blake takes another step back, running his hand along the back of his neck. "Well, you know. You're so young, for starters," he says, flipping his hand out in front of him.

"Nice save," I say, nodding as I stick out my tongue.

He shrugs sheepishly.

"Well, sorry to disappoint you, but despite my aversion to flying, I've actually traveled a helluva lot. Thank you very much."

His lips tug down as surprise flits through his face.

"So, has Aiden sent over any more details? Do we know where in Greece we're headed? I know the place pretty well. I might be able to get a clear read on things if I have some more specifics. It could narrow down our search. Well, assuming you don't get in the way."

"See, this is why I have a hard time fully believing in the whole psychic thing. There's always the convenient out," he shakes his head, "Anyway, yeah, the traffic cams and facial recognition caught them en route to Mount Parnassus. Out by Delphi, I guess. Do you know where that is? We're not sure if they're using the ancient sites out there as a cover for a meet-up and exchange, or if there's something else out there drawing them. Aiden seems to think there are a number of caves out that way they could be using to smuggle the girls."

I nod, "There are."

I cast my gaze to the floor, shaking away the bizarre sense of déjà vu. The hairs on the back of my neck and arms tingle.

Being lost in one of those very caves is the first memory I have of my life as I now know it. You don't know darkness until you're lost inside a cavern with no source of light and no way of knowing how to get out. It's utterly petrifying.

To be brought back there now—*for this*—I dunno, it means something. The universe is rarely so lazy.

A shiver runs up my spine and the memory of me stumbling out of the Korykion Cave, as it's known now, penetrates my mind. It's been centuries since I was last in Greece —centuries since I even considered my origin story.

Suddenly, despite the proximity to Blake, visions of green lights flash in my mind and the memory of the cavern shifts from me then, to present day. I watch as four girls are herded into the innards of the cavern system, led by a single flashlight held by a man much older than they are.

Fear permeates the atmosphere. They know they're on a death march, of sorts, with no way out.

"Shit," I mutter, shaking away the remnants of the vision.

"Whoa—your eyes. Uh, something wiggy just happened.

They just went completely white. What the hell? Were you just—?" Blake stutters.

I wave away his question—there's no time.

"I know where they're taking the girls. We need to leave. *Now*," I say, slipping my feet into my shoes and grabbing my carry-on.

"Okay, look I need a minute to process—" Blake says, raising his hands and shaking his head. "I mean, was that a thing you do? Do you roll your eyes for that effect or—?"

"Blake for the love of God, just trust me. This is why we're here. It's why you agreed. My abilities don't need to make sense to you right now. You just need to take the leap. If we sit around here wasting time, the girls are gonna vanish —or worse. We have to move quickly. They're already there and it's gonna take us half a day to get there."

"Where's there?"

"Korykion Cave. It's within walking distance from the ruins at Delphi, but it's still a hike."

Blake nods, finally turning around. He grabs his cup of coffee, downing the contents and grabbing his coat.

"I hope you're right about this," he mutters, shaking his head.

"Only one way to find out."

The urgency from the vision tells me we'll need to plan this down to the minute. The time it's going to take us to get to Greece from Rome is far too long for my liking but I wouldn't have been given the information unless there was a chance we could do something about the situation. That's one thing I've learned for sure.

As soon as Blake reaches for his carry-on, I head for the door and walk out.

We're gonna need to haul ass to catch another flight.

Catching the 10:40 a.m. flight from Rome to Athens just as it was boarding is more than simple coincidence—it was providence. However, the two hours in the air is still pure torture. Sitting mostly in silence, I continue to stay with the stillness, so I can check in with the cave and the girls. A compulsion has taken hold of me. I need to maintain a read on them and their whereabouts. Luckily, the lack of booze has cleared my head and allowed me to use my abilities properly again.

Plus it helps that I'm acutely aware Blake and I are their final hope of ever getting away from these monsters.

So far, nothing has changed for them, but I'm not sure if it's the truth of the matter—or if being in close proximity to Blake is disrupting my vision in a different way. A strange energy about the whole thing pulses around me. Something I can't put my finger on. There are blind spots and I'm not sure what it means.

Only time will tell.

The second the plane lands, Blake stands up, reaching for his bag.

I take a deep breath and ground myself.

"We're gonna need to catch a taxi or grab a rental," I say, finally breaking the silence.

Each of us were deep in thought through the whole flight, but now it's time to get down to the nitty-gritty.

Blake nods. "I don't know the area. What do you suggest?"

"If we—no, scratch that—*when* we get the girls, we're probably gonna need to get the hell outta there fast. Don't you think? Best to get a rental, I suppose. I can drive," I say, grabbing my bag and heading down the aisle once the seatbelt light turns off and the flight attendant flashes her signal.

"I don't wanna just get the girls. I want the men apprehended," Blake says, his tone heavy. "I don't wanna come all this way only to have them do it all over again."

"Okay, you do the apprehending, I'll focus on the girls. Deal?"

"Deal," he says. "Damn, I wish my case woulda made it with us."

"See? Pack light, man," I say, shaking my head. "When you have less to rely on, there's less that can go wrong."

"You're not kidding. I'll make a call to Interpol once I know for sure what we're dealing with," he says, shifting to his other foot.

Reading between the lines, he means once he verifies my story.

I roll my eye and continue to the front of the plane.

Blake follows behind, giving me the space to take the lead. I can tell it's not his strong suit, but he acquiesces, just the same. I only wish he'd give in that easily with my abilities. Or at least give it a try.

Minutes tick away as we hurry to pay for our rental car and get the hell out of Athens. The drive to Delphi could take us another couple of hours, but I know I can shave time off with a few tricks up my sleeves. It all depends on how much the terrain and roads have changed over the years.

As soon as we get in our rental car, I step on the gas and instinctively head toward Delphi. Blake pulls up the sat nav, trying to help us find the best route. Everything is a strange juxtaposition of the same energy and vibe from years ago, all overlapping with new buildings, roads, and landscape changes. Large trees and old sites that once stood are nothing more than ghosts in my memory as we speed toward our destination.

"You know, for someone who doesn't overly seem like they like to drive, you sure do know how to handle this vehicle," Blake says, breaking the silence.

"When needs must," I mutter, refusing to remove my eyes from the winding road. The mountainous landscape is far different from the relatively flat one back home. One glance away could be disastrous. Especially at my speed.

"I'm gonna check in with Aiden to see what he knows," Blake says, doing something on his cellphone. "Dammit. No signal out here."

"Can't say I'm surprised."

"What about you? You picking up on anything?" he asks, trying to sound like he means it.

"Only bits and pieces," I say, shaking my head.

"I hope you're right about all of this Diana. I really do."

"Me, too," I say. Now would not be the time to be wrong, that's for sure. "How are you planning on apprehending the guys once we're there? Have you managed to work out a plan yet?"

"I've got a few things in the works, but it will depend on the situation once we're in it. Those guys likely know the area a helluva lot better than we do, and that's definitely to our disadvantage. Without my gear, I'm gonna need to be extra cautious," he says, then adds, "You will too."

I risk a quick flick of my eyes over to him. His gaze is dark and serious.

"You don't need to worry about me. I can handle myself."

"Yeah, well, as true as that may be, you're still a part of my team and I have to worry about you, too. Like it or not, you'll need to be a little more cautious than you were back at the creepy old man's place by the river."

I tip my head in acknowledgment. Once a military man, always a military man.

"I think our best bet will be to get to Delphi, then hike to the caverns to see what we can find. I'll get us as close to Parnassus as I can though. If we're lucky, there might be a place to get wifi or at least a better signal before we pack up. You could check in with Aiden then. I'll do my thing while you do yours," I say.

Blake nods. "Sounds good to me. I just hope we're not too late."

"So do I. I can't imagine how those girls must be feeling right now."

"How anyone could be this way—do this to innocent little…" He shudders. "They've gotta have something evil inside them."

I shiver away his words.

He has no idea just how right he is.

15

*B*LAKE STOPS FOR A MOMENT, casting a hand over his eyes to shield them from the blaring sun. Red and gold glint from within the strands of his dark hair.

"I thought you said it was close," he says, eyeing how much further we have to go to the cave's entrance.

"Pretty sure I said it was within walking distance," I correct.

Sweat pools at the small of my back and I know Blake's feeling the same as I am.

We need to move faster.

I glance down at my watch. It's been nearly five hours since we left Italy. Five freaking long hours.

Blake does the same, shaking his head in what I can only imagine is disgust.

"Anything coming through on if the girls are close—or still alive?" he asks, his voice cracking slightly.

I shake my head. "No. Ever since we arrived, everything has gone dark. Almost as silent as when I try to read you."

"That can't be good."

I cast my gaze on him. Silence is definitely a mixed bag.

"I'm hoping once we get to the cavern, things will click into place. Sometimes I need to come into contact with items, or the location before things makes sense. There's probably a lot of interference, energy-wise."

"All right, let's keep moving, then," he says, reaching out and taking my hand.

I grab hold of his and take another big step forward.

The terrain is rocky, and the elevation is much higher than back home, making it harder to breathe as we forge on.

Avoiding the tourist groups and their occasional stopping points, it still takes us another twenty minutes before we reach the mouth of the cave.

"Wow, there's a lot of people here," Blake mutters, placing his hands on his hips as he takes in the scene.

I walk up, eyeing the massive cave opening. He's right. It's a hub of tourists interested in learning more about Delphi, Greece, and the ancient ways people honored Apollo and Pan. Clusters of people huddle around tour guides who are all giving their own variations of the stories. Some speak in Greek, others in English or Italian.

I shake my head. This isn't what I saw in my vision. There was no bustle of people and the cavern mouth wasn't as wide and open as it looks in person. Yet, I know it was this cavern. I can feel it.

"They must have taken the girls deeper," I say, leaning into Blake.

"Could they do that without being noticed?"

"Sure, if they did it in the middle of the night or something. Hell, anything is possible. In my vision, there wasn't anyone around when they all came through. They may have taken a different entrance or something. It wasn't this wide."

"Are you absolutely certain it was this cave?" Blake says, his eyes narrowing.

"I'm sure," I say, staring him in the eyes.

But now that I'm standing here defending myself, I'm totally not sure.

What if the weird sense of connection—the fact this place was where I began my journey—has been clouding my judgment? Could I have let it all get in the way and taken us off course? It wouldn't be the first time.

I shake away the memory of the ritual with Demetri and the way the Violet Flame transmuted more than it should have—all because of me.

"Then, c'mon. We need to look around the cave a bit," he says, walking beyond a small group of tourists and heading deeper into the cavern.

When no one comes running after us, Blake takes his flashlight out of his pocket, switching it on as we go beyond the mouth of the cave and into the rear cavern opening. I stand back, trying to pull a read off of the energy in the space—the rocky walls, the unique way the stones and stalactites have turned green, before following him through the narrowed opening.

Small flashes from the vision seem to mesh with where we are, but I'm not sure. Things are in flux and shifting around. I shake away the confusion, pushing myself to go forward.

"Does anything look familiar?" Blake says, cautiously shining his light around the space.

"Everything—and nothing," I mutter.

Blake turns around, the flashlight blinding me as he shines it in my direction. "Are you okay?" he asks, concern suddenly surfacing.

"Yeah. I don't know. Something's not right. I think I'm going to need to you to leave."

"Excuse me? I don't fuckin' think so," Blake says, snorting indignantly.

My eyes widen at his cuss. It's the first time I've heard

him swear like that.

"Please. We both know there isn't much time and if I can't get a read on the girls—" my voice drops off, "well, you know. I need to eliminate this feeling that it's you muddying up the water."

Blake's left-hand raises as he presses his thumb and middle finger to his forehead.

"Okay, look—I'll give you ten minutes. That's it. I don't feel comfortable leaving you alone. Especially not here—not with these men on the loose."

"Ten minutes should be more than enough to know if it's you or not."

I take a seat on one of the nearby rock outcroppings.

Sighing heavily, he drops his hand and rubs his mouth. "All right. I'll be just outside the cavern entrance. Will that be far enough?"

I shrug. "I would think so, but I honestly don't know how this shit works anymore. It's all-new territory. Sometimes I read stuff just fine with you nearby—but other times, it's like the messages get scattered when I'm near you. Let's just give it a try."

He nods. "Ten minutes—but stay put. Okay? Right here so I can find you."

"Oh, believe me, I'm going nowhere. Getting lost in this cavern is the last thing I wanna do."

I shudder away from my very first memories of stumbling out of this cave—lost, starving, and totally dehydrated.

Blake nods again, stepping forward to hand me his flashlight.

"Keep it," I say, waving it away. "I have one, too."

Tugging the tiny flashlight from my pocket, I tap the button, and the LED springs to life.

Giving me a final glance, Blake's lips form a thin line, but he puffs up his chest and walks out.

The moment he leaves my immediate vicinity, it's like a breath of fresh air wafts through the cavern. My mind clears as the strange fog subsides.

Licking my lips and shaking away my daze, I pull my legs in to sit cross-legged against the rocky wall. I flip off the flashlight, allowing the darkness to settle around me. People's voices bounce around the cavern walls, mixing with the slow drips of water as it continues to form more stalactites and stalagmites, as they have for eons.

Blowing out a breath, I center myself and search the cavern space for the girls.

At first, nothing happens.

My perception is filled with the scent of cold, wet dirt and rocks. Then, something shifts…

Flames erupt in my inner eye and I begin to catch snippets of a conversation elsewhere in the cavern.

"Finally got the word. We make the exchange at 2:00 a.m.," a man says.

I can't see his face, but he has long reddish hair in the light of the small fire. On the floor, the girls huddle together, trying to make themselves as small as possible. Their clothes are torn and dirty and an air of abuse already lingers around them.

"Why so fucking late?" another man says, kicking at the dirt. "I ain't no damn babysitter."

Anger spikes in the first man. "I'm not paid to ask questions— and neither are you. We're just damn lucky we were reassigned here instead of being caught by the police."

"Guess none of these people ever heard of sleep. So, where's the damn drop happening? We gonna have to meet him, I suppose?"

"Yeah, as if he's gonna make his way through this labyrinth," the first man snorts. "Moron. Of course, we're gonna meet him. We'll start making our way to the entrance at midnight. The tourists should all be gone by then and we can do what we need to

do without prying eyes. Plus, we can dump 'em when we have our money and get on our way."

"Yeah, that'll be good," the other man says. "Looking forward to being done with this one. They've been more trouble than they're worth if you ask me."

"No shit. It went sideways from the minute we got mixed up with that little girl back in the States. It'll be nice to finally be rid of this lot. Gonna lay low for a while until it all blows over."

One of the girls on the floor whimpers, fighting back tears.

"What the hell's wrong with you?" the first man snarls, walking over to them.

Instinctively, the girls cower together.

"I said, what's wrong with you?" he repeats, kicking the girl closest to him.

The girls cry out, jarred from the contact. They bow their heads, refusing to look up at their captors.

"Babies," the guy mutters, walking away. "Next one of you who cries is gonna get something worth crying about. Ya hear?"

Again, the girls huddle in to the point of practically being on top of one another—almost as if they could vanish if they just merged into one person.

Suddenly, the vision of the girls and men shifts—dragging me from their location as I desperately try to stay with them.

I float through the cavern tunnels, hovering over an open space with standing water. Then through another tunnel with etchings in the stone face. As I try to lean into it and get a better view, images of the symbol from Blake's dreams and drawings juxtapose themselves over and over in my mind, blocking me somehow from seeing anything else.

"Diana—Diana, oh god, are you okay?"

My eyes roll, as I try to ground myself to the here and now, and my own body. Without warning, everything goes limp and I slump forward. Blake's arms wrap around me before I can hit the ground.

"What in the hell was all that? You—you were glowing. Like, on your own, bright purple—glowing. And your eyes—they were. I just—I can't—" Blake's words drift off, but I can't find a way to my voice just yet.

The visions—two separate, but clearly equally important visions—have depleted my body.

I should have brought chocolate, or something to eat in case something liked this happened.

Stupid.

Blake pulls me in close, his broad chest becoming my platform for stability and relief. Everything around me is spinning and I know if I'm not careful, I'll lose consciousness. Who knows how long it would be before I awoke, and neither of us can afford that kind of detour.

I close my eyes, focusing on the sound of his heartbeat as it thumps away. It's my metronome to stay here and now.

His left-hand slides up beneath my hair, resting on my neck. The warmth of his palm radiates through me, making me shiver.

"I'm sorry, Diana," he says, his voice low and husky. "I still can't believe what I saw. I mean, I know I saw it—and I know something was clearly going on with you. But I still. How do you explain something like this?"

Even if I wanted to, I couldn't explain what happens to me. I've never experienced it from the other side when the stronger energies take over. I just know what it does to me afterward.

Blake must sense how much this has taken out of me because he stops talking and instead shifts to a more comfortable position and simply holds me. Nothing in this world—and I mean that literally—nothing has felt so good as being in his arms.

After a few minutes, the world stops spinning, and my head begins to feel more centered. Unfortunately, my ass is falling asleep. I shift slightly, just to release the cramp.

"How are you doing now?" Blake asks.

I don't open my eyes but remain firmly in place—a permanent fixture on Blake's chest for the time being.

"A little better. Thanks," I whisper, taking a deep breath through my nose.

"I didn't know this took such a toll on you. It didn't seem like such a big deal before."

"It's okay, Blake. It's not always like this. Just—sometimes it's more… powerful than others."

"You're not kidding."

"Besides, you wouldn't be the first to think I was spewing BS," I say, taking slow, deliberate breaths.

"After seeing you glowing, though… I feel like a complete ass. I mean, holy shit, that was intense. Why did you feel like you needed to prove anything to me when you clearly have something crazy unique going on? You should be studied at MIT."

I swallow hard, trying to fight the feelings snaking their way around my insides.

"Lots of reasons," I finally say. "It was partly for the sake of the girls. Blake, they're alive, by the way. They're all still together and alive. They're planning on moving them tonight, and from what I got, they're going to be coming back through here in the middle of the night."

For a split second, Blake's hand stops moving.

"You're certain?" he finally says.

"Definitely. They'll be doing the exchange at 2:00 a.m."

I close my eyes, trying to fade out the memory slightly of the man kicking the girls.

"All right, so we can set up our trap," he resolves. "I'll get Interpol involved in a little bit."

"Okay." I sigh, leaning into him.

We continue to sit for a moment, listening to the sound of water droplets in the cave make music against the rocks.

"What about the other part?" he says after a few moments of silence.

"What are you talking about?"

"You said part of the reason you wanted to come along was for the girls. But that wasn't to prove anything—it was to get them out alive. So, what did you have to prove?" he urges.

I bite my lip, trying to decide what to say and what to keep to myself. I'm only just starting to parse it all out and I'm not sure what any of it means yet. I don't understand after all this time why I'd want to open myself up again. Why him? Why now?

"I don't know. I guess not being able to read you, it's made me curious. There isn't much I don't know and what I don't already have as knowledge, I pick up pretty quickly."

"Okay?"

I sigh. "I guess I wanted to spend time with you to understand what makes you so different."

His body relaxes a little and his fingertips start to caress the side of my neck. I close my eyes again, focusing on it.

"And what have you found out so far?" he asks.

"Not sure. I guess I'll need to keep digging."

"Oh, you're digging, huh?" He chuckles.

He's trying to give me something to think about—something other than the dizzying effects of my vision.

"Sure, why not?" I laugh. It feels good to laugh, ushering in some lighter energy.

"Warn me when you find something out, would ya?"

"You'll be the first to know."

"Wonderful," he says, twisting his fingertips through the tendrils of hair at the back of my neck.

"What about you, Blake?"

His fingertips halt their playfulness and his back stiffens. "What about me?"

"What made you want to prove me wrong—or to be near me? Did it really have anything to do with wanting to prove I wasn't who I said I was? Honestly, after getting to know you more, I don't think you're really that kinda guy."

I pull my head from his chest to look him in the eye. My head lolls listlessly to the side, but I take a deep breath, holding it upright.

Warmth rushes through his cheeks, even in this dim light I can see it, and his gaze narrows.

"Honestly?" he finally says.

"No, lie to me," I say, sticking out my tongue.

Blake rolls his eyes and shoots me a sexy smirk.

Butterflies escape from my solar plexus and I bite my lip.

"I think a part of me always knew you had something special. But it wasn't about your psychic stuff. There was something about you—the woman you are. Being around you, it's like... I can't even describe it. It's like finding something you didn't know you were looking for. Like there was something you misplaced, but it had been so long since you last had it, you forgot it even existed. I know that sounds stupid—"

"What? You weren't looking for all this?" I say, brushing my hands along my body, and shooting him a dorky grin.

He laughs again, returning his fingertips to their dance along my neck. "Not even a little bit. I was perfectly happy just living in my own little bubble with Aiden. But now..." his voice trails off.

"Now?"

"Well, I'd like to see where this could lead," he says.

I sit up so I can get a better look at him. He smiles, shrugging sheepishly.

"Glutton for punishment, I see." I poke him in the rib and raise an eyebrow.

"Guess you could say that."

"Poor fool," I say, shaking my head and grinning.

"I'll be the judge of that," he says, holding my gaze for a beat. His eyebrows flicker up and down as he processes whatever's flashing through his mind.

"Will you do me a favor, Blake?"

"Sure, anything," he says without hesitation.

"When we're through with all this—when it's all said and done and we're back in Helena, can we grab that cup of coffee you asked for? I mean, for real this time."

Blake's dimples emerge in a slow, deliberate smile. "Yeah, I'd like that."

I nod. "It's done, then."

"So it is." His chin dips in acknowledgment.

My strength feels like it's returning and I adjust again.

"You do know, this means having an actual conversation, though. Right? Telling me more about you and not freaking out about it. We've been through a lot, but I'd like to learn more about the real Blake Wilson."

"Deal. I'd like to learn more about the real Diana Hawthorne, too." He smiles. "Magical psychic stuff notwithstanding, I'm sure there's a lot more to you than meets the eye."

I raise my eyebrows. "Oh, you have nooo idea."

Even in the low light of Blake's flashlight, the weight of his gaze pulls me into it, making my breath hitch in my throat. Something has magnetized me to his eyes and even if I wanted to, I can't look away. The hints of green and gold hidden in the depths of his eyes are so—*familiar.*

The familiarity gnaws at my insides, like a memory you're trying desperately to cling to but no matter what you do, you just can't recollect it.

"I—I don't know what this is between us, but I'm happy I deliberately bumped into you," Blake says, the magnitude of his words drawing me in.

My heart thumps awkwardly, skipping beats as I try to stay grounded, but I'm losing grip fast. This time, it has nothing to do with my abilities.

"I am, too. But—I just—I mean, we're in a weird situation right now, you know, trying to find the girls. We should be focused on—" my voice drifts off as his face moves, almost in slow motion, toward me.

Those big brown eyes of his close and the intensity of his pull is like the oceans rising to meet the moon. We've somehow managed to create a gravity all our own and even if I wanted to stop this collision course, I wouldn't be able to.

I suck in a breath and close my eyes, bracing for impact.

His lips graze mine, gentle, but self-assured. There's no doubt what he wants from me and he knows I'll give it to him. In this moment, I'd give him my whole life. I'd lay it all down on the floor at his feet, if I could.

My inhalation catches in the back of my throat and I lean into him, placing my right hand on his chest. His scent permeates my reality and all I want to be consumed by… is him. There's something so familiar in his touch—in the energy and essence of him, yet it continues to slip through my awareness the way sand slips from open fingers.

Blake leans forward, placing both hands alongside my face as he draws me closer, building urgency to his kiss. It's as though his essence and mine are bound somehow and we're only now beginning to realize it.

Hungrily, his tongue parts my lips, creating the gateway the ancients used to say could merge souls.

Suddenly, my memory cracks open, and flashes of times long past—recollections I've never had access to begin to flood my awareness.

16

*S*PLIT APART *from the present moment, I'm suddenly viewing myself from the outside as I walk these same long cavern tunnels. Tears stream down my face, and my heart is shattering into a billion pieces.*

Clutched in my hand is a small dagger, sharp enough to claim a life, but I sense that's not my intent. Even then, even in the ancient past, I know I can't die—even if I'd want to. Instead, I'm painfully aware of my eternal life, but there's no way I can live with this type of heartache. The pain of this loss is too unbearable.

I try to focus, to see who or what has caused the heartache, but the memory is still clouded—aspects of it shielded from me.

Staying with the vision, I continue to follow myself as I meander the cavern tunnels to the location I'm seeking—the area with the most potent power so it can assist me in what I have planned. Not only is the pathway an energetic vortex, but it's not easily accessible. This is good. I can't risk having everything destroyed.

As I reach the tunnel, at last, I don't hesitate. Instead, I immediately begin the chant and start my plea to Mnemosyne. To what purpose, I'm not entirely sure. I only know I have to complete the sacrifice and carve out the sacred symbol before any of Apollo's servants can stop me.

The fissure in my memory seals back up—closing whatever gateway granted me a glimpse of what was.

I pull back from Blake's kiss—my eyes wide and heart thrumming loudly in my chest.

"What is it? What's wrong?" Blake says, mirroring my surprise.

What the hell do I tell him? Oh, hey, by the way, I just had a vision from a past I've been trying to get access to for as long as I've been alive. Yeah, and just so you know, I'm over two millennia old.

Screw that.

"I uh—I just had another vision," I say, thinking up something fast.

"What was it? What did you see?"

"Blake, you'll need to make your call to Interpol right away. Get them here and ready, they're considering making their move sooner. In the meantime, I need to go back in—try to get more info," I say, hoping it will mean him having to get outside to find cell signal.

"Are you sure? Shouldn't I wait until we know you're okay?" His eyes search mine, concern permeating all of his features.

"I'm sure. I'm okay," I say, nodding. "I'll be fast. In and out to get the information I need."

Blinking wildly, Blake finally nods to himself, letting his hands slide down to my arms. He pauses a moment, tugging his eyebrows in just before he leans forward and places his lips against my cheek. "Okay, I'll go make the call. Just—please, be careful. Or better yet, wait for me to come back?"

I shake my head. "I'll be okay, I promise. I've been doing this my whole life."

Taking a deep breath, he finally nods.

I lean forward, placing my hands alongside his face and pulling him to me. More present and aware this time, I put my own desperate fervor into the kiss. Enjoying the fleshy part of his bottom lip, I tug gently at it with my teeth before parting his mouth and sliding my tongue inside.

He shudders breathlessly but pulls me closer to him and hungrily returns my advances.

I don't know what it is about him—*or why*—but for opening my memory, even temporarily, he deserves a kiss and so much more.

Blake groans, his hands sliding to my back as he takes a seat and lifts me onto his lap. My arms wrap around his neck and I press myself into him.

"Get a room, guys. This is a public place," someone hollers out.

Startled, we both break apart and look around.

A group of three pimply teenage boys stand and gawk from a few feet away. They snicker and point—one with their phone out, no doubt SnapGramming, or whatever the hell it's called.

My hand flies to my mouth in an attempt to keep myself from telling them where to shove it. Instead, absurd giggles erupt from my lips and Blake's boisterous laugh joins in the chorus.

"Dude, talk about robbing the cradle," one of the boys says before they all walk out.

Blake snorts but casts a sideways glance in my direction.

I roll my eyes and shake my head.

"Whatever. Ignore them," I say.

Honestly, they'd probably all be mortified to know they're right—but not the way they're thinking now.

The thought makes me laugh again and I climb off of Blake's lap, reaching for his hand to help him to a stand. He reaches for my offering and grabs hold of his flashlight beside him on his way up.

Dizziness tickles at my temples, but I ignore its commands and instead, lean into Blake. He wraps his arms around me and places his cheek against the top of my head.

We both release a strange, blissful sigh of contentment.

"All right, looks like I have a phone call to make. I'll be right back, okay?" he says, not actually moving.

Sighing one last time, I nod. "Okay, I'll be here."

Blake leans down, brushing my lips gently before sauntering out. I stand back, watching his perfect ass move in a whole different light—a far dirtier one, for sure.

Shuddering to myself, I pull out my flashlight again and flip it on. I'm gonna have to make this excursion quick, or it's gonna freak him the hell out.

Clambering over the rocky outcroppings, I follow my inner guidance and cling to the remnants of the vision for where to go. I don't feel like it's all that far, but I need to see for myself if the place in my vision was real. If it is, then maybe it will help me unlock more of my memories.

My insides claw at one another, the further away I get.

I shouldn't be doing this.

I should have backup, or at the very least, I should have told Blake I was going to check something out. I should have given him that much. Another part of me is feeling totally guilty I'm searching for my own stuff while there are girls in this cave who need to be saved. Another strange part doesn't give a rat's ass if I'm being a bit selfish—because my god, this is all I've ever wanted my whole miserable, multi-millennia existence.

Racing down one rocky tunnel, then another, I'm acutely aware I'm not being cautious enough. I should probably be mentally mapping where I'm going so I can find my way back out but I feel like I'm being divinely guided somehow. I'm not even afraid of the darkness. Perhaps it's cellular memory. Whatever it is, I trust it and just go with it, hoping it will be enough to get me back out.

The hunch pays off.

As I turn the final bend, squeezing through a small opening barely large enough for my body to get through, my mouth drops open as I shine the flashlight along the rocky surface of the walls.

There, etched into the cavern face, is an enormous rendition of the symbol from my vision—the same symbol from Blake's dreams. In fact, this entire location and everything about it is very reminiscent of his drawings.

Goosebumps flash across my skin and I know there's so much more to this I have yet to uncover. Blake is somehow intrinsically linked to me—to all of this, but I just don't quite understand how. How can he be?

Walking up slowly to the wall, I take in the sights and sounds as I try to invoke the memories in my buried past.

What is this symbol for? What was this all about?

Reaching out, my fingertips graze the etchings.

"Hello, Pythia. Have you returned to accept your fate?"

The words are inside my head and in ancient Greek—yet my mind translates them easily.

I take a step back from the cavern wall, my hand still raised to the level of the symbol. The flashlight trembles in my other hand, making the space feel ominous.

I never thought, never anticipated after all this time, coming here to help on this case would lead me to this—to everything I've been hunting for. I'm so close to finally having some answers.

My mind strays to Blake and our last exchange… It's even led me to a few things I didn't know I was searching for.

Instantly, guilt tremors through my body. I shouldn't be here. I shouldn't be worrying about myself or hunting for answers to my own mystery. There's plenty of time for this later. I should be focused on saving the girls. I should be honest with Blake.

And yet, a few glimpses of insight wouldn't hurt. Would it? Blake is trying to get Interpol involved, after all. I'm sure the call will take a bit of time to explain things.

There's time.

Taking a deep breath to instill a sense of calm, I step forward and return my hand to the symbol. Closing my eyes, I let the images and feelings inundate my senses.

No longer seeing things from outside myself, I get a first-hand glimpse at a memory through my own eyes.

I run through these cavern tunnels. Uncontrollable sobs heave in my chest and make it feel as though my ribcage may crack apart.

My tunic is splattered in blood and pulls awkwardly at my hips as I try to rush to this place of power—the vortex of Mnemosyne. The space is lit, but in my memory, I can't tell how. It simply glows in soft light.

Pulling the dagger from my belt, I raise it to the cavern wall and begin my incantation without a moment's hesitation. My fingers tighten around the hilt and my knuckles turn white as I etch the symbol into the rock. The blade's tip digs in, grinding at the stone and casting away debris as if it were wiping away grains of sand. The act begins to charge the air, invoking Mnemosyne's power. The power to forget. The power to wipe from my mind all of which can no longer be carried.

My hands work quickly, assuredly, despite not being able to see through my raging tears. My heart and body ache, as though I may never be whole again.

How can the universe be so cruel? How can it take him from me? How could she take him from me?

Images of my husband, the man I married upon the approval of Apollo himself, lying limp in my arms—it will not escape my mind. They circle my every thought, my every breath—every uneven thump of my heart.

He was meant to stay by my side for all time. We were going to be together forever. A promise was made to us by the God himself. But now—now all is lost, and I'm left alone for all time.

All because—

We knew the rules. We knew we were breaking the standard Delphic Pythia decrees when we were married under the full moon. But I'm Apollo's Oracle, and this role of mine, I was meant to be the first to be gifted a soul mate. Our love was meant to ease this burden of everlasting life of servitude and devotion.

He was never meant to die.

Sobbing uncontrollably, I clutch at my side and fall to my knees. Pebbles from the wall continue to fall, peppering the ground the way rain hits the water. My tears strike the fabric across my thighs, mixing with the blood of my beloved.

I slam the blade into the ground and without hesitation, I begin reciting my incantation.

"Mnemosyne, mighty Goddess of mind and memory, wash away all awareness of Anastasios from my mind, body, and soul. Abolish all traces so not even the smallest of specs may slip past my gifts. Grant me the ability to begin anew and walk through this life oblivious to what I have lost."

Bending forward, I sink into child's pose—my head resting on the rubble of the dirty cavern floor. My arms lay outstretched in reverence—in the hopes the Goddess will hear my pleas and take pity on me.

When nothing happens, I repeat the incantation.

Suddenly, the light cast upon the space extinguishes, and for a brief moment, a potent mixture of fear and relief floods my body.

The air fills with the kind of static electricity only a God or

Goddess can produce. The scent of jasmine and rose petals permeates my senses and I thrust my hips back, sitting on my feet.

"Daughter of Apollo, your pleas have been heard and a judgment has been made," the voice of Mnemosyne echoes in my mind. "If erasing all evidence of Anastasios from your awareness is truly your wish, drink from the well of Lethe and all will be forgotten."

With that, the Goddess's presence is gone.

The dank, earthy smell of the cavern returns, as does the low lighting. As I turn around, a small pedestal raises from the ground. With a few tentative steps, I lean over the edge and look inside. In the center of the stone pedestal, a golden bowl the size of a small shield has filled with water so clear I can see myself in the bottom.

Not wanting to dwell with a second more of this despair, I dunk my hands inside, forming a cup and scooping up as much water as my hands can carry to my lips. Droplets of deep red blood splash back into the bowl, tainting its clarity. Without hesitation, I drink the cool, clear liquid in, trusting it will wash away all the agony and sorrow as it hits the back of my tongue.

When the water enters my stomach, I buckle over, groping at my midsection. Pain courses through my insides and the impulse to gag threatens to regurgitate the memory-stealing liquid. I crumple down, lying on my side, as I hold on for dear life—not wanting to lose the ability to forget...

My eyes pop open.

Ripped from the vision, I pull my hand back and cast my flashlight to the floor. Even after all of these years, the rubble made by my own hand still lays against the cavern wall, just like it was in my memory. I swear, I can still see the place where I rested my forehead against the ground in prayer to Mnemosyne.

Taking a deep breath, the realization I had a husband lingers with me.

Anastasios.

The name circles my mind, but still holds no significant weight. Not really.

Yet, the unfurling of its weight takes hold and my stomach clenches. Flashes of insight flutter behind my eyelids and I begin to realize the far-reaching extent this decision has taken form.

My lower lip tucks under my teeth as I close my eyes and witness Anastasios' soul lifted from his body. Then, I follow it through the ages. Lifetimes morph before my eyes as I become a spectator to the myriad ways he's walked this earthly plane since the moment we parted.

I never even considered, never in my wildest dreams foresaw, that he would be reincarnated and find his way back to me. No wonder reincarnation has been another blank spot for me. It was still a part of *him*.

All these years, I could have had him by my side, even if it meant finding him anew every time he died.

Tears well in my eyes and my heart begins to crack under the significance of this revelation.

I'm given the smallest glimpse of what could have been— of perhaps what could still be as a face flashes through my mind.

Blake.

It's no wonder we're connected. No wonder his dreams are eerily similar to my visions.

He is Anastasios' latest incarnation.

Stepping back in a daze, I blink wildly at the epiphany.

My god, how could I have been so stupid? The blind spots in my past, my inability to form attachments… The inability to see or read Blake—it was all me. I'm the cause of it all.

I deliberately blocked everything about him, so I wouldn't have to go through eternity feeling his loss. And all I did was keep myself from ever finding him again.

How idiotic.

I'm no better than all those lovesick women and men who've been coming to my shop all these years. I've been healing their wounds and answering their questions and all the while judging them for being so attached in the first place.

I place my hands over my face and take a deep breath.

"A choice befalls you, Pythia," a voice rings out in my head. The Ancient Greek is eloquent and rings with the majesty of godly energy. Jasmine and rose tickle my senses. Mnemosyne has returned. "Choose now to relinquish the entirety of your gifts and you shall walk through the remainder of your days, a mortal—having forgotten who and what you truly are. You will be free to live and love. Or choose to further unlock your mind so you may keep your gifts and see things more clearly than ever before. By drinking from the well of Mnemosyne, all memories, awareness, and reach will flood back into your being. All broken memories and boundaries will crumble. With this choice, however, you must accept your immortality as you fulfill your higher calling to the aid of Apollo."

My eyes widen.

Gain more potentially painful memories in order to keep my immortality and gifts? Or go about my life as a mortal and forget I ever had them? What kind of choice is that?

Taking a deep breath, the realization of what this could mean washes over me.

I can finally be free. Free to live my life the way everyone else does. I can finally live and die. I could love without restraint. No more unbidden flashes of insights, or knowledge I shouldn't have. My head can finally be as silent as it is when I'm with Blake.

My mind swirls with the heaviness of this choice—and

yet, an immense weight feels lifted from my shoulders in anticipation of my answer.

I'm going to relinquish my gifts, so I can be with Blake and live a mortal life.

After all these years, it's an absolute no-brainer.

17

STANDING UP, I take a deep breath and take a final glance around the dimly lit space. I need some time to think and get a grip on everything I just learned.

Shaking my head, I leave the sacred vortex. I set aside the partially unlocked memories and the realization of what I'm about to do.

I've lived a long time. Decisions like this shouldn't be made lightly, as there can be far-reaching consequences, obviously. Besides, there are more pressing concerns. Like getting back to Blake before he realizes I'm missing and freaks right out.

My heart trips over itself.

For the first time in my life, I will be free to love. Free to embrace a relationship and not fear the impending conversations. Of having to leave before they realize I don't age. Or staying with them and watching them grow old and die. Pretending to be a daughter, a granddaughter, neighbor, or friend just so I can continue to be near them.

Blake and I could have a real, normal chance at something, if that's where this is all leading. And how could it not? He's my *soul mate*, after all.

My footsteps are light as they carry me purposefully through the tunnels. With my new memories, I don't have to remember the way I'd come. My body instinctively knows and does the work for me.

It takes less than ten minutes to return to the place I'd left Blake, but the closer I get, the more concern creeps over me.

How long have I been gone? Has he come back for me already and wondered where I am?

Glancing down at my watch, I realize it's been nearly forty-five minutes since I parted with him.

Much, much too long.

Running the last leg of the journey, I come to a screeching halt when I get to the location and it's completely empty.

"Blake?" I call out. My voice cracks slightly. "Are you here?"

The echo of my words against the cavern walls is my initial response.

"I can be Blake for you, darlin'," a man says, leaning casually against the cavern opening. His ruffled-up plaid shirt splays open, drawing the eye to a stained wife-beater beneath.

Shuddering, I ignore him completely and walk out into the main opening of the Korykion Cave.

There aren't as many people milling about as there were earlier. My eyes scan from crowd to crowd, searching for his dark hair or perfect ass—anything to guide me to him. There are still enough people standing around that it takes me a few moments to verify Blake isn't amongst them.

Racing out into the lower hanging sunlight, I draw my hand to my forehead and scan the surroundings.

Do I tell him about what I've learned? Do I freak him the

hell out with my revelations? Or do I wait until we're more comfortable with one another?

God, he's gotta be so pissed I left without telling him where I was going. But wow, I'd still say it was worth it.

Craning my head around, I shield my eyes from the setting sun and survey the area for any sign of Blake.

But he isn't here, either.

He's literally nowhere in sight, and I know without a doubt, this is not like him. Even if he thought I was missing, he would have started with local authorities and made sure he was standing nearby in case I still met up. He wouldn't just leave.

My heart thumps unevenly in my chest and begins to skitter off like a deer running from the sound of gunshots.

What if something happened to him? I can't lose him now —not after everything I've just learned.

I sit down, closing my eyes as I try to use my abilities to find him. The familiar energy of accessing my gifts begins to rise up my spine, tingling along my neck and making the tiny hairs stand on end.

At first, my mind circles around the cavern and tunnels leading in and out and around the area. Everything looks so familiar as I view all the places I've just been to. But I'm suddenly blocked by the big flashing Mnemosyne symbol as it blocks my mind from accessing anything related to Blake and his whereabouts.

"Dammit," I spit, hitting the ground with my closed fists. "There has to be a way to find him—or contact him. He wouldn't just disappear like this."

Raking my fingertips across my forehead, I can't help but swallow back the rising hysteria.

His cellphone. He had his cellphone on him.

Blinking away my dread, I stand up and rush to the

nearest tourist with a cellphone in their hand. The man stands back, taking a photo of the view from Mount Parnassus and I tap his shoulder.

"Excuse me? Do you speak English?" I ask, desperation bleeding into my words.

The man nods. "Sure. I'm from Kentucky."

"Do you mind if I use your phone for a moment? I've lost a friend and I need to find him."

"Why don't you use your own damn cellphone?" he asks, clutching the device close to his chest and giving me an indignant look.

"Well, I would, but I don't have one," I say, biting back my inner bitch so I can get what I want.

"You're not one of those anti-technology freaks, are you?" the man says, eyeing me nervously.

I throw my hands up in exasperation, "Ugh. I just need to find my friend. Can I have it or not?"

The guy actually snorts in my face and walks away, muttering under his breath. "I ain't a phone booth, bitch. Didn't your momma teach you manners?"

My jaw slacks open wide and I search for anyone else with a phone in their hand. A woman downslope has her cellphone out as she takes some photos of her kids against the backdrop of the skyline.

Racing down to meet them, I skid to a halt. "Excuse me," I say, trying to catch my breath. "Do you—do you speak English? I need to find a friend. I was wondering if I can use your phone to try and locate him. I'm getting worried something happened to him."

The woman and two kids turn to look at me. Their dark, heavy eyebrows kiss their hairline as they stare back at me in surprise.

"Please?" I repeat, pointing at the phone.

The woman looks down and nods—clearly not understanding anything else I've said but understanding what I need.

"Thank you, thank you," I repeat, walking a few steps away from the three of them.

Taking a deep breath, I clutch the device in my hand. I stare down at it, trying to figure out how the hell to turn it back on.

Dammit, I really should have figured these stupid things out by now.

Blinking back tears, I start pressing every button on the sides of the black box. The woman walks up to me, gently resting a hand on my shoulder and pointing to the middle circle.

Through her touch, I get glimpses of her life. She and her two children are here on vacation from Turkey and this is the first time they've been to Greece. Though I can, I don't need to speak her language, because the energy binding us all is universal.

I touch the button and the screen flashes to life. My body trembles, but I nod my head.

"Thank you—er—teşekkür ederim," I breathe.

The woman presses something on the screen and the dial pad pops up.

Taking a deep breath of relief, I freeze. I don't know Blake's number.

"For fucksake," I spit. "Can't anything just go right?"

Why didn't we think of this? Why didn't we have a plan in case we got separated? How idiotic are we? I don't even know Aiden's number.

"Aiden—" I practically scream.

The woman beside me steps back, surprised by my sudden outburst, but I can't worry about that now. I need to connect with Aiden and lift his number somehow, or a way to reach him.

Closing my eyes, I reach out to the universe, asking for guidance back to Aiden. I hone my senses so they narrow down all the information beginning to assault my awareness. A Helena telephone number raises into my perception and my fingertips instantly start dialing.

The first attempt ends in a screeching sound, telling me I need to add a country code to dial out. A new, longer number flits in my mind and I redial.

Clutching the phone, my fingertips dig into the sides of the metal and plastic as I wait in anticipation.

Finally, the phone rings—a breakthrough in communication for me.

"Hello?" Aiden's voice fills my ear.

Relief washes over me and I breathe out. "Aiden? It's Diana. Quick, have you heard from Blake? Or do you have his number?" I blurt everything out as quickly as possible.

"Diana? Wha—what time is it?" Aiden says, his voice groggy sounding.

"Oh my god, I'm so sorry. It's still the middle of the night over there," I say, shaking my head.

Aiden clears his throat. "It's okay. What did you need again?"

"I can't find Blake. We split up for a bit and now I have no idea where he is. Stupid me, I didn't think to get his number in case of emergencies. Do you have it?"

"Are you both okay?" Aiden says, alarm playing at the edge of his tone.

"I'm fine, but I really need to find Blake. You haven't heard from him, have you?"

"No, I haven't. Okay, you got a pen and paper? I'll give you his number."

"I don't, but I'll remember it. Go ahead," I say, eyeing the woman whose phone I'm borrowing, as she edges a little closer. Impatience is starting to take root in her aura and I'm going to need to make this quick.

Aiden rattles off the number and I curse myself for not having a pen. I really should write it down, just in case I can't pull the recall, thanks to Blake being a blind spot.

"Thanks, Aiden. I gotta go."

A tiny protest echoes from the phone as I pull it away from my ear, but he's not my concern. I have to call Blake before this woman gets pissed.

Hitting the red button, I turn to her and hold up my index finger. "One more call. I'll be super quick," I say in Turkish.

Her eyebrows scrunch in and she takes a step away, saying something to her kids as she jabs a thumb back in my direction.

As quickly as I can I dial the number again. Kicking up dust as I pace back and forth, I wait as the connection picks up and the line starts ringing.

"C'mon, c'mon," I mutter, clutching the phone tightly.

The ringing stops and I cease pacing as I hold my breath.

"Hi, this is Blake Wilson. Sorry, can't come to the phone right now, but feel free to tell my answering machine whatcha need. It can't keep a secret, so I'll find out about it eventually."

"Fuck," I hiss, waiting for the BEEP.

As it sounds, I grip the phone close to my face and say, "Blake, so help me, you had better be okay. I'm sorry I wandered off. I didn't mean to be gone so long. I'm by the cavern entrance. Please, please just come find me."

Pressing the off button, I turn sharply and start racing back to the cavern.

The woman and her two kids chase after me, yelling

something at my backside. Their arms are flailing in midair and their faces are red with anger as they point at the cellphone I still have gripped between my fingers.

"Shit, I'm so sorry," I say, stepping toward the woman handing it back to her. "Rahatsızlıktan dolayı özür dileriz. Hadi bakalım."

She snatches the cellphone back and skins me alive with a look before throwing her arms around her kids and rushing away. They speak frantically in Turkish, clearly pissed.

"I said I was sorry," I call out after her.

Well, that's me scarring her and her kids for life. Way to go, Diana. They're never gonna help another poor soul like me again.

Taking a deep breath, I butt the palm of my hand to my forehead and turn back to the cave.

Where in the hell would he be? Better yet, how the hell am I gonna find him?

The tourist groupings have dwindled to only a small handful of people as the sun continues to set. Without the ability to reach out and find Blake with my abilities, I'm truly lost. We only have a few hours before the girls are moved and I don't even know if Blake managed to get in touch with Interpol.

What if he hasn't? Holy crap, could this seriously get any worse?

How am I meant to split my allegiances between saving the girls and finding Blake? Hell, for all I know, he needs saving too.

I am so in over my head.

I curse myself again for not having a backup plan with Blake in case we get separated.

Christ, you'd think after all this time I wouldn't be so dense.

On the verge of hyperventilating, I hunch over, trying to slow my breathing. My fingertips dig into my scalp as I wrack my brain.

There has to be a way to find him.

A young man's voice filters into my awareness as he says, "Yeah, Mom. We're on our way back to the hotel. Seriously, you should have come out this way. You would have loved it. The Temple of Apollo is amazing. Plus, we hiked to this cave by the site—"

I stand up, suddenly revitalized.

Of course! I'm Diana freakin' Hawthorne. Even if I can't get a read on Blake, I can get a read on everyone else.

My eyes flit to the young man just a few feet away. Reaching out with my abilities, I search his recent memory for any signs of Blake to see if he may have seen what happened. I might not get a full idea, but perhaps snippets the way I was able to with Aiden. Unfortunately, it's all clouded with make-out sessions with the redhead he's standing next to.

Immediately, I turn to the next person—an older gentleman with a broad, worn smile and kind eyes. He's been here a while, but unfortunately, his eyesight isn't very good, and he spends the majority of his time listening to his tour guide who's been urging his group to start heading back to the tour bus.

The tour guide hasn't seen anything unusual. She's been too hell-bent on rounding up the stragglers, so she can meet up with her boyfriend for a romantic dinner in town.

I switch from person to person, hunting for the information I'm looking for but no one, not a single person witnessed anything about Blake I can use. Unless of course, I'm being completely blocked.

"Dammit," I whisper under my breath. "Okay, okay… There has to be something I'm missing. Or someone."

Trekking the last bit up to the cave's opening, I walk inside and have a look around. A man and woman with one small child are all that remains inside. I take a seat on one of the stones resting at the entrance and close my eyes, allowing my senses to reach out and find their way to the man first.

He's enthralled with the geological formation and the way the cavern was created. Clearly, someone with far less imagination than the others I've surveyed, as he doesn't overly care about the sociology or history. His wife stands by his side, nodding her head and holding the young child's hand. She acts engaged with whatever the man's saying about the rock, but her mind is back at the hotel as she longs for a bath and a glass of wine—*alone*. She's been the one chasing the three-year-old all day and all she wants in this whole wide world is for a few minutes to herself.

Releasing a sigh, I open my eyes and bite my lip.

Nothing. Not a damn thing.

How is this even possible? How can a grown-ass man just disappear?

Ugh. He could have been thinking the same thing about me. I wandered off into the—

My gaze flits back to the cave's opening.

No… he wouldn't have gone deeper into the cave without knowing where I was. Would he?

Suddenly, I get flashes of a police car and a puppy—the name Chase comes to mind. It switches to a disjointed image of a mask and a cartoon-like cops and robbers imagery, but still with dogs. Something like Papatroll comes to the forefront but I have no idea what the hell that means.

I sit up straighter, trying to find the source of where the images are coming from. My eyes rest on the little boy whose eyes are trained on the dark abyss leading deeper into the cavern. It's freaking him right out.

The images change again to a brightly colored water gun

pointed at the middle of a man's back. It switches to a man, with arms raised like the cops and robbers imagery as he gets edged toward the back of the cavern.

The little boy shudders, remembering...

"And just what do you think you're doing here?" the man with the gun says. "Make a scene and you're dead. Start walkin'. You're comin' with me."

The three-year-old's parents are nearby, but they're too busy talking to each other. The toddler hasn't been allowed to do much of anything, so he's been watching others closely and making up his own stories.

Even though he's much lower to the ground, I push myself to dig deeper into his mind, trying to parse out reality from whatever fiction he's associated with what he saw. I never get a glimpse of the men's faces, the little boy is too engrossed by the gun, but then I catch it—the clue I'm looking for. Blake's signature ass. It's at the perfect height for the little boy to take in fully as Blake gets shoved past him and pushed into the darkness beyond.

My eyes pop open and I'm on my feet.

Racing into the gaping entrance to the rest of the cavern, I pluck my small flashlight from my pocket and enter the pitch darkness. Pressing the button, the LED springs to life, illuminating the pathway ahead. At first, the tunnel is wide and direct, but the further I jaunt, the more turned around I get. Tunnels and offshoots splay out in every direction—some larger, some extremely narrow—and without a good read on the man with the gun, I can't hone in on Blake or where he's been taken. And I sure as hell can't go ask the boy for more details. I'm lucky I got what I did.

My feet hit the dusty ground in rhythm with my heart-beat—rapidly.

What if I can't get to Blake in time? How long has it been?

Would the man kill him?

Could he already be dead?

I pull up short in the middle of a larger opening, with five offshoots branching out in front of me. Clenching at my side, I shine the flashlight to the ground, searching for any signs of footsteps—or a clue to the direction Blake was taken.

"Dammit, he's gotta be here somewhere. But which one —" I curse aloud, raking my fingertips through my hair. "C'mon, Diana. Where did they go? Which direction?"

I take a breath, trying to calm myself and use my gifts. My tongue brushes my lower lip, as I close my eyes and concentrate. Instantly, I'm overcome with the sensation of dizziness and nausea as the Mnemosyne symbol flashes in my mind—still blocking any access to Blake himself.

"Dammit," I mutter, dropping to my knees.

There's still a way to find Blake, but it means losing everything.

"This can't be happening. It can't be the only way."

The fingertips of my left-hand press against my lips as I clutch the flashlight firmly with my right. My heart thumps unevenly as I weigh my really shitty options.

I've waited for this day for longer than I can remember—the day where I knew I could finally grow old and die. And before I can even accept, it's being pulled out from under me.

What kind of sick joke is that?

On the other hand, Blake's insanely capable. What if he's already managed to get out of the situation? Or used his background to overtake the asshole with the gun?

I could be throwing it all away for nothing.

I bite my lower lip.

But what if he hasn't?

Is that a risk I'm willing to take?

I shake my head, my nostrils flaring.

What if he just needs a diversion. Or a little help? What if by holding off, I get him or the girls killed?

The musty odor of the cavern triggers the newly gifted memories from before.

I can't lose Anastasios's soul again.

Sighing in defeat, I know exactly what I have to do.

ACING BACK TO THE VORTEX and the place where I carved Mnemosyne's mark, I come to an awkward halt as I trip over my own two feet and slam my right shoulder against the cavern wall. My ripped skin aches, but it doesn't matter—it will heal, and I'll live on. I can't say the same for Blake or the girls if I don't take immediate action. I need to locate him and there's only one way I can force it to happen.

Rubbing my shoulder, I widen my stance and take a deep breath. Lifting my head high, I call out into the black abyss, desperation permeating every word.

"What good are these gifts if I'm left blind and helpless when it really matters? Come on Apollo, or Mnemosyne, whoever it is I need to bow to or kiss ass. Give me something to work with. People are in danger here and I can't sit on the sidelines," I say, lowering my head and whispering, "I can't lose him again."

I flare my nostrils and clench my fingers, curling them so tightly into my palms they begin to lose blood flow.

One at a time, as if held up by invisible torches, purple

flames burst from the walls. They cast an eerie light, not dissimilar from the Violet Flame invocation weeks before with Demetri. Stumbling backward, I cry out in surprise and the sound reverberates off the cavern walls.

My senses are suddenly inundated with Mnemosyne's trademark scent of jasmine and roses and I know she's heard my beckoning and come to me.

"What's done cannot be undone without expressed permission, Pythia. You know this to be true. To unlock that which you seek, it requires a decision to be made. One which may only be made by you. Do you accept your immortality and responsibility in the aid of Apollo? Will you secure your role as the rightful Oracle of Delphi?"

Blinking back the tears burning in my eyes, my heart folds in on itself. I'm so close. I could have it all. A life, a love of my own. I could finally age and die.

But if I don't regain my gifts fully, I can't help Blake and I may lose my chance with him altogether. Hell, maybe I already have.

Chewing on my lip, I flip back and forth between my decision.

This is not the way I like to make decisions—impetuously, impulsively. Not anymore. But what choice do I have?

"I accept," I say, the words stinging my tongue as they tumble out.

I can't believe I'm throwing it all away, but there's no other option. A new sense of purpose—of direction emboldens my being. If I can unlock my memories and the rest of my abilities, I'll be able to see everything more clearly. I'll be able to help Blake, and in turn, help the girls.

Suddenly, from the center of the room, the same style of pedestal from my memory rises from the ground. This time, instead of a golden bowl of water, the large bowl in the center is pounded silver, reminiscent of the way moonlight pools along the water's edge.

Jasmine and rose continue permeating the air and while I see no one, I sense the power and presence of the Goddess.

"You have performed powerful magic, Pythia. More potent than you realize. The water from my river will return to you that which you've forgotten and lift any blockages to the memories they shield back. Be ready for the deluge. It will give rise to a power you perhaps didn't realize you were holding at bay," Mnemosyne says, her words echoing within and around me.

Swallowing down my trepidation, I nod. "I understand and I'm ready."

"Drink, and it shall be done." Mnemosyne's voice is like music on the wind as it tinkles with its own air of magic.

Stepping forward to the pedestal, I take a deep breath and peer within. The water ripples gently around the edge of the bowl and my mind flashes back to the last memory I was gifted. To think it all comes full circle. I was here, crying out to the universe, to Apollo and Mnemosyne, to take my memories as I wished away the despair I felt for losing Anastasios.

And now, I'm right back where I started, desperate to have everything returned so I can save his reincarnated soul.

Never in my wildest dreams would I have believed I'd be here. Especially since reincarnation never seemed plausible.

Holy shit. That's another way this spell affected what I could see.

Shaking away the mild revelation, I cup my hands, dipping them in the cool, clear water and raising the liquid to my lips. I drink in the power and energy from the Mnemosyne River—or at least a small offering gifted to me by the Goddess herself. I allow it to wash away all the blockages I've placed upon myself, knowing full well there's no turning back now.

I will live my life eternally and in the servitude of Apollo —for whatever that means.

It also means I will watch Blake live, grow old, and die. If I'm lucky.

When nothing happens from the first sips, I dip my hands in again and continue to consume as much of the water as I can bear. I'm acutely aware of the clarity and cleanliness in the motion this time around. There's no blood on my hands, no tears. But the same fierce determination stirs inside my belly.

Without warning, the cavern itself rumbles. The walls and ground both quake with the energy of Mnemosyne's magic. Stones unhinge from their hiding places along the walls and ceiling, crashing to the floor around me. From behind me, deep crevasses eek across the wall where I carved Mnemosyne's mark, fracturing the stone and forcing slabs of rock to slam to the ground, annihilating the symbol and any power it possessed.

An outburst of energy explodes from the stone slabs and I'm thrown forward in the momentum. Swirls of purple, blue, and white streaks circle around me, unbinding me from the pull of Mnemosyne's mark. Dropping to my knees, I steady myself on the floor, my fingertips digging into the rock and dirt beneath me as I'm suddenly overcome by the urge to heave. Just like before, I clutch at my stomach, doubling over as whatever magic imbued in the water releases its torrent within me.

Memories flood into my awareness, bursting through and inundating all of my senses—every single one. All of my experiences; sight, sound, taste, smell, touch. I recall every glance, every embrace, every stolen moment with Anastasios.

There was a reason I lost my entire first twenty-four years.

He was there, with me, every step of the way. He and I were inseparable from the moment we could crawl, walk, and talk. There wasn't a moment where Anastasios wasn't somehow intertwined with my life and it was clear, even to the Gods, how intertwined our souls were.

As small children, we would play down at the Gulf of Corinth, carving small boats in the driftwood and racing them together. We would sneak out at night, playing in the moonlight and telling each other ghost stories. Then, when adolescence followed us, we would sit by the same water's edge, watching the sunset between stolen kisses. I remember the smell of his skin as his lips lingered on mine and the way he always tasted like grapes.

I close my eyes and touch my lips.

His eyes were the same color as they are now—a deep, passionate brown with more flecks of colors hidden in the intricacies of his irises.

When I was tapped to become one of Apollo's priestesses —we didn't know I would become his sole prophetic vessel. Neither of us knew I would become immortal—not at first. But as this news arose, Anastasios was there with me when it rocked my world.

He held me and kissed my forehead as I swore to Apollo, then and there, that I would never serve a master who would be so cruel. I didn't want the burden of being alone forever, but Anastasios promised me he would remain by my side in whatever way he could. Even if it meant we could never really be together.

He joined Apollo's guard, just so he could protect the Temple and all of the priestesses inside. But everyone knew he was really there for me.

He was strong, and capable, and loyal like that. There was

no one else—not a single soul I could ever have imagined myself with. Even Apollo himself took second place to the love I felt for Anastasios.

But the day my sister took him from me…

Iphitheme.

My eyes widen with newfound enlightenment as the full memory returns.

He didn't die of natural causes. It wasn't the natural course, or the plan Apollo had laid out. Instead, it was my sister—a priestess in my inner sanctum who took matters into her own hands. How could he have seen her betrayal coming when he swore an oath to protect her?

The jealousy that lingered in her gorgeous blue eyes cripples my heart as I see it again in my mind's eye. Tears pool behind my eyelids before streaming down my cheeks. My heart shatters all over again, forcing me to double over and place my head against the ground as I give in to the potency of the memories and the fallout from their revelations.

As the cognizance takes hold, it demolishes any sense of tranquility or self-assuredness I had, replacing it with doubt, agony, envy, anger, and grief at all I've lost. At the betrayal of it all.

The recollection of my sister and her actions rips me apart. Long gone, Iphitheme's body is now nothing more than a dusty memory of the legacy of the Temple of Apollo. I wish more than anything I could confront her and ask her to take it all back.

Her motivations become clear as the discovery unfolds in tandem with my gifts. She didn't want Anastasios to soil the reputation of purity for the Oracle of Delphi. She feared for the sanctity of the priestesses—and all that she worked so hard for.

But in her actions, in her fear—she destroyed it all. Both

the Oracle and the priestesshood's venerableness. Not to mention, the Temple of Apollo. *Everything.*

After what she did, it all crumbled and fell apart because the Pythia was no longer operable. Not when the Oracle up and vanished.

I up and vanished.

When the memories bring me back to my starting point, the energy begins to slow down and the revelations cease. The pain and heaviness of the past bears no weight now— not when Anastasios's soul is alive and well in Blake.

I have to find him.

Kneeling, I place my hands on my thighs and straighten my back. I'm no good to anyone—not Blake, not the girls—if I'm a big puddle of mess on the floor. I force the memories inside to go into deeper waters. To calm themselves by burying them in an undercurrent so I can bring the matters at hand to the surface.

Blinking back my tears, I wipe them away with the back of my hand and take a deep, cleansing breath.

"Diana, you would not have been given these gifts if you weren't capable of bearing their weight," I say aloud, shaking away the inundation of emotions and images. "It's time you stop hiding and start doing what you're put on this damn Earth to do."

Without skipping another beat, my resolve hardens, and I place my hands on the cavern floor, knowing I will need grounding. The space rumbles, jostling pebbles and loose stones free. This time not from Mnemosyne, but from the power and magic residing within me as I unleash my gifts.

I will find Blake before time is up.

White-hot energy shoots from my fingertips as I splay them wide. Suddenly, my vision blanks out entirely and I'm consumed by blinding white light. Though I'm acutely aware of my surroundings, my abilities see and sense the white light as if it's the only thing that really matters. As if all particles, atoms, subatomic particles—*everything*—exists solely in the clarity of the light.

My thoughts drift to Blake and my vision abruptly and instantaneously shifts.

My awareness spreads out, concurrently searching for Blake and the girls. Memories weren't the only thing unlocked by releasing Mnemosyne's symbol. The power driven by Apollo unleashes itself and I see through the lens of Godlike eyes as his prophetic vision is left unhindered and coursing through me.

I breathe a sigh of relief.

Blake is alive but bound by gunpoint further in the cave. Interestingly enough, he's not far from where the girls are being held. Rocking back on my feet, the worries, reasoning, and thoughts of everyone in the vicinity meander into my mind as if beckoned by a lover's hand.

"Told you it was him," a man says.

Beside him, another man snickers.

My mouth drops open in surprise. The men who have the girls also have Blake.

I take another breath, digging deeper into the minds and memories of the two men.

One of them had been sent ahead to scout the area and radio back when tourists had left. But he had spotted Blake and acted. The grungy old man from the blue cabin back home had a surveillance system installed in his house and they had our faces. Each of them were on alert for being followed—just in case.

I dive deeper, allowing my senses to truly dig in and listen.

"There—all tied up and secure," the first man says, wiping his hands across his green shirt. His lips curve into a sneer.

"That's great. Really. What in the hell are we supposed to do with this asshole?" the second man says, kicking at Blake's limp body as it rests on the ground.

Blake's mind is blank, clearly not conscious enough to tap into yet. But his energy signature is alive and well.

"I dunno—but I couldn't just leave him out there. As soon as I spotted him, I knew I had to act. You know what happened with the little girl back in the States. He and that bitch stole her right out from under us. Who knows what the hell he was planning to do."

"What if he's got backup, moron? Or maybe he's been tagged with some sort of GPS locator. You coulda led the police right to us for all you know," he spits. "We gotta distance ourselves from him and quick. Start rounding up the girls."

I don't actively go searching for personal details and yet they come to me freely. The man with the dirty green shirt and gung-ho attitude's name is Peter Johnson. A completely ordinary name for someone so vile, and he didn't want to be on this mission in the first place. At least, not after Blake and I got involved. But his boss wouldn't let him out of the deal—someone by the name of Lester Lewis. The other man goes by Brady, but his real name is Ralph Anderson, and not even Peter or Lester's aware of this sleight of hand.

The white light takes form and almost as if a virtual map loads in my mind, the fastest route appears to where they all are. Leaving the present behind, I cast my mind into the future, trying to see the possible outcomes and uncover my best way in.

I could go raging in there, but without Blake, my scope is limited. I don't have a gun or anything to apprehend them—that was Blake's play. It's his area of expertise, not mine.

Stealth it is.

I'll need to get to Blake without the men seeing me. Then, I need to get him back up and operational, so he can do his part of the job. Together, we can overtake them and get the girls. Easy peasy.

Easing myself to a stand, I sigh in relief. This will all be over soon.

Blake and I will have a lot to discuss. I can't keep all of this from him. He'll have to know.

Following my inner compass and the pathway of light in my mind, I walk the cavern pathways. It's an odd feeling, almost like sleepwalking, as I'm guided closer to where Blake and the girls are being held. In an ironic twist of fate, Ralph Anderson, or Brady, was right. Blake has been tagged, just not with a GPS locator the way they know it.

From where I am, the tunnels leading deeper aren't entirely walkable. Some require strength and skill to climb up, over, or through narrow passageways. I've never been one to overly love spelunking, because the thought of getting lost in the pitch black—or worse, trapped without a way out. Even my abilities, at least in the past, have had their weaknesses and that was enough to instill caution. Yet, now there's never a moment where those thoughts arise and give me pause. I know exactly how to get to where I need to be and the most efficient way to do it.

I'm surprised by the way my awareness is more vast than it was before—encompassing movements, thoughts, and placements all in real-time and without much effort at all. Before I had to truly focus to get the information I wanted, all while sifting out the details just causing noise. But that's gone now.

I place my tiny flashlight between my teeth, climbing up and into a narrow passageway, as I begin the next leg of my journey. The space is tight, forcing me to crawl on my stomach for a good distance. This isn't the only way to Blake's location, but it's by far the fastest and right now, I'd rather be faster and ensure Blake's safety, than take my time to protect my own.

A source of water must be nearby because I can sense its stagnation and feel its vibration. The dank air in the cavern begins to close in, flooding my lungs with the memories of long past. Not much in this space has changed over the millennia.

Nearing the end of the narrow tunnel, I scrape my knee against the side of the rocky wall as I push myself forward, rushing. The rough surface shreds through the fabric on my jeans and though I don't even have to look at it, I already know it's drawn blood.

"Dammit," I hiss, biting my lip to keep myself quiet.

Sound echoes in these enclosed spaces and alerting the men I'm coming is the last thing I want to do.

Finally, I reach the end of the crawlspace and I clamber through the opening; flopping out onto the dusty cavern floor. Beside me, a small pool of water glimmers in the low light as I release my flashlight and let it fall to the ground.

The way the light hits the liquid and bounces around the enclosed space instantly reminds me of some of Blake's drawings and paintings and I know why. Pulling up short, I hunch back onto my heels and take a look around. This pocket between the crawlspace and the next tunnel can't be any larger than four hundred and fifty square feet, and yet, I'd remember it anywhere.

It's where I found Anastasios's body.

19

DREAD AND DESPAIR overtake me, and I'm suddenly consumed in the memory of what was. As much as I try to push it under, the stone left to the side—it's the one smattered in his blood, even if it now looks like it's simply covered in rust.

I flashback to the way I found his crumpled body as he took his last breath in my arms. I hear his final labored words when he told me who did this to him.

My shoulder and knee throb, my own blood trickling down my leg, but I don't make a move.

Instead, my mind twists to my confrontation of Iphitheme.

She didn't even try to deny it—as though murder was a completely acceptable action for a priestess of Apollo to take. I watched the way her eyes glinted like cold steel and I cried out to Apollo for refusing to let me see this fate before it took place. I cursed his name. I cursed everything about him. I cursed Iphitheme. I cursed this eternal existence.

A vision captures my attention, pulling me from the past and hurtling me into the near future.

"He's nothin' but trouble. We need to get rid of him before he fucks up this whole operation. I'm telling ya, this whole thing stinks," Brady—also known as Ralph—says. He garnishes his handgun, pointing it at Blake's head.

Blake sits up taller, his arms bound behind his back and his mouth gagged. His eyes widen slightly, but his mind is wielding through scenarios faster than I can keep up.

"What in the hell is he gonna do bound and gagged, Brady? We ain't gotta be killers," Peter says, throwing a look of disgust.

My stomach lurches. As if murder is the greater of the two evils when they consider child prostitution and kidnapping.

"Maybe you ain't—"

The sound of the gun loading a bullet into the chamber snaps me from the vision and I'm on my feet running.

Apollo may not have warned me before—but he's warning me now.

It's a gift I will not take lightly but accept gladly.

My feet hit the ground in soft thuds, but I don't stop. There isn't time for super stealth or elaborate plans now.

The place where everything is about to unfold is coming up fast and I pray to Apollo and Mnemosyne that they'll all be safe—the girls and Blake—until I get there. I pray with every fiber of my being I've been given enough time to change the course of this.

The terrain is uneven and close, but I'm getting closer.

I round a bend and hear hushed voices speaking in frantic angry tones. The hairs on my neck rise. I've only got seconds to react.

"The guy's coming to, I think. Want me to knock him out again?" Peter says.

"He's nothin' but trouble…"

The exact words from my vision—the ones I've been

dreading since I saw them have been spoken, and I race forward before the rest can continue to unfold.

"Hiya there, gentlemen," I say, stepping out of the shadows.

Blake's eyes widen, and his face turns ashen. He shakes his head frantically, nodding back toward where I came from. His eyes are nothing more than slits as he flares his nostrils wide.

I grin apologetically at him with a 'sorry-not-sorry' kinda smile, as I edge further inward.

Beyond the two men, the small group of girls huddles together, but their faces are bright with curiosity and...*hope*.

"Hey, who in the hell are you?" Peter says, standing up quickly. His green eyes are wide with shock and his lopsided mouth gapes open. "Oh, damn. It's the bitch from the cabin."

Foresight flashes into my mind. The other guy, Brady, will try to over-power me by leaning on the element of surprise. As he lunges, I sidestep his power grab, and he falls flat on the floor as his momentum carries him down.

While I have the element of surprise to myself, I pull Blake to a stand. Without missing a beat, he drops his arms down, stepping through them so they're in the front of his body. With a swift movement, he throws his bound hands in the air and brings them down across his knee, breaking the duct tape. Casting it aside, he rips the tape from his mouth and lunges, as Brady attempts to stand back up.

The girls scream and squeal as they scoot back, trying to avoid the scene unfolding in front of them.

Peter stands in the middle of the space, halfway between the girls and the three of us. His jaw still slacking open, I suddenly get the vision of him coming to his senses and grabbing on of the girls.

As Blake lands an elbow across Brady's cheek, splitting it open, I sidestep the two of them and tackle Peter. Of the two of them, he's the one I feel I could most overpower using my gifts. His height and weight almost match mine, but I have something he doesn't—Apollo's aid.

Wrapping my arms around Peter's torso, we both free-fall backward, landing hard against the cold ground.

He hits with a sickening "Ooof" as his back thumps against the rocks.

The girls scream again, but this time, they all climb to their feet and edge further down the cavern tunnel. Their hands are bound in similar fashion to how Blake's were, but they're also bound to one another with some sort of coated wire.

Peter entwines his fingers in my hair, pulling hard. My chin tips upward and he plants a knee in the middle of my thigh. Sparks of pain explode in the muscle. Rolling off of him in surprise, he twists around, throwing me down, as he straddles across my body.

A sick, creepy grin slides across his lips and I immediately bring a fist into his groin before he has the opportunity to pin my arms down.

Screaming in agony, he slumps off of me, groping at himself.

I slide out from under his weight, kicking at him again to push myself further away.

"Blake, gun—" I scream, seconds after seeing Brady ditch their fight in lieu of the weapon.

Blake lunges forward, kicking the gun out of his reach just as Brady makes an attempt for it. The gun clatters against the walls as it hits the rock face.

"Thanks," Blake says breathlessly, as he lands his fist against Brady's cheek and the bridge of his nose.

Blood splatters the ground as a fissure separates across Brady's face. He lets out a howl, groping at the wound. Blood gushes between his fingers, and Blake brings his elbow down on the back of the man's neck. He drops instantly and doesn't move.

Without missing a beat, Blake yanks Brady's arms behind his back and pulls rip ties outta thin air. At least he had those, despite the missing luggage case. He clicks them in place, then moves on to restraining Brady's feet.

I'm mesmerized by the way Blake moves—such precision and power. There's no doubt in the way he maneuvers as his training and muscle memory kicks in. It's only the second time I've gotten to see this side of him, yet this time immediately brings back memories of the way he was as an Apollo guard. He didn't mess around then, either.

Images of Peter rising up and landing a blow to my face pull me from my admiration of Blake and I scramble to my feet. Instead of retaining his opportunity for a punch, things shift in real-time as Peter lunges forward. Before I know what hit me, we're on the ground as I struggle to breathe—the wind effectively knocked out of me.

Stars and bursts of light invade my vision and I'm suddenly spinning in a sea of abstracts.

Blake's voice is far away, saying something, but I can't quite grab hold on the words. My body feels weird, as if it's being moved, but I'm not really in it.

Maybe if I rest for just a minute...

No sooner does the thought flash through my mind, I feel myself sinking. Sinking through the earth beneath me—sinking into a place of utter cessation. The beauty in the stillness of this space is something I never knew could exist—and yet, it feels vaguely familiar. Almost as if it's the place from which we all spring from.

Whatever it is, it's a restful, peaceful place I could totally get used to. Yet, somewhere in the back of my being, I know it's all temporary. Rest and peace have never been in the cards for me.

A blast somewhere nearby extracts me from the tranquility and forces me back into my body. My eyes pop open at the sound of gurgling beside me. Breathing takes effort, as I struggle for each inhalation. Slowly, the pain eases and I twist around, taking in my surroundings.

"You shot me," Peter screams in agony. "You fuckin' shot me."

Less than a foot from me, Peter clutches at his shoulder, blood streaming from beneath his palm.

A few meters away, Blake drops the gun to his side, then tucks it in the space between the small of his back and his jeans.

"Are you okay?" he says, rushing to my side. Blake drops to his knees, placing his left hand on my shoulder.

I nod, unable to find the energy or breath to speak.

Returning the acknowledgment, he stands up, making his way to Peter. Without a single warning, Blake lands a blow across the man's face, and his body slumps to the dusty floor. His limp hand slides from his wound, and Blake grabs hold of it, twisting him over to apprehend him in the same manner as Brady.

"Holy shit, Diana. You are either the dumbest person I know, or the bravest. What in the hell were you thinking? How did you even find us?" Blake says, shaking his head and dragging Peter's limp body closer to Brady's.

Sitting up, my gaze strays past him to the group of girls hiding in the shadows. Swallowing hard, I shake my head and point to the girls.

I don't have it in me yet to talk. Besides, the priority should be the girls now. It's what we came here for, after all.

Blake's eyes linger on me for a moment, concern and conflict creeping across his features.

"Are you sure you're okay?" he asks.

"No, not really. But I'll be okay. Go help the girls," I whisper, my voice scratchy and labored.

Nodding, he shoots a quick glance at the apprehended men and walks off down the cavern tunnel. Shining his flashlight toward the girls, they tentatively step out into the light.

"Are you… Are you here to save us?" a redheaded girl no more than ten asks, clutching to the arm of the brunette next to her.

Blake stands his ground, not chancing to go any further, as he bends down on one knee.

"Yeah, Diana and I—we've come a long way to make sure you're all safe," he says, his tone soft and gentle, pointing my direction when he says my name. "Are any of you hurt?"

Each of their faces flit through a series of emotions as they each try to decide what to respond with. Their pain isn't necessarily anything that can be seen, but none of them are one-hundred percent okay with how the past few weeks have transpired.

A blonde girl in the back raises a pointer finger to the men beyond and says, "They're not the ones in charge. There's another man—"

"Lester, right?" I say, forcing myself to an awkward stand. The words tumble out as my body screams from the movement.

The blonde girl nods.

Blake throws a glance over his shoulder, his eyes bright and curious.

"Well, we need to get outta here before Lester comes looking," he says, walking to me and holding an arm out to grab onto. "You sure you're okay?"

"Yeah, just had the wind knocked out of me. I'll be fine in a bit," I say, forcing air deeper into my lungs.

Turning back to the girls, Blake says, "I'm going to get you all out of these restraints, okay?"

He lets go of my arm gently, waiting for me to grab hold of the cavern wall. Once I've steadied myself, he walks to the grouping of girls, and takes out a small pocket knife.

"So, what's everyone's name?" he asks, keeping his voice calm and gentle as he cuts through the cord binding them all together. "Mine is Blake."

The small redhead is the first to speak. "I'm Torie."

Her hand waves quickly in front of her body.

"I'm Haley," the blonde says.

"Rebecca," the brunette says, rubbing at her newly freed wrists.

The last one, a tall, dark-skinned, dark-haired girl steps out of the shadows. She doesn't say a word, but instead, embraces Blake in a full-on hug.

"That's Kaylee," Torie says.

Blake waits a moment, allowing Kaylee to feel safe and calm. He rests his hand on the back of her head, holding her close.

"It's really nice to meet you all. This is my—uh, this is Diana," Blake says, waving a hand to draw me closer to the group. "I wish we were all meeting under better circumstances, though."

"How's everyone feeling?" I ask, walking closer. Breathing is much easier, but it's still hard to get words out.

"I'm starving," Haley says, her eyebrows tugging in.

"It's been almost a day since we ate," Torie says, nodding as her tummy rumbles.

Blake tips his head in acknowledgment, "Reinforcements are on their way, but we need to get outta here. As soon as we're out, I'm sure food will be a top priority. Is everyone able to walk?"

They all nod in tandem with one another.

"Allow me to lead the way. I know the way out," I say, taking my time to step out front.

I turn my flashlight on and take my time, allowing insights to flood into my awareness so I know exactly the right way to take. I push my mind further, going into the future so I know we'll be safe in whatever pathway we choose.

Light extends out in front of me, acting as our virtual GPS as I follow its lead to bring the girls out of the cavern and to safety.

For a long while, none of us talk. We simply walk in silence, each circling the recent events in our minds and hoping for the best. Blake's thoughts encompass a myriad of topics—the safety of the girls, wondering how I found him, wondering where I was in the first place—the phone call to Interpol—then they flash briefly back to our kiss. Some of his thoughts are garbled, as he tries to parse them out and I take a step out of his mind to give him some privacy.

Each of the girl's minds weigh heavy between the events of recent days and their fears over what it will be like to go home. They'd all resigned themselves to the horrors awaiting them, so this change in direction is a welcome one.

"Your parents will be so relieved to have you back," I offer, responding to their thoughts.

Kaylee's eyes brim with tears, but she flares her nostrils and nods with resolve. The other girls link their arms, tugging each other in tightly. This was by no means a good circumstance, but the sisterhood they've developed between the four of them is strong. I can already tell it will last through their entire lifetime.

"Is it very much further?" Haley asks, her eyebrows furrowing.

I stop walking so I can close my eyes and get a better read on the distance before we're out of the tunnel. From what I sense, the walk isn't much further. Another five minutes or so. I open myself up, searching for details on when, or if, the Interpol Agents will find us.

Luckily, it seems at least one has entered the cavern in search of us.

"We're very close," I say aloud, picking up the pace.

I can't wait for this horrifying life experience to finally be over for them, so they can move on with their lives. Not to mention, I can move on with mine. Whatever that's about to entail.

The girls stay close at my heels, with Blake taking up the rear. I sense his alertness as he makes a mental map on how to get back to the two men, while simultaneously being alert for danger. He doesn't need to do it, though. I can easily get him back to the location, but he wouldn't be the man I know and love if he didn't.

As we reach the last bend out of the tunnel, I take a tentative look around, trying to get a gauge on where we're about to exit. The location is different from the main mouth of the Korykion entrance. More to the side, this opening is obscure but easier to escape and be found by the authorities.

The light from my flashlight ceases as it finds the opening of the cave and shines out into the wilderness beyond. A man dressed in field gear steps into the light just as we're reaching the end.

His flashlight shines up beside his head and he calls out, "Interpol—don't move."

The girls and I stop, waiting for the signal we're all clear. Blake, on the other hand, steps forward, dropping his flashlight to the ground and raising his other hand.

"Blake Wilson—United States, ex-Special Forces. I'm the guy who called," he says, making his way to the front of the group.

"Glad to see you, Mr. Wilson," the man says, keeping his

flashlight beside his head. "I see you located the girls. Everyone get out okay?"

"Yeah, We got 'em out. The two guys are back—"

Seconds too late, I realize my guard was down just enough. I was too focused on those around me and not focused enough on the legitimacy of the man in front of me.

I lift my gaze, just in time to see the glint of the gun and receive the insight from my gifts.

This Interpol Agent is legit, *but he's also Lester.*

20

*H*EAT RISES FROM SOMEWHERE INSIDE ME as Lester raises his gun, pointing it directly at Blake. Nothing about how this is about to play out is good, and I curse myself for being such a gullible nitwit to let my guard down.

I should have known better. People are still people after all. They mostly still suck.

"So glad I'm the one who found you first," Lester says, with a slight lilt to his voice. "I'd hoped to head you off before you reached the others, but I had contingencies just in case. I have to admit, this is so much better."

Recognition dawns on Blake and he doesn't hesitate. He reaches behind his back to garnish his own weapon—the gun confiscated from the other men.

Neither of them is the kind to take long pauses to think things through. They both share the 'kill or be killed' mentality.

Suddenly, my gifts flash me forward. Though the insight is almost instantaneous, it sure did take its sweet ass time to kick in.

Though both men pull the trigger—Lester is a split second faster, having already had his weapon ready. Racing toward their intended targets, Blake's bullet grazes Lester's ear. Lester's bullet, on the other hand, makes an accurate purchase—lodging itself directly into Blake's heart.

Blood gushes out of the wound, staining his grey dress shirt as it streams down his torso. Before I can will my feet to move, I watch in horror as my soul mate drops to the ground, his mouth contorted in a large-o of surprise.

I don't follow the vision any longer. Instead, I blink it away and spring into action.

"Get down," I command to the girls, throwing my arm out and pointing to the ground.

Their eyes are wide as screams of surprise escape their lips, but they hit the floor without needing to be asked twice. Before I have time to truly think about it, I step out in front of Blake just as the bullet leaves Lester's gun. With my arms splayed wide, I jump in the way, putting my body between Blake and the bullet.

The impact as it rips through my torso is enough to slow my momentum and force me backward instead of continuing on my sideways trajectory. My body slams against Blake, but his strong arms encircle me as we drop.

Blake's bullet flies wildly off course, thanks to my fall, and it lodges itself in the rocky cavern wall.

Instead of Blake's shirt stained crimson, it's my own. As I hit the ground, my hands fly to my wound, trying to keep the blood inside my body, as pain sears through me.

Blake's nostrils flare wide and his lips press tightly together. He doesn't say a word. Instead, he lays me down gently and returns his focus to Lester.

His mind is a whirling cyclone of fury, worry, and 'what if's'—but he also knows he can't dwell there. Not yet.

Standing up, he picks up his fallen weapon, then clutches the gun tightly in his hands.

I grope at the place where the metal invaded my body, mesmerized by the way the dark liquid is warm as it rushes through my fingers, just below my rib cage. The bullet is still lodged somewhere inside, and I can feel the entire trajectory it took as it ripped apart my insides.

Dizziness takes hold of my consciousness, yet I still catch the split-second surprise in Lester's eyes as they then slide into a satisfied glint when he realizes his bullet still hit a mark.

He feels this worked out more in his favor anyway because it will make Blake weak—*fearful*. Or perhaps, sadness and devastation will make him easier to overcome.

Another shot fires, and this time, Lester's gun drops from his left hand as the bullet strikes the place just under his left collar bone. Blake steps forward, hovering just over Lester's body. His mind is consumed with thoughts of rage and revenge.

His lips are pressed tight and his nostrils flare as he begins to squeeze the trigger again—this time, to end it.

I'm flooded with the vision of things going sideways. Of us being detained and big problems arising because this is an Interpol agent, not just some random kidnapping mastermind.

"Blake—don't do it. I know you want to, but please, we need him alive," I sputter, blood leaking from my mouth. Shaking, I wipe it away, and the deep crimson smears across the dirty flesh on the back of my hand.

Blake turns his head to look at me, pain and despair clinging to his unguarded eyes.

Lester tries to scramble backward as he clutches his shoulder, his eyes trained on Blake. Silently, Blake returns his gaze to Lester and lowers his gun. Then, without another moment's hesitation, he shoots Lester through the fleshy part of his right thigh.

The man screams, clutching the new wound with already bloody fingers.

Behind me, the girls squeal, but I feel one small hand suddenly rest on my shoulder.

"Does it hurt?" Kaylee asks, her dark hand contrasting against my shirt's light-colored fabric.

"A helluva lot," I say, trying to force a grin.

Before I realize it, Blake is at my side.

"How bad is it Diana?" he asks, kneeling down.

"She's lost a lot of blood," Kaylee whispers.

I glance down at the ground beneath me. She's right. The puddle is growing fast.

Flipping open his phone, Blake dials someone on his keypad.

"Please, we need some help. A civilian—she's been shot and I have the culprit in custody. Interpol should be nearby. Can you get a fix on my coordinates?" he says, not even trying to hide the panic fraying at the edges of his voice. "We need a medic immediately."

Voices the size of ants chatter in his ear, but I have no idea what they're saying. I concentrate, instead, on the place where his hand gently rests on my arm. It's warm and pulses against my skin like a metronome.

My eyelids are heavy, and it's a struggle to keep them open. Commotion beyond my periphery tries to stir me from the black abyss encircling me, but I can't find the will to focus on it.

If I just close my eyes, maybe I can…

Darkness beckons me and instead of lingering here, I slip into its comforting embrace.

"I think she might be coming around," a voice says somewhere in the vicinity of my head.

Everything is so heavy. Like I fell asleep when I shouldn't have—or I used my gifts and pushed them too far again.

My eyes pop open and I bolt upright. Pain shoots through my abdomen and I clutch at it, trying to claw the pain out.

Realization hits me.

"That son of a bitch shot me—" I say, more to myself than anyone who might be nearby.

I grip at my torso, my fingers searching for the point of entry. Instead, I find a new shirt has been put on and my wound has already begun its accelerated healing process. The gaping hole is now much smaller, thanks in part to the new set of stitches.

"Lay back down for christsake," Blake says, his hands suddenly on my shoulders and easing me backward.

As my back touches the bedsheets, I cock an eyebrow and try not to snicker to myself. It would take a helluva lot more than a bullet to keep me down.

A rush of emotions suddenly wells up, kicking me right in the gut as I stare into the wells of his dark, concerned eyes. I fight off the tears as they brim to the surface, making my eyes sting and my stomach clench.

He's alive. I'm alive.

Blake takes a seat beside me, scooting his chair in closer so he can take my right hand. His thumb caresses the back of my hand, comforting me in more ways than I can even express.

"She sure is a fighter," a nurse says to my left, her face buried in my medical chart.

Without a word, he nods. Instead, his eyebrows crumple inward, then flick up in the middle. "How are you feeling?" he asks, his words soft.

I don't know how to tell him I feel fine. Or that in a

couple of days it will be like nothing ever happened at all. It's not the sorta thing you talk about, especially with the nurse standing by.

"I've been better," I say, my lips curving upward in a slow smirk.

"I bet," he says, nodding. His thumb continues its siren song on my body—both relaxing me and making me hyper-aware of where his body touches mine.

The nurse sets down her chart and says, "I'll be back in a minute. Are you hungry for anything, dear?"

I shake my head. "No, not yet. My stomach feels a little queasy."

The nurse nods, turning on her heel to walk out of the room.

Turning back to Blake, I search his eyes for details. "How are the girls? They okay?"

"They're all fine—safe. Lester's been apprehended as well."

"Good. I hope he rots," I say, fire spitting from my lips. Not only for being the disgusting kind of human that traffics children in multiple countries—which in and of itself is horrifying. But also for shooting me—and aiming for Blake.

Blake's eyes fall to our hands, his lips curving slightly but not enough to force his dimples out of hiding.

"What about you?" I say, waiting for him to return eye contact with me.

He glances up. "What about me?"

"Are *you* okay?" I ask, raising an eyebrow again.

He takes a long, deep inhalation and leans back slightly in his chair. For the longest time, I take in his mannerisms, trying hard not to invade his mind but his thoughts begin to tumble out at me easily.

He's been beside himself with worry. With the amount of blood I'd lost, he doesn't understand how I could even be alive. Much less as healed as I appear and even talking with him now. He has his own questions and he has no idea how to ask any of them.

I watch as he finally licks his lower lip and nods. "Yeah, I've been better, too. Everything was very touch-and-go for a while. I was worried you weren't going to stick around to have that cup of coffee you promised."

"You can't get rid of me that easily. You should know that by now," I say, smirking.

"Very true. You can certainly be a stubborn pain in the ass when you want to be," he says, his dimples finally shining through.

"You're one to talk."

I take a moment, deciding how much to say right now. There's nothing I want more than to blurt it all out—that we're soul mates, he's my reincarnated husband and we have to make up for lost time. That I screwed up my memory because I couldn't stand to be without him. All of it.

I bite my lower lip. "He was gonna shoot you, you know."

"Well, yeah. I did actually get that," he says, his nostrils twitching to the side in deflection.

"No, I mean—" I take a deep breath and lock eyes with him. "You would have *died*."

I wait for the revelation to seep into the creases of his eyes. When they widen, I tip my head in acknowledgment.

"So instead, you took a bullet for me?"

"Yeah, well… I guess I also knew I wouldn't die," I say, settling on a partial truth.

He lets go of my hand, pressing his fingertips to his mouth.

Sighing, he leans forward, dropping his head to the place beside my hand. Reaching out, I run my fingertips through his dark strands, playing with the length.

"You shouldn't worry so much," I say.

"Easy for you to say. You can see everything," he says, his voice muffled by the fabric of the bedding. Abruptly his head pops up. "Hey, wait… How did you know I would have died? Did you—see me die? As in, your gifts…"

Blinking back my apprehension, I nod. "Yes, I did."

"Hang on, I thought—"

"Think, process. I'll give you a minute," I say, rolling my eyes playfully.

"But—how? I thought I was a blind spot to you?" he asks, his eyes narrowing.

"It's really a long story. And I want to tell you all of it—I do," I turn my head toward the nurse who reenters the room with a new bag of saline.

Without needing to explain any further, Blake nods. The look in his eyes alone tells me he gets where I'm going with this.

"When you're feeling better, then," he says, nodding.

I bow my head, keeping my gaze trained on him. "Agreed."

Casting his eyes to the floor, he leans forward again in his chair—shifting his elbows to his knees.

"Really, there will be time," I say, reaching out and placing my hand over the top of his forearm.

"I know. There's just been a lot to contend with these past few weeks," he says, sighing. "You really are a surprise, you know?"

"Thank you?" I say, quirking an eyebrow.

"No, no—it's a good thing."

A gentleman I've never seen walks into the room. The air around him exudes authority and you don't need to be psychic to know he's an agent of some kind. Though my gifts immediately tell me he's from Interpol and his name is Bruce Dexter. He's 50 years old, has a wife he adores, and four kids all entering college.

Blake stands up, shaking his hand.

"Good to see you again," Bruce says, as he releases his grip.

"You as well," Blake says, nodding.

"So, this must be Diana. Nice to see you on the mend," he says, walking over to me and extending his hand. "I'm Bruce—"

"Dexter. I know," I say, unable to help myself. Sometimes it's just fun to see the look of surprise on someone's face.

He blinks rapidly, but nods, "Right. Did Mr. Wilson tell you about me?"

"He must have," I say, smiling sweetly and throwing a sideways glance at Blake, who simply scratches his forehead.

"What can we do for you, Agent Dexter?" Blake says, returning to his seat.

"After all the commotion, I wanted to check-in and make sure you're all doing well. We sure do appreciate the help on this case. I'm sure it goes without saying, but we've been looking for a way in on this ring for a while now. They've been hard to pin down because they never go to the same place twice. Sure as hell didn't think one of our own was involved—or that it would be Americans who cracked the case."

Blake smiles sardonically. "I'll take that as a compliment."

The Agent slips into a sly smirk but doesn't say a word. His thoughts on the other hand—he doesn't typically trust Americans further than he can throw them. And he has a few of his own concerns over how we happened to unravel everything when they've spent years on the case. It's not that he isn't grateful—he is, but he's still skeptical.

I shake my head, my lips twitching into a smile. "I'm not entirely American. I just live there now."

My mind casts itself back to the ruins of the Temple of Apollo. I suppose one would say I'm Greek.

Agent Dexter's eyebrows flick upward in surprise, but he smiles. "Where are you from originally, then?"

"Here, actually," I say, letting my gaze fall on Blake. His face flashes through surprise but settles on rolling his eyes.

"Really? Where were you born? Did you grow up with one of my kids?" Agent Dexter asks.

"I seriously doubt it."

"Huh. Well, what are your plans once everyone is back to health? You planning on staying in Greece for a while? Or heading back to the States?"

"Probably head back to the States," Blake says at the same time I say, "Stay here for a bit."

Surprise floods Blake's features.

"You plan on staying?" he says.

I shrug. "I dunno. Maybe?"

"Well, I can see you both have a lot to talk about. I don't mean to cause any havoc. But if either of you are ever this way again, please give me a call," Agent Dexter says, brandishing his card to both of us.

Blake takes the offering, glancing at the face of it briefly, before nodding.

"Thanks," I say, taking the card and immediately place it on the rolling side table used to deliver meals.

"Well, whenever you head out, have a safe flight. Until next time," Agent Dexter says, shaking hands with Blake and shooting me a quick wink.

"Thanks for stopping in," I say, waving with my fingertips.

As soon as he's left the room, Blake turns back to me and repeats, "You plan on staying?"

"Well, as it turns out, there's a lot here I need to rediscover."

"Like what?"

I take a deep breath. For whatever reason, this isn't the

time to have this conversation. Instead, my insights flash me forward to a different time and place—one that will help deliver the information in a way that makes sense in Blake's mind.

"Blake, I'm actually feeling really tired. Can we—is it okay if we talk more about this later? I think I need to rest."

His eyelids flutter, but he nods. "Of course. I'm sorry. I don't know what I was thinking. You must be exhausted. Do you want me to get you anything?"

"No, I'm good. I just need to close my eyes for a few minutes, if that's okay."

"It's more than okay. Do you want me to go—or?"

I pull his hand back toward me as he makes a move to stand.

"Don't even think about it. There's room here," I say, patting the minuscule spot on the bed beside me.

Without batting an eye, he grins and slides onto the bed right alongside me. I curl on my side, resting my head on his broad chest. As I drift off, my mind is consumed with the memories I've shared with his soul—spanning across time and space.

21

"WHERE ARE YOU TAKING ME?" Blake asks, his eyes filled with curiosity.

"You'll see," I say, playing coy. He never was good at surprises.

"You don't know, do you?" He laughs.

"Of course I do—and you should, too. If you'd have been paying attention," I say, gripping the steering wheel tight rounding another bend in the road.

As Mount Parnassus begins to take center stage, Blake leans back in his seat.

"Ah—you're bringing us back to the cave," he says.

"Not exactly, but warm," I say, smiling.

"Hmmm..."

He adjusts in his seat, looking out the window and hunting for clues of his own. Part of me hopes this place jogs some of his own cellular or psychic memory, but even I'm not sure if it works like that. The other part of me worries about whether or not he'll believe a word I'm about to tell him.

After a few minutes of driving in silence, I turn left on the last leg of our journey. The view of the Temple can be seen—though not nearly as impressive as it once was. Pulling into the tourist parking lot, trepidation begins to flood my veins. I want him to understand. No, I need him to understand.

"The Temple of Apollo?" he says, pointing to the sign.

"Yup." I pull the handle and kick the driver's side door open.

Blake follows after me, confusion playing across all of his features as he surveys the surroundings.

"You know this place is closed for the night, right?" he says.

"Temples never close, silly," I say, smirking and walking ahead.

I try to settle my racing heart by breathing in deeply the smells of home. I didn't realize how much I missed these smells—a mixture of olive branches and earth.

"Wait up for me," he says, jogging to catch up. The moonlight glows off the top of his head, giving him an ethereal vibe suiting to the man who broke my heart—and healed my memory.

Standing still, I reach out, taking Blake's hand. I lead him away from the parking lot and toward the ruins of the Temple of Apollo and the theatre. There's so much we need to discuss and I'm not sure exactly how to break the news to him that he's really the reincarnated soul of my super-late husband.

How will he respond? Will he think I'm nuts? Or will he accept this as another weird quirk?

"Where are you taking me, Diana?" Blake finally asks, as we meander the footpaths to the sacred site.

The moon has risen—full, proud, and beautiful—and it casts its light upon the entire sanctuary. Shadows dance through the once magnificent structures. Now, they echo with the haunting memories of times past. I could have brought him in the daytime, but this will mean more. I know it will.

Sliding my tongue between my lips, I sigh.

"Blake, I need to talk to you and truthfully, I dunno how you're going to take some of the information. Frankly, you're gonna probably think I've tipped off my rocker when you hear it."

"Oooh, intrigue," he says, tilting his head. His lips shift into a half-smirk.

I let go of his hand, walking into the main Temple of Apollo. Meandering toward its hestia, I pause, taking in the scenery and the way everything has changed from its original glory.

It's strange to be able to see ancient locations with these eyes. My new modern perception overlays the freshly returned ancient memories from when it was once a thriving venue. Not that the Temple doesn't still bring its draw of people, it does—just for far different reasons.

I wonder if Apollo is pleased or appalled.

Blake walks up beside me, searching my face for answers. My forehead creases and I look away. How do I explain everything that's happened to me without sounding utterly and completely insane?

Blake's intense stare pulls me from my own thoughts and he pulls my hands into his.

I'm suddenly inundated and overwhelmed by the love he feels—the trust and loyalty—devotion, even. He doesn't have the words to express what he's feeling or why, but I know destroying Mnemosyne's mark has opened up more than simply my own memories. Something new is arising in him. Perhaps he'll be able to take what I say after all.

"Diana, I'm not going to say I understand everything you do. Or everything we've been through," he begins, "but what I do know is this feeling I have for you—it's deeper than anything I've ever felt before. I want to know why. I need to know what's going on with you. Why the secrecy and mystery?"

His eyebrows tug in and the pulse in his hands throbs against my fingertips.

"Blake, you know those dreams you've been having your whole life? The ones you had to start drawing in order to get them out of your mind?"

"Of course," he says, scrunching his eyebrows in.

"You're right—you and I have a deeper connection than most," I say, shaking my head.

I sound like a moron.

"Go on," he urges.

Pulling his hands closer, I lead him to one of the benches placed out for tourists. It's not part of the original structure, but I'm grateful for its functionality.

"I believe the reason you've been having those dreams—is because of a past life," I say, watching him closely.

"Hmmm." He takes the news with stride but sets his hands in his lap as he considers.

"I know it sounds a bit strange to start it like this, but I need to for the rest to make sense," I say, biting my lower lip.

"Okay, so what's the rest?" he asks, narrowing his eyes.

"The dreams were memories for you—*traumatic memories*. You—well, the person you once were, anyway—you were murdered in the cavern where we found the girls a long, long time ago."

"How long?"

"We're talking Ancient Greece times," I say sheepishly.

"All right," he says, skepticism permeating the word, "and I was *murdered*? How would you even know? Is this a vision thing?"

"No, not a vision," I say, shaking my head. "I was with you."

"So you have your own reincarnated memories?" he says, trying to understand.

"Not exactly. I was there with you. You and I—we were married," I say, holding his gaze. If he could only see it in my eyes—if he could only feel my soul—maybe he'd know.

Blake snorts. "But that's impossible. It would make you—"

"Two-thousand-three-hundred-eighty-four," I say, my eyebrows arcing high.

"How in the hell?" he says, his words coming out slow.

"I'm—oh hell, there's really no other way to say it, so I'm just gonna spit it out and sound like a lunatic. I'm the Oracle of Delphi. Like, as in, *the Oracle*. This is my rightful place and you were once one of the guards for the Temple of Apollo. You were sworn to protect me and the Pythia's sisterhood—the priestesses who were a part of my inner sanctum because they didn't have the gift of immortality, the way I do."

His eyes widen. "You're…immortal?"

I nod, my lips tightening. "It's kind of a shit deal, if you ask me. Definitely not something I would wish upon anyone else. Though, I guess it has its perks. I heal fast," I say, winking, then placing my palm over my recent bullet wound.

His eyes brighten with recognition. "Whoa—hold up a minute. You're telling me, you knew you couldn't die when you got shot because you *can't die*—and you didn't tell me?"

I shake my head in surprise. Of all the things he's concerned about, it's that I didn't tell him not to worry over me.

"You're right. I should have told you I heal fast. Maybe it would have prevented some of your dismay. But honestly, there were more pressing concerns, don't you think?"

"Not overly. The girls were safe. Lester was in custody… And hang on a second. I thought I read once, or maybe it was a History Channel thing… the Oracle of Delphi was stoned to death?" Blake says, tilting his head. "If you're her and can't die—I'm so confused."

"There was a time when I was forced into hiding by the Christians, but they never caught me. I have no doubt they would have tried their best to kill me, though. In reality, those stories, in my opinion, originated to explain my disappearance."

"Why did you disappear?" he asks, his eyes trained on me.

"That's where you come back in," I say, gently.

He makes a face.

"One of my sisters didn't believe our bond was gifted by Apollo. She felt it was tainting the reputation of the Pythia, as I had handed my innocence over to you. We were married in secret and didn't flaunt it. There was no need—but naturally, everyone knew anyway," I say, remembering back to the way everyone was so happy for us—thrilled we had found a way to be together, despite the odds. "You were meant to be with me forever. You weren't meant to die. Apollo approved of our union, but Iphitheme was jealous and heartbroken. She wanted to prove to me—to all the other priestesses you were mortal, just like they were…"

"So, a priestess murdered me?"

"Yes," I say, my mind instantly flashes back to the standing pool inside the cavern—the blood on my hands. His blood. His limp body. I relive the rushing memories from his consciousness as they departed his dying cells. His shock, desperation, and horror when he realized what was happening.

"Wow. This is—it's a lot to take in," he says, staring out at the mountain view in front of him.

"It really is."

We sit in silence for a few moments, absorbing the revelations and taking in the moonlit view. I wish I could gift him some of the memories I have—some of the insights and feelings I know to be true.

"Because I lost you, I couldn't deal. I was completely heartbroken. It was as though my whole world was imploding because what I was experiencing—it no longer made sense. My world no longer made sense."

Blake tilts his head, watching me from the side of his eye, but doesn't say anything.

I continue, "I was—distraught. I enacted a powerful ritual to remove my memories—*all memories* of you. All traces of you that I could. The symbol in your dreams—the symbol that continued to haunt my mind and put an immense drain on my abilities—it's Mnemosyne's mark. I didn't expect it to be as powerful as it was and I certainly didn't expect how far-reaching it was. I mean, I couldn't get a single read on you at all."

"Ah, this mark—that's why you struggled with reading me."

I nod.

"Talk about weird physics. Or metaphysics?" he shakes his head. "I meant to ask you—how is it you can read me now? Or know any of this? What happened to you in the cavern?"

"I was being pulled another direction. The entire time we were in the cave, it was as though the ritual was calling me back," I say. "It was powerful."

Suddenly, memories from the full moon ritual with Demetri flood my consciousness. I see the circle we cast, the Violet Flame of Transmutation, Morgan and Gabe, and her map to find her final five guardians. I didn't think it had worked for me, but I was wrong. The intentions of how we manipulated its magic to transmute and transform the energy surrounding my memories—it had worked all along. It just needed to guide me to my path so I could fulfill its purpose. Time had to run its course and free will had to play its role.

"So, you... went hunting for something? Is that why I couldn't find you?"

"Yes. I know I should have been focused on the girls, but when you've spent millennia trying to unlock your mind, and you realize you might be close..."

Overwhelmed by the intense desire to bring him current, to explain myself in a way that can't be explained by words, I take a breath and allow the full capacity of my God-granted gifts to flow through me. These abilities—they've always been more than just a simple psychic ability—they're powers in their own right and I've never even given them the attention they deserve.

Placing my middle two fingers alongside Blake's temple the way Morgan did for me, I close my eyes, summoning the power to relay some of the details I've lived through these past few weeks.

The hunt for Esther, the realization there were other girls. I show him the ritual with Demetri, Morgan, and Gabe —the Violet Flame. The insights to Mnemosyne's symbol and the ritual of drinking from the River of Lethe. My heartache as I found him dead in the cave and the way I feel now that I know.

The memories rush through me, flooding from me into his consciousness. I show him the thread tying his soul through the ages—directly to back to Anastasios. I gift him the years of memories we shared together—our childhood. The time we spent together by the Gulf of Corinth—first as young children. Our first kiss by the water's edge. Our moonlit wedding and the gifts granted by Apollo. Everything I feel and have felt throughout the long, lonely existence of my life.

Blake pulls back, his eyes wide, but dazzling in amazement.

He takes my outstretched hand, placing it over his heart.

"I—I don't even know how to describe—" he begins.

"You don't have to. I just, I needed you to see and feel what I do."

I search his eyes, wanting to see at soul-level what impact this may have had.

After a moment, he licks his lower lip and takes a deep breath. "That was—an experience I will never forget. Well, obviously. I mean, I had no idea. No clue something like that was possible, let alone everything you've been through. I mean, I was following you. I heard what you were saying about being the reincarnation of your husband and while I understand and felt something, I dunno, resonate in your words… I guess, it's nothing like the experience of it."

A slow smile slides across my lips. "Tell me about it."

His eyes fall to the ground, as he clutches my hand to his body, his eyes going distant and far away. We sit in silence for a moment, taking in the moonlit sights and sounds.

"I think I might hold a missing piece to your puzzle," he whispers.

"What do you mean?"

"When you—well, whatever you just did knocked some things loose for me. Memories of my own. At least, I think that's what they are." His eyes narrow as he stares at the rocky ground.

My heart hitches and I lean forward. "Can you explain?"

"I remember you—*us*. I remember our connection and my side of the exchanges you sent me. But… I was never gifted immortality, Diana. Or should I say, Amara?" he says, looking up at me from under his eyebrows and grinning.

Hearing my birth name—or rather, his nickname for my birth name, *Amarantham*, pulls me up short. It's been eons since I last went by that name. Tears brim at my eyes and my forehead crumples as I deal with this proclamation.

Blake's eyes are wide and sympathetic as he waits for the news to settle and his hands refuse to drop mine from his heart.

"But we were told—" I sob.

"We were only told I would be by your side forever. That's all," he says, raising his eyebrows.

"And how is that not immortality?" I say, splaying my other hand out wide in front of us.

"Because the only way a human soul can walk alongside an immortal is…"

He holds the silence, waiting for me to catch up.

My eyes widen. "Reincarnation. Oh my God. I'm so stupid. How did I not realize? How did I not pick that up?"

My fingertips graze my lips and I sit in horror at the revelation. Sure, it would have sucked to locate him again, to have to go through years of childhood and adolescence before he could be with me again—but my gifts would have easily brought him to me. Instead, I forced myself into two millennia alone. I forced him into two millennia reincarnating without me. All that time lost…

"You weren't meant to know. It was my burden to carry and a promise I made to Apollo in exchange for his approval. He knew we'd continue to find our way to one another and he wanted the timing to be right for you to learn the truth."

"Why would timing even matter?" Tears stream over my cheeks, dropping to my lap.

"I don't know, beautiful. It wasn't my place to question a God," he says. "Holy shit—I've dealt with a God." His eyebrows tug in and he shakes his head. "Until now, I've been a hundred percent atheist."

"I'm sure under the circumstances, Apollo will forgive you," I say swiping at the tears and chuckling despite myself.

"Sure as hell hope so. I mean, wow. How many people can say they've had that sort of interaction? Well, and not been locked up for it?" he says, scratching at the back of his neck with his right hand.

"Not many." I laugh. "I thought for sure you'd have me committed after this conversation was over."

Blake shakes his head. "No way. We're in this together."

My heart lightens, as my burden of loneliness is lifted from my being. For the first time in forever, I feel light as air and smile with the light and love of Apollo.

"Besides," he adds, "we can't have our first true 'official' date at the coffee shop when you're strapped down to a bed. Well, okay—that could come after, if you're into that sorta thing now."

His grin is infectious, and his lopsided dimples emerge in a way that instantly melts my heart.

"You'll have to wait and find out," I say, pushing at his shoulder playfully.

"For you, I'll wait forever and then some."

His right-hand slides beneath my hair, tugging at my neck and drawing me closer. I close my eyes, feeling his lips as they press against my own in a strange mix of memory and magic. I breathe it all in—embracing the present moment and all the beauty it has to offer.

At first, all I perceive is his fragrance of grapes hidden in the depths of his cologne, but it twists into something else.

Mnemosyne's scent of jasmine and rose floods my nostrils, taking over everything.

"Pythia, it is time. Are you ready to resume your role as the rightful Oracle of Delphi?"

IS THIS THE END?

Diana Hawthorne's story continues, starting July 2021! Stay tuned for preorder links, coming soon!

Oracle: *Book 1*
Amends: *Book 2 (coming July 2021)*
Immortals: *Book 3 (coming December 2021)*

AMENDS: BOOK 2 SNEAK PEEK
(CHAPTER 1)

THE ORACLE OF DEAD GODS

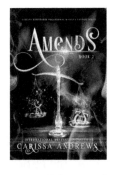

There's no way in hell I'm allowing them to trap me here.

I shiver from the cold sweats brought on by this morning's vision. They're coming at me now with more frequency. More *urgency*.

That's why I had to get out of the hotel room and come back to the source. I need to sit inside the vibrations of the temple again, just I can be sure.

Luckily, the drive to the Temple of Apollo isn't more than a few minutes from where we're staying.

I bite my lower lip and clutch the steering wheel tightly.

I'm almost positive I know what the visions mean, but I'm not sure how to lean into them. Not when I'm so close to having everything I've ever wanted.

My jaw clenches and I cast a gaze over my shoulder. Blake's soft breathing pulses up and down softly like a metronome to my every existence. He has no idea what awaits.

There's movement in the old space. It feels like the old gods are preparing their return and I've become the linch pin to their plan.

But I've come too far to sit on a pile of rubble, telling fortunes to the rich and powerful while they rouse the troops. Because let's face it, once word gets out that *the* Oracle of Delphi has returned, those in power will come for me the way they did before. Humanity hasn't changed all that much.

Plus, with the advent of social media, I shudder to think how quickly the information would travel. I'll become a spectacle—some sort of dancing monkey—and the privacy I've come to know and love will be lost.

Then, rather than being accessible to all the poor, sad souls of the world, I'll be fashioned into a weapon. One they can use to their advantage.

Then, the fanatics will come. First, they'll try to kill me. But when they find out they can't a worse fate will come. I'd probably be locked in a vault under the Vatican somewhere with everything else that scares the hell out of humanity.

Fuck that.

I practically growl as I shudder at the thought.

It's bad enough I have to be an oracle for dead and buried gods. I should at least be able to pick and choose where I go and how I serve.

Come on, Apollo. Give me at least that much.

Swallowing hard, I put the rental car into park. I leave the car running and slip out into the cool morning air. As gently as I can, I close the driver's side door, and peer inside. Blake's arms are pinned by his arms and his dark eyelashes flutter under the weight of his dreams. Hopefully they're better than mine.

I don't fully understand why he wanted to come with me. It's not like he's a morning person. He could still be warm and comfortable in the hotel bedroom. I know that's where I'd rather be.

My heart flutters and I can't help but smile.

Turning around, the wind whips my hair in a cyclone around my head. It's a dazzling display with the varying strands of gold and pink as the rising sun bleeds its welcome into my hair. Despite all of this, I reach for the ponytail holder in my pocket and tie my hair back. I need to be focused and centered now. Taking my time, I meander the trail to the ruins of the Temple of Apollo.

It's been two days since the arrest of Lester and his cronies. Two days since I got my memories back.

Two days since I gave up a mortal life to continue on with the insanity of this supernatural one.

When I reach the location, I take a seat on a stone wall and sigh.

It's also been two days since my soul mate was returned to me.

Blake is so excited to be uncovering our past, one memory at a time. His life as Anastasios was just as locked to him as my past was to me. At least we have that much in common.

But this undercurrent of anxiety clouds my elation.

I exhale my trepidation and settle into the energy of the space. My gaze lifts, settling on the horizon. At this time of the morning, the view is almost the same as it was millenia ago. However the beauty does not thing to shake the terrible revelation that while I have regained so much, my life is no longer my own.

While not exactly the most idyllic of circumstances, the past two millennium have moulded me into the woman I've become. How the hell am I meant to revert back to someone I no longer am?

That woman was shed a long, *long* time ago.

This never-ending existence has left me jaded. Sure, I might be more of a prickly pear these days, but I'd also like to think the rougher edges have left me with a little more depth. And certainly a little wiser to the world as a whole.

Being psychic can only get you so far. You still need experience to accurately unpack everything.

Inhaling deeply, the crisp morning air clings to my lungs until I exhale the breath in a soft plume of frozen water droplets. I lean forward, placing my elbows on my knees. Bringing my hands to prayer position, I press the edge of my index fingers to my lips in an effort to silence my mind.

Blake may be recalling bits and pieces of our past life together, but he doesn't remember everything. He doesn't have the recollection of all of his past lifetimes, and I'm not sure what to make of that. Maybe it's a byproduct of me meddling with our memories. As long as he's happy with what he remembers, maybe that's all that matters.

My one concern is that he doesn't understand the restraints I now wear, and all for the sake of saving him. If he knew what I gave up to do it, he'd call me a damn fool. But then again, he doesn't know all that I've endured without him by my side.

There have been so many decisions I've made that would shock him. So much I've seen and done that I'm not proud of throughout these years alone. Rather than being set on a course and following it to its destination, my life has been a tangle of events that would leave others crawling out of their skin.

Maybe even Blake.

And it's certainly something the gods could use against me, if they really wanted.

My stomach constricts and I swallow back my uneasiness.

I'll cross that bridge when—or if—it ever comes.

For now, though, I need to find a loophole to this prison sentence before it becomes my reality.

As much as I love the memories of growing up here, and the time of being with Anastasios, I no longer have any desire to live in Greece. That time has passed. Sorrow lingers here like a layer of fog that won't dissipate. I can feel it now, even as I sit here.

This is where everything went wrong… Where two-thousand plus years of self-loathing began.

No, I don't want to be stuck here. Blake and I found each other again in Helena. It's where we belong now. Besides, it's not like he'll want to uproot Aiden and his entire life to move to Greece.

Arms wrap around my neck from behind, making me jump. Not an easy feat, all things considered.

"Didn't mean to startle you." Blake's words are gruff, but hold a smile at the edges of his tone. His thoughts tumble through various things to say, but they're garbled by the early morning. One thing is clear, though…he's amused that he caught me off guard. He kisses the top of my head and takes a seat beside me on the bench. "It's easy to find you—you're always in the same place."

My lips twitch, but don't fully form into a smile.

"Uh oh. What's wrong?" he asks. His eyebrows draw down, darkening his features as he puts on his investigator hat.

I straighten my shoulders and shake off my apprehension. There's no point in worrying him until I have a plan. "Nothing," I mutter.

The creases around his brown eyes deepen and he grunts. "Mhm."

Shaking my head, I stand up and stretch nonchalantly. "No, seriously. It's nothing to worry about."

"Then why won't you tell me what's going on?" he asks, arching an eyebrow.

I press my lips tight and give him a knowing look. "Because it's nothing to worry about. I've just got a lot on my mind. We've been through hell and back these past few weeks."

His expression is firm and he refuses to remove me from underneath his scrutiny. I hold firm, trying to lighten the energy between us. Finally, he leans back a bit and says, "Yeah, if you would have told me a month ago that I'd be having past-life memories about being married to the Oracle of Delphi, or that I've made a pact with the god Apollo, I would have said to lay off the acid."

I chuckle, dropping my gaze to the sandy ground. "Right?"

So much has changed.

A little over a month ago, I had been trying desperately to understand my past. If I'm completely honest, I don't think I really expected anything to come of it. After being let down time and time again, how could I?

But the Violet Flame invocation came through.

Demetri came through.

My stomach constricts again and a fresh wave of guilt and anxiety rolls through me. I exhale, trying to release the tension. Instead, the realization that I'm the reason Demetri's powers were stripped from him punches me in the feels.

His powers are gone and mine have grown. Oh, he'll *love* that.

I again press my fingertips to my mouth and turn away from Blake.

"See, now I know something's up. What's going on with you?" Blake says, as he presses his hand against my back, letting me feel his presence.

He's genuinely concerned for me—I can sense it in every

molecule of his being—but I've been alone so long, I don't quite know how to open up completely. Even with him.

He's fragile and human… and I could still push him away if I'm not careful.

I close my eyes for a moment, allowing my abilities to survey the landscape of our new relationship before proceeding. "When you mentioned where we were at a month ago, it got me thinking about what was happening in my life around that time… I'm just worried about a friend back home," I admit, hoping it will be enough for him to let things go.

"Is something wrong with him?" he asks, narrowing his gaze.

My eyebrows pull in as I try to put things into the right words. It's way easier when I'm just the vessel, delivering universal information. But when I'm at the center of it all, shit gets so damn complicated and messy.

"You could say that, yeah. He was helping me with a ritual and it backfired." I shake my head. "Well, sort of."

Blake continues to watch me, giving me the space to process through what I want to say without interruption. It's who he is—the watcher. It's why he's such a good private investigator.

I inhale slowly and let my shoulders drop. "He's psychic as well, but after the ritual, the blow back cost him his gifts. I don't think he's very happy with me."

"Is there anything that can be done?" Blake asks, switching gears into fixer mode.

I shrug. "Honestly, I don't know."

"Well, I fully admit that I'm new to this whole supernatural thing, so correct me if I have this wrong," Blake begins, narrowing his gaze, "but you're connected to some pretty powerful beings. I'd be surprised if you can't pull a few strings for him."

I mull over his words for a moment. Would the gods help Demetri? I suppose they could, but then it would be one more thing they could hold over me. If they even felt it was something to bother with. The gods and their plans...

I glance at Blake, then back out over the valley. "While technically true, the gods don't look kindly on trivial requests. I should know. And this...would definitely be considered trivial." Besides that, in a way, it's a direct consequence of my selfishness all those years ago. It's serving not only to punish him—but me. And maybe I *should* be punished.

"Well, I have faith in you. If there's a way to fix this for him, you'll figure it out. So, stop worrying, would you?" Blake says, grabbing hold of my arms and spinning me to face him. He lifts his right hand to my cheek, brushing back a strand of my pink hair that's slipped loose from my ponytail.

I inhale sharply, suddenly tuned into every movement he makes and the proximity of his body to mine. While we may have been married in a past life, everything about this relationship we have now is so new. I can count the times we've kissed on one hand...and that's as far as we've taken things.

I've had relationships in the past that existed solely for sweaty entanglements—and nothing else. No names, no shared experiences beyond that. But this...

Blake's eyes linger on mine, holding my gaze so long my heart begins to race.

Can he see into my soul? Can he feel my thoughts?

My breath catches and I try to shake this horrible feeling niggling its way into my consciousness. Love is a beautiful, strange thing. I love him so deeply, even though we've barely met in this new lifetime. His essences is the same.

Yet, I've changed so much.

What if after all these years, he finds out I'm no longer worthy of his love?

Those worries puddle at my feet when Blake slowly bends in, brushing his lips against mine. The whiskers in his peppered goatee tickle the edges of my lips, making my skin hum.

As much as I try to stay clear of reading his thoughts, they still come to me with fervor. Despite his gentleness, he wants the exact same thing I want. Only, he's just as nervous to reach for it as I am.

I lean into his kiss, wrapping my arms around his neck, and entangling my fingers into his dark locks. The wind whips around us, echoing through the branches nearby and the ruins themselves. Hidden in the undercurrent of the breeze, I swear I can hear someone calling my name.

Only, it's not my name anymore…

The Grecian accent is thick, but my mind translates them instantly."Amarantham? Is that you?"

I wish I could tell you the past never comes back to haunt you…but I'd be lying.

Because I'm staring straight into its gleaming brown eyes…

Preorder Amends, Book 2 in the Diana Hawthorne Supernatural Mysteries now! Coming July 23rd 2021!

CAN'T WAIT FOR MORE DIANA?

Diana Hawthorne seems to get around. (No, not like that. Get your mind out of the gutter.)

If you're waiting for Diana's supernatural mystery series to continue, here are a few additional places you can get your fix:

The Final Five
Awakening
The Windhaven Witches

ABOUT THE AUTHOR

Carissa Andrews
Sci-fi/Fantasy is my pen of choice.

 Carissa Andrews is an international bestselling indie author from central Minnesota who writes a combination of science fiction, fantasy, and dystopia. Her plans for 2021 include continuation of her Diana Hawthorne Supernatural Mysteries. As a publishing powerhouse, she keeps sane by chilling with her husband, five kids, and their two insane husky pups, Aztec and Pharaoh.

For a free ebook and to find out what Carissa's up to, head over to her website and sign up for her newsletter:
www.carissaandrews.com

facebook.com/authorcarissaandrews
twitter.com/CarissaAndrews
instagram.com/carissa_andrews_mn
amazon.com/author/carissaandrews
bookbub.com/authors/carissa-andrews
goodreads.com/Carissa_Andrews

CPSIA information can be obtained
at www.ICGtesting.com
Printed in the USA
LVHW080244210223
740036LV00014B/783